Marilyn Lee Presents

Loving Large 2:

Yours, Now And Forever

Marilyn Lee

©2011 Marilyn Lee

All Rights reserved

This is a work of fiction. Names, characters, places, and incidents are products of the author's imagination or are used fictitiously and are not to be construed as real. All service marks, registered trademarks, and registered service marks are the property of their respective owners and are used herein for identification purposes only.

All rights reserved. No part of this book may be used or reproduced electronically or in print without written permission, except in the case of brief quotations embodied in reviews. Copyright laws prohibit trading, selling, and or giving away ebooks.

Chapter One

"Oh my god, Neida. Your tall, sinfully handsome brave has noticed you. He's looking this way!"

Oneida Armstrong's heartbeat increased. She swallowed quickly before she looked across the room and into the dark brown eyes of the handsome man seated alone at a table on the opposite side of the restaurant.

A shock of desire and emotion overwhelmed her senses. She felt as shaken as she had after their gazes met and briefly locked on Monday morning. Then, as now, she knew she looked at her ultimate fantasy. His raw, sensual masculinity stroked her most primal passions and needs. Something deep in his dark, compelling gaze whispered to her heart.

He's the one. With him you'll know either heartache and pain or endless nights of bliss and a long life of shared love and devotion. He's the one. Don't let him slip out of your reach. Do whatever is necessary to get and keep him.

She sucked in a breath. Did he feel a sense of destiny as he looked at her? Did his heart and sensual desires recognize her as his soul mate?

They locked gazes for several more moments.

She felt as if he were probing her most secret desires. Instead of shaming her, the thought excited and aroused her. She felt beautiful, sexy and hungry to satisfy his deepest passions. Did he feel her need for him? If so, did it stroke his cravings?

He abruptly rose. Keeping his gaze locked on her, he put several bills on the table and moved in her direction.

"Here he comes. Get ready to bat your gorgeous eyes and to flaunt that outrageous rack of yours at him so he's knocked right off his big feet."

Neida dragged her gaze away from the handsome stranger's and turned to give her best friend Betty a frantic look. "I can't."

"Yes, you can!"

"He's out of my league."

"The hell he is! You're beautiful. He's gorgeous! I'm so sure he's your Mr. Right, I can almost hear the beautiful babies you'll make together calling me Auntie Betty."

Neida's gaze was drawn back to the object of their discussion. With the exception of her first crush and love, her most intimate fantasies had always revolved around Native American men. She loved their skin tone, their high cheekbones, their glossy brown hair, and the mystique surrounding them.

Although a lot taller than the men populating her sensual desires, the sexy hunk strolling towards their table might have stepped right out of her most erotic daydream. She moistened her lips imagining herself slowly peeling the clothes off of his big, buff body. She loved a man who possessed a muscular build without the appearance of an overly muscled weightlifter.

She swallowed, envisioning stroking her hands over his wide shoulders, down his massive chest and his rippled abs to cup his cock. As he hardened against her fingers, she'd part her legs and welcome him inside her body. A rush of moisture filled her thong at her erotic desires.

Get a grip, Neida. What are the chances he's attracted to plus-sized black women? He didn't ask your name on Monday and he's not going to ask it now.

"Neida!" Betty nudged her foot under the table. "Here he comes! Snap out of it already. Say something witty or at least smile at him."

Even as an inner voice urged her to seize the second chance she'd been given to capture his attention, the fear of rejection kept her silent and unsmiling.

"Neida!"

The man with the sinfully dark, compelling eyes slowed his stride.

Betty reached across the table to give her hand a hard squeeze. "Smile at him and give him a reason to stop."

He paused at their table.

Neida sucked in a slow breath, unable to look away from him. Her heart thundered against her ribs.

"Good morning ladies."

Her imagination ran wild at the sound of his deep, sexy baritone. *Undress me with your eyes. Stare at my lips and my breasts. Give me a sign you feel some of what I feel.*

"Good morning!" Even as Betty smiled at him, she gave Neida's hand a vicious squeeze.

"Good morning," he said, his gaze still locked on Neida.

She gave herself a mental shake. "Good morning."

He glanced at her left hand before raising his gaze to her breasts. "It is now."

Neida swallowed hard.

His gaze lingered on her breasts for so long her nipples hardened.

Finally, he looked into her eyes again. The long, searching look in his dark, sensual gaze pinned her to the seat.

She parted her lips and drank him in with her eyes. He must have been at least 6' 5" or 6' 6". The most attractive male she'd ever seen in person, he exuded confidence and sex appeal. *Was he married?*

Noting her gaze shifting downward, he lifted his left hand. He turned it slowly, allowing her to see that it bore no signs of having recently been adorned with a wedding band.

Cheeks burning, she looked into his eyes again.

He treated her to a sudden slow, sensual smile. "Ladies," he said and walked away.

Neida and Betty sighed in unison and turned to watch him walk out of the restaurant and into the warm early June sunshine.

He walked with all the confidence of a sexy predator. Neida moistened her lips, imagining his tight ass clenching and unclenching as he repeatedly thrust his hard cock into her wet pussy. Her stomach muscles churned and she burned with desire.

Outside the restaurant, he turned, catching her staring at his ass. A slight smile curved his lips.

Neida leaned forward. It would be too delicious to nibble at his sensual bottom lip before kissing her way down his chest and over his abs to his genitals. The thought of slowly drawing his hard, bare cock between her lips and into her mouth filled her with an almost insatiable need.

Betty squeezed her hand. "Don't just sit there like a dolt. Wave or smile at him. Do something to give him a reason to come back inside to ask for your number!"

Lost in a lust-driven haze, it took several seconds before Neida could rouse herself. She'd only half raised her free hand when he turned and walked away.

Oh. Damn. You blew it, Neida.

Betty hissed and tossed her hand back at her. "I suppose now you're satisfied."

"Satisfied?" She could almost taste her disappointment. She dragged her gaze from the restaurant window to stare at Betty. "You're either kidding or nuts."

"*I'm* nuts? I'm not the one who just allowed her Mr. Right to walk out of her life never to be seen again!"

Neida and Betty treated themselves to breakfast at Becky's Place twice a month. They'd arrived at Becky's on Monday morning as the handsome stranger exited. It had taken Betty four days to talk Neida into returning to Becky's in the hope of encountering him again.

"You can say that, knowing how much effort it took for me to come back here today?"

Betty leaned across the table to stare at her. "Well, you're nuts if you think I'm going to stand by while you let this one get away," she warned.

"Oh Betty, it's over."

"It's over? Not damn likely."

"Betty—"

"Don't push me or I'll give you a good, old-fashioned, teeth-rattling shake you'll feel for a week!"

Neida's lips twitched with amusement. She looked down at her full-figured body before arching a brow at Betty's size six frame. "Feeling your oats today?"

"You think this is funny?" Betty demanded.

As her best friend, Betty took an intense interest in

Neida's love life and felt each emotional setback almost as deeply as Neida did. They had cried and brooded together for weeks after Neida's first love had left the U.S. to work in Africa. She shook her head. "Of course I don't think it's funny, but he's gone, Bett. Get over it."

Betty stared at her. "I don't know how or why I put up with you, but I'm going to get you happily married to him if it's the last thing I do."

Neida's knowledge that men generally found her attractive offered no comfort because his was suddenly the only male opinion which mattered. She'd never met anyone quite like him. Surely a man with his looks and sex appeal wanted a supermodel thin trophy lover. She shook her head. "Get real, Bett. He didn't even ask my name."

"That's because you didn't give him any encouragement." She pointed a finger at Neida. "But you'd better make more of an effort the next time you see him."

She stared at Betty. "You're serious."

"Of course I'm serious. I know he's your Mr. Right and I'm not going to let you blow it with him."

Neida blinked. "I think you need to be realistic and—"

"Never mind trying to throw road blocks in my way. We might as well go," Betty said, sounding aggrieved.

She nodded. "Yes. We might as well."

Betty treated her to the silent treatment during the three-block walk to the middle school where they both taught.

"You're impossible," Neida told her as they stood outside her classroom door.

"*I'm* impossible?"

"Yes! You're behaving as if I didn't sit in Becky's with you hoping he'd come in and notice me."

"And when he did notice you what did you do to encourage him?"

"Betty—"

"You're not getting any younger, Neida. You'll be 27 soon."

"So? The last time I checked, that wasn't exactly considered over the hill."

Betty waved a hand in dismissal. "Whatever, Neida. I don't want to talk about this anymore."

Neida blinked in surprise. "You don't want to discuss my love life or lack thereof? Holy hell, the sky must be falling."

Betty compressed her lips.

"I never thought I'd live long enough for you to lose interest in spearheading the search for my Mr. Right, Bett."

"Well, what do you expect when you stubbornly refuse to cooperate? You…" Betty's voice trailed off suddenly. She was silent for several moments before she went on in a more cheerful voice. "All isn't lost. I have an idea."

Neida tensed. "Before you come up with another scheme, you should know I'm not going back to Becky's," she warned.

Betty tossed her head, sending her long, dark hair cascading around her slim shoulders. "Neida Headstrong, you are nuts if you think I'm going to stand by while you let your dream man slip through your fingers!"

"The name is Armstrong and I'm not going to

make a fool of myself by stalking a man who isn't interested in me."

"Why do I waste my time with you?" She cast her gaze ceiling ward in a Lord-give-me-the-strength-to-deal-with-this-lunatic manner.

"Because I'm so damned pretty?" Neida suggested, hoping to disperse the mounting tension between them.

She nodded. "You're very pretty and intelligent, Neida. Try to remember that when you see Mr. Tall, dark and handsome brave again."

Aware that she had not sparkled or done or said anything to impress him, she sighed. "I doubt I'll have to worry about seeing him again."

"Oh you'll see him again." Betty gave her a sweet smile. "I feel it in my bones and you know they never lie."

Betty did seem to have a certain intuition. That was one of the reasons Neida had allowed herself to be talked into going back to Becky's that morning. "I know that, Bett, but you have to acknowledge that not all men like full-figured women."

"You're not just full-figured. You're curvy and voluptuous!" Betty retorted, her smile vanishing. "What's not to like? No one's going to convince me that a six-foot plus hunk like him wants a tiny, 80-pound woman in his bed!"

Oh if only she could spend a few hours in his bed. "What are the chances he likes his women full-figured *and* black, Bett?"

"Judging by the unmitigated lust he projected as he looked at you, I'd say the chances are very good." She hugged herself. "Can't you just imagine him bare-chested astride a big stallion chasing you across a prairie with lust in his heart like the heroes in all those capture romances we devoured as teenagers?"

"Yes, I can," Neida admitted.

Betty smiled. "I knew it!"

She shrugged. "Before you get too excited, remember most of the heroines in those capture romances were tiny blondes with pale skin."

Betty waved a hand in dismissal. "You're not going to discourage me, Neida Headstrong. That was fiction. This is real life. I'll bet you anything he got a hard-on staring at your breasts and lips. I know he'd love to have a beautiful, curvy black woman like you to share his bed. So don't try to discourage me or give me any grief."

"So now I'm beautiful?" Neida smiled. "At this rate in a few more seconds you'll be entering me into a plus-size beauty pageant."

Betty gave her a cool stare before she stalked down the hall to her own classroom.

Thankful to have escaped without another tongue lashing, Neida entered her empty classroom. Seated at her desk, her thoughts turned to all the capture romances she'd lost herself in over the years. After all those romances she'd finally met a Native American hunk. Well, not met exactly. Seen. And oh what a beautiful sight he'd been.

She shook her head. Get real, Neida. So he stared at your lips and breasts. If he'd really been interested, he'd have introduced himself.

The bell rang and her students wandered into the classroom. She reluctantly turned her attention to teaching. There would be plenty of time to daydream later when she was alone.

Chapter Two

Late that afternoon, Braden Elkhorn looked up from his laptop as his brother Raven, walked into the living room of the extended stay hotel suite they shared. Normally, they would have stayed in their brother Seneka's penthouse condo while they were in Philly. Although Seneka and Autumn had extended the invitation, he and Raven knew better than to make a third and fourth wheel with a couple who had only been married eleven months and still found it difficult to keep their hands off each other.

He sat back in his chair, flexing his shoulder muscles. Raven, a corporate lawyer, headed the team of attorneys negotiating the possible acquisition of a small software company Braden wanted to acquire.

"How did the meeting go?" he asked.

Raven tossed his suit jacket over the back of the loveseat and sank down onto the other cushion. "It's going to take a few more meetings before things get interesting." He stretched his legs out. "How did your day go, Bray?"

"Lousy." He glanced at his watch. "It's after three and I haven't accomplished a single damn thing all day." And there was plenty he should have been doing. In addition to paying attention to the negotiations for the possible acquisition, he also needed to decide if he'd buy a house or rent an apartment in the Philadelphia area. Then there was the problem of getting his key people to agree to relocate to the East Coast when he moved his headquarters from the West coast—after they'd chosen a site for the new offices.

"Nothing? Did you see her?"

Braden hesitated. As the eldest of four sons, his parents had impressed upon him the need to set the proper example for his younger brothers. That included centering his romantic attentions on Native American women. He lately felt a pressing need to marry a Native woman since Seneka, two years his junior, had again fallen in love with a non-Native woman. Seneka's first wife had been Caucasian. His second was Afro-American.

"Bray?" Raven prodded.

He ran a hand through his hair and nodded. "Yes. I saw her."

Raven sat forward. "So? When are you taking her out?"

He'd have to be content to lust after her from afar. He shook his head. "I have no intentions of asking her out."

Raven sat back on the loveseat. "Why not?"

Although five years younger, Raven had always been his confidant. Still, he felt he'd erred in telling Raven about his juvenile reaction to the beautiful woman who had dominated his thoughts since their brief encounter four days earlier. He, who never ate breakfast, had stopped in the restaurant for coffee and fallen into an instant and painfully powerful lust.

"She looks about fourteen years too young, she lives in Philly and she's not Cherokee." He shrugged. "Take your pick from those three reasons why I didn't ask her out."

"The last time I checked, 26 is legal. Philly isn't the end of the world. And even if it were, we'll all be relocating here in a few months. And Mom and Dad's wishes notwithstanding, not every woman you date has to be Cherokee or even Native, Bray. You're allowed to date who you like—just as the rest of us do."

Braden had never wanted to buy into that argument more. In high school and college, he'd dated black women exclusively. After his thirtieth birthday his mother started to laud the virtues of Cherokee women and lamented the many Native men who married non-Native women. She reminded him how his late father had counted on him to set a good example for his brothers.

After careful consideration, he'd started dating Native American women hoping to fall hard for one. During the ensuing ten years of dating women his mother approved of, he'd never fallen in love or even into deep lust with any of those mom-approved women. He had in fact lost the only woman he'd ever loved—his former lover and assistant, Kania. Then, after he'd partially recovered from the end of their intimate relationship, he'd met Seneka's new love, Autumn. He'd had a few uncomfortable days when he feared he'd fallen for her.

His thoughts turned back to Kania. Kania. He'd come very close to proposing to his beautiful, full-figured former assistant. But they'd foolishly allowed their individual circumstances and obligations to conspire to keep them apart—until she fell out of love with him.

When he closed his eyes, a vision of a tall, statuesque beauty with warm brown skin, lush lips, alluring curves and eyes so deep he'd longed to lose all his inhibitions within their depths imprinted its self on his lids. Everything about her felt right—even her name, Oneida, which loosely met eagerly awaited one.

He shook his head, opened his eyes, and met his brother's dark gaze. "Mom's not getting any younger and she's not going to live forever."

"I'm aware of that. What's your point, Bray? If you're about to say she wants grandkids before she's too old to enjoy them, let me remind you that Autumn's three months pregnant. Isn't that why we've all decided to relocate to the East Coast so the first Elkhorn baby in thirty-one years will be surrounded by an adoring grandmother and doting uncles?"

"We can't expect Neka to carry the family obligation by himself. He and Autumn are giving Mom her first grandchild. One of us has to consider giving her a Native daughter-in-law. Since that's not likely to happen with either you or Shane, that kind of leaves me. Doesn't it?"

Raven narrowed his gaze. "I love Mom as much as you do and I'd like nothing more than to make her happy, but I don't plan to marry until I meet a woman who completely blows me out of the water. Hell, who knows? By some miracle, she might even be Native. If not, I'm sure mom will learn to love her anyway — just as she now does Autumn. I'm not going to marry for any reason other than feeling a love so deep and intense it consumes me — as Neka's love for Autumn does him. You shouldn't settle for any less than that either, Bray."

"None of my lovers have ever elicited an emotion anywhere near what you describe." He sighed. "I think I'm incapable of romantic love."

Raven lowered his lids, concealing his expression. "None of them? What about Kania? Don't tell me you didn't love her."

Braden sighed, aware of an insistent regret for the loss of the only woman he'd ever loved. He closed his eyes. "I did love her. Hell, I might always love her." Much as Seneka would probably always love his late first wife.

"But?"

"But I didn't feel the same deep-seated need for her Neka feels for Autumn." *Or I wouldn't have allowed another man to steal her away from me.*

"Are you sure? When she married another man, I…"

Hearing the disquiet in Raven's voice, Braden opened his eyes. "You thought I'd lose it?" He inhaled slowly. "Honestly, when she told me she was pregnant and had already married another man, I'll admit, it hurt like hell and I…damn. It hurt. It still hurts. There's a part of my heart that she owned that feels bruised and battered beyond repair."

Raven swallowed and raked a hand through his hair. "It's only been seven months. That's not a lot of time to recover from losing the only woman you ever loved, Bray—especially when she's pregnant with a child that should have been yours. I know you're still hurting, but you can't give up on love."

If he hadn't been foolish enough to think she'd wait indefinitely for him, he wouldn't have blown his one chance with her. Since he had, he had little illusions or hope of ever falling in love again. Hell, he'd go out of his way to guard his heart so he didn't. Losing love hurt and he sure as hell had no desire to repeat the experience.

"I'll admit my heart is still a little bruised and I'm not great, but I'm not miserable either. I'll get over her."

"Then? Or should I say but?"

"But now that she's out of my reach, I'm not interested in having my heart torn to shreds again. As ridiculous as it sounds, I think I'm one of those men who only loves once. And Kania was it for me."

"I know you loved her, but you can love a woman without her being your wyanet."

"What?"

"If she'd been your wyanet, you wouldn't have allowed her to slip through your fingers." Raven lowered his lids briefly and glanced down at his nails. "Unless there's a really good reason to suppress your feelings."

Braden narrowed his gaze. "Ray? Are you speaking from experience?"

Raven inhaled slowly before he raised his lids and shrugged. "Some conventions are sacrosanct."

"Such as?"

Raven shook his head. "It doesn't matter. My point was that once you meet your wyanet, she'll heal your heart and you'll find you have the same capacity to fall in love again as any other man. Sometimes love starts out as a deep and overwhelming passion, much like I know you're feeling for the current object of your desire."

Raven's use of the word wyanet, the endearment the Elkhorn men used as an endearment for the special women in their lives, surprised Braden. Yet, the woman from the restaurant's breathtaking beauty certainly made the term, which roughly translated as legendary beauty, appropriate—at least on a physical level.

He sighed. "She is beautiful."

"But?"

"But she's also young and very shy."

Raven smiled. "Young and shy sounds like charming qualities in a woman."

"She's also inexperienced."

Raven arched a brow. "Never say you think she's a virgin."

Noting the spark of interest in his brother eyes, Braden shrugged. "I don't know if I'd go that far. However, I'm fairly sure she's hasn't had many lovers."

"Young, beautiful, shy and a near virgin? I don't see a downside, Bray."

"I'm not so sure about that. She probably deserves a man who—"

"Wyanet deserves a man who can fully appreciate her beauty and skillfully draw her out of her shyness and introduce her to a world of sensual delights. Imagine having the opportunity to indoctrinate her into the joys of love and deep devotion."

Braden inhaled quickly at the picture the words conjured in his mind. But he had to marry a Native woman. He had to. He shook his head.

"You'll have a troubled spirit until you satisfy your needs with her."

Even as he hungered to get to know her and to make love to her, the thought of pursuing her solely to satisfy his carnal passions felt wrong. He shook his head again. His ability to make the right decision when it came to women lately had been sadly deficient. First, he lost Kania to another man. Then he'd nearly come between Neka and Autumn. And now he hungered for a woman his instincts told him he should leave alone—given his determination to marry a Native woman.

"I don't think she's into casual sex and even if she were, I have no desire to use her."

"Commendable. What's her name?"

"What makes you think I know her name?"

Raven shrugged. "Oh I don't know. Maybe the fact that you've spent the last four mornings haunting the restaurant where you first saw her — even though you don't eat breakfast."

"Her name is Neida."

Raven stared at him. "Oneida or just Neida?"

"Oneida," he admitted.

Raven smiled. "There you go. The spirits have spoken."

Maybe so, but they didn't feel the burden he felt to marry within his own cultural and racial group. "I can't get serious about her, Raven."

"Yes you can."

"No. I can't. I'm going to marry a Native American woman."

"Even if a black one owns your heart and passion?"

"She definitely has me hot, but that's lust, Ray. Not love."

"Fine. If you don't love her, have a fling with her."

"I told you I don't think she's into casual sex."

"Have you ever met a heterosexual woman who didn't enjoy spending time with a single, rich male so consumed with desire for her that he's prepared to pamper and adore her as if she were the only woman on earth worth knowing?"

Braden sighed. "It shows, huh?"

"How many years have you spent dating Native women Mom approved of but who clearly were not your wyanet? It's time for some selfish, lust-inspiring dating, Bray."

"This isn't the time to lose my head over a woman. Not when we're so close to getting a deal done on the acquisition and—"

"Do what you do best, Bray. Design software. Let me do what I do best. Leave the acquisition to me and pursue wyanet or should I say sheenea?"

"I didn't say I felt she was my sheenea, Ray. Hell, I don't even know if I believe in the concept. I leave that mystic shit to the Grayhawks," he said of another family of area Cherokees they'd known for years. "They must be rubbing off on you."

"Surely you agree that the concept of a sheenea is an intriguing one. And you have to admit Layton, Randall, and Peyton seem very happy with their sheeneas. I'm thinking the Grayhawks know how to land the right woman. Besides, I've never seen you obsess over any other woman other than Kania."

Bray ran a hand through his hair. "We know how well my obsession for her worked out."

"We know why it didn't work out," Raven countered. "Because you allowed your feelings of cultural obligation to outweigh your emotional needs and debt to yourself, Bray. You could have been the father of the baby Kania's having."

"Well, I'm not and if you don't mind, I'd prefer not to discuss her." Or her child who would never call him dad.

"Fine. Let's discuss Oneida. Despite all the other women vying for your attention, you want her. Why? I think your spirit knows she's the one person in the world who can help you get over Kania while completing you." Raven arched a brow. "Wouldn't that make her your sheenea?"

"I'm not going to be held hostage by lust."

Raven laughed. "Oh give it up, Bray. We both know we're not just talking about your average, garden variety lust with her."

Aware that Raven knew him better than anyone else, he narrowed his gaze. "Are you implying I feel something more than lust for a woman I've never even spoken to and only seen two times?"

"Do you?"

"How can I when I don't know her?"

"Don't think I didn't notice that you didn't actually answer my question, Bray, but not knowing her is easily remedied."

He sighed. "Please don't do that, Raven."

"Don't do what?"

"This is a time when I need you to encourage me to do the right thing."

"I've rarely known you to do otherwise, Bray."

"I've never been nearly as perfect as you've given me credit for. I nearly interfered with Neka's relationship with Autumn and—"

Raven held up a hand. "You're giving yourself way too much credit. There's no way in hell you were going to take Autumn from Neka. Yeah, you beguiled her for a few days but why in the hell would she have settled for your lust when Neka had that and so much more to give her? Those two were born to love and adore each other. So don't let Oneida's charms make you lose your grip on reality."

He laughed. "That's exactly what will happen if I see her. When I look at her, I lose my ability to think rationally and everything is shot to hell. Then, even though I know it's not wise, I just want to do what feels good."

"Then do. You're entitled and she's an adult. Who's to say she wouldn't be interested in a casual affair with you?"

"My instincts."

Raven shrugged. "I know they generally serve you well, but there's a first time for everything. I have an idea. Send her some sexy lingerie. Something that will leave her in no doubt as to what you want. If she doesn't slap you or give you a piece of her mind when you meet again, you'll know she's not necessarily averse to a casual affair. Assuming, of course, that's really all you're interested in."

Before Braden could respond, the phone rang. He picked it up. "Hello?"

"Mr. Elkhorn?"

"Which one did you want?"

"The tall, hunky one who had breakfast at Becky's this morning. You know the one with gorgeous dark brown hair and a tight ass."

He didn't recognize the female voice. He hesitated and then decided to yield to the inner instinct which rarely led him astray. "I was at Becky's this morning and I have brown hair," he spoke in a guarded voice.

"Is your brown hair gorgeous and do you have a tight ass?"

He laughed.

"I'll take that as a yes. I knew I'd find you."

He arched his brow, intrigued. The woman on the other end sounded Caucasian, so she wasn't Oneida. But she might be her companion. "Was I lost?"

"Droll. Very droll. A sense of humor, however

misplaced, can be a charming quality in a sexy, single man. You are single. Aren't you?"

"Yes. I am."

"Thank God!"

He remained silent, although he was nearly certain he was speaking to the woman who had accompanied Oneida at the restaurant.

"We need to talk, Mr. Elkhorn," the woman went on.

"About?"

"I'll tell you when we come up to your suite." She hung up before he could ask who *we* included.

"Who was that?" Raven asked when he put the phone down.

"A woman."

Raven sat forward in his seat. "Wyanet?"

Didn't he wish? "No."

"Then who?"

Braden shrugged and stood up. "We'll find out shortly. They're on their way up here."

"They?" Raven smiled. "One for each of us?"

Braden shook his head. "You can have them both."

"Lost all interest in sex with other women already?"

"I wouldn't count on that, Ray."

"Then why the outright dismissal?"

"I'm forty, not twenty, Ray. At some point a man has to learn he doesn't have to fuck every willing woman he meets."

"That's not what you said at Max Stoner's last fuck jam."

Recalling the three women he'd slept with during that long weekend, he gave Raven a cool look. "Fuck off," he said, straightened his tie, and waited for the knock at their suite door.

Chapter Three

Late Friday night, Neida lay staring up at the dark ceiling in her bedroom for longer than usual before she finally drifted into a series of wild dreams that culminated in her lying bound to a bondage rack while the sexy stranger from Becky's mounted her and fucked her until she couldn't stop sobbing with pleasure as she shuddered through multiple orgasms.

She woke in the morning with her lips parted, as if pursed to receive a kiss that never came. The bottom of her pajamas was wet. Her pussy ached. She groaned and rolled onto her stomach. *Neida, girl, yes, you need a fuck, but you have to get a grip. You're not going to see him again. Deal with it and don't think you're going to become obsessed with him.*

The certainty that she wouldn't see him again only served to fuel her desire to lose herself in endless fantasies which all ended with him fucking her with wild abandon. Slipping out of bed, she tried to rein in her daydreams by telling herself he'd probably been in Philly on business and might have already left. But even if he were still in town, there was bound to be some lucky tiny woman who'd already staked a claim on him.

After a quick shower, she dressed and had a light breakfast. Then her thoughts turned back to him. Thinking of him with another woman sent a shock of despair through her. She paused in her cleaning to imagine herself held in his arms as they slow danced to music soft and sensual enough to put them both in the mood to spend the night making love.

It had been so long since she'd had sex she felt

ready to burst. Her last relationship with a police officer ended a year earlier when she realized he was on the verge of proposing.

She and Pete Tyson had dated exclusively for two years. He'd been a kind and considerate lover of whom her parents had approved. If not for Neida's hidden yearning to have at least a one-night stand with a man of Native American ancestry, she could easily have fallen in love with Pete and happily bore him the children they both wanted.

Unwilling to risk hurting him, she'd broken up with him and had since been lonely and sexless. Now that she was fixated on the handsome stranger from Becky's, she knew ending her relationship with Pete had been wise. If only fate would be kind enough to somehow arrange things so that she got to spend one night or even a few hours with the object of her lust.

Yeah. Right. Like you have a hope in hell of that happening. You can't have him, but you've never had any trouble having any other man you want. Don't get greedy, girl. Settle for the men who want you and stop wasting your time and energy pining for those who don't.

Her apartment bell rang. She put her dust rag aside and went to answer the door. The delivery man handed her a large, flat package and two shoe box-sized ones.

"Who are these from?" she asked as she signed for the packages.

"The name on the large one is Discriminating Lingerie. The smaller is from Sassy Shoes."

Only wealthy women could afford to shop at the elite lingerie boutique or the equally outrageously priced shoe store. Neida sighed and pushed the boxes back at him. "Then you have the wrong address."

"You're Neida Armstrong?"

She nodded.

He placed the boxes back in her hands. "Then these *are* for you. Have a good day, ma'am."

Back inside her apartment, Neida placed the shoe box on the hall table and stood turning the other beautifully wrapped box with black and maroon wrapping paper, over. The card must be inside. She frowned. Her birthday had been in January. Who would have the money or desire to send her anything from the outrageously priced intimate apparel boutique and exquisite shoe store?

For a moment, she wondered if Pete had sent them. It had taken him several weeks to accept her decision to end their relationship as final. She shook her head. Even if he'd decided to make another attempt to restart their relationship after eight months of silence, he couldn't afford a present from even one of the stores. Who did that leave?

Open the boxes and find out.

She tore the wrapping paper away and lifted the lid from the larger box. Inside, on white tissue-like paper, laid an apple-green piece of lace lingerie. She lifted it and held it up. The chemise felt soft and silky. It had scalloped lace trim, lace-up sides and spaghetti straps. She held it against her body and moved across the small entranceway to the mirror hanging above the hall table.

The sinfully soft and decadent piece of underwear would highlight her breasts and long legs. Staring at herself and imagining how she'd look in it, she suddenly knew the stranger from Becky's had sent it to her.

As the certainty filled her, her cheeks burned and her heart raced with excitement. Yes! She smiled at her reflection. *Neida girl, it looks like he's at least interested in a one-night stand with you wearing this beautiful chemise.*

Still smiling, she laid the garment on the table and went back to the box to look for the card. It nestled among the silk tissue paper. Her hands shook as she read it.

From an ardent admirer left bereft of words by your exquisite beauty.

She sucked in a breath, her smile turning into a wide grin. Her exquisite beauty? Most of the men she'd known had considered her worth a second look. Some had called her pretty. Others had thought her attractive. None had actually called her beautiful.

She sank down into the chair by the hall table to open the other box. Oh hell yeah! It contained a pair of designer patent leather black shoes with open toes, ankle-high straps and 3" heels that she knew cost roughly five times what she normally paid for shoes.

The remaining box contained a black and gold matte suede bag with a golden shoulder strap that she knew cost as much as the exquisite shoes. She read the accompanying card.

This bag and the accompanying shoes are almost superb enough to grace your feet and showcase your long, lovely legs. BE

How soon would he call her? What did BE stand for? What tribe was he from? Navaho? Apache? Would he expect anal sex? Would BE spank her ass until it stung? How many times would they be able to have sex during their one-night stand?

Sitting there imagining herself posing before him in the chemise and shoes while he stood facing her, naked and erect, with his hand raised to spank her ass, aroused her.

She licked her lips. Though shyness had prevented her from confessing her most intimate needs and desires to her two lovers, she had a feeling her tall, dark, gorgeous brave would fully satisfy her. He might even know what she wanted and needed without her having to ask for it.

Would he want her to do all the things her mother had warned her that ladies never allowed men to do to them, including spanking her ass and insisting she suck his cock?

Giving herself a mental shake, she reached for the phone on the hall table. She called Betty to tell her about her anonymous gifts.

"The shoes and bag probably cost nearly $2,000 dollars and the chemise…what? About $200 or $300? Oh Neida, there are definite benefits to capturing the attention of a handsome, rich man."

"We don't actually know he sent the presents."

"Oh yes we do."

"He doesn't know my name or where I live."

"I wouldn't be so sure of that, if I were you, Neida."

She frowned. "Why do you sound so certain?"

"Because I am."

"Dare I ask why?"

"No. You don't dare because you probably don't want to know what I've been up to."

She bit her lip. "Good or bad?"

"Good. Believe me."

"Fine. How do you know he's rich?"

"Do the math, Neida. Both times we saw him, he wore an expensive suit that was clearly tailor made and must have cost a fortune. And did you notice his shoes? They probably cost a good $700 or $800 dollars. He's rich all right and he has the hots for you!"

"Bett—"

"Oh Neida. I knew you were gorgeous enough to land a really worthwhile man."

"Mark is worthwhile," she protested.

"Of course he is, but that wasn't fated to work out."

Betty was probably right. "Well, Pete was worthwhile too."

"Oh don't get me wrong, Pete's a great guy, but we both know you didn't love him."

"I'm not in love with this BE either."

"Maybe not, but you can't deny he inflames your passions in a way Pete never could. And before you toss Mark's name at me again, let's be honest. You're older now and more passionate. Your handsome brave speaks to that passion as no other man in your life has. I'll bet just the thought of being alone with him gets you hot and wet."

"You have no idea," she admitted.

"Oh yes, I do. Just thinking about Jack naked and aroused is still enough to make me burn with need. The longer we're married, the stronger my love and desire for him and I know he feels the same way."

Neida sighed. "You're so lucky to feel that way after five years of marriage, Bett."

"Yes, I am and you'll get a chance to feel the same about your BE, Neida."

"He sent me sexy underwear and hooker shoes. He

wants sex, Bett, not a relationship."

"You know hooker heels are much higher than the ones he sent you. So let's not go there. Now please tell me you're going to give it to him."

God help her. "I am."

"Now you're talking, Neida. He may only want a one-nighter now, but if you sex him up good enough, he'll keep coming back for more until he realizes he's hooked and wants you all for himself—forever."

Forever? Be still my heart. "That's not going to happen, Bett. I have to concentrate on getting up the nerve to spend a wild night with him. If that happens, I'm going to keep my eyes open and my expectations real."

"Oh Neida. You can't settle for a one-nighter. You deserve more than that—at least in the long run."

"I know I deserve more, but sometimes you have to settle for what you can get. And I'd happily settle for a one-nighter with him."

To her surprise, Betty sighed and said goodbye.

* * *

Neida finished cleaning, had a light lunch, and then settled down on her sofa with her smartphone to finish reading an erotic romance from her favorite online publisher. Within minutes of starting the first love scene, she closed her eyes and imagined herself as the lucky heroine lying over the hero's naked thighs, gasping with delight as he repeatedly brought his large palm down onto her ass cheeks.

Then, with them stinging, he lubed his finger and slipped it down her crack. Feeling his finger pressing against her ass, she moaned. "Oh…please…"

"Please what?"

"Stick it in me," she pleaded. "I need to feel some part of you inside of me before I burst."

"We can't have that." The hint of laughter in his voice teased and pleased her.

As he eased his finger into her, he bent to press his warm lips against her neck and shoulders. He finger fucked her slowly while nibbling and licking at her neck, sending shivers of longing and anticipation through her.

He continued sliding his finger in and out of her ass until she started to rub her wet pussy against him, in an agony of need.

"Please," she begged.

He lightly bit into her shoulder before sitting her on her feet and slowly rose.

Naked and aroused, he was the most beautiful man she's ever seen. With her passions aroused and her knees knocking, she leaned against his chest.

Neida lapped at his nipples and slid her palms down his abs. Feeling his pubic hair against her fingertips, she paused for a moment. She allowed her excitement to build before she trailed her fingers down his body in search of his cock. Just as her fingers were about to close around his hard flesh—

Brring!

Neida sat up with a jolt, her eyes opening. For a moment she was confused. She heard the phone ring again. Glancing down, she saw her smartphone lying on the carpet by the sofa. Oh hell. She'd fallen asleep. A dream. It had been a dream.

The phone on the end table near the sofa rang again, startling her. She reached for it, glanced at the caller I.D. screen and answered it. "Hello, Bett."

"Were you asleep?"

"I was reading and drifted off."

"Boring book?"

"Just the opposite."

"Oh? Well, never mind your book now. I'm calling to invite you to dinner tonight."

Neida, eager to lose herself in the book again in the hopes of drifting back into another erotic dream, shook her head. "Thanks, but I'm in the middle of reading this sexy romance I want to finish."

"You can read anytime, Neida. Tonight, you're having dinner at our house."

She shook her head. "Not tonight, Bett—"

"I'm not taking no for an answer."

She smiled. "When do you ever take no for an answer?"

"Never mind the smart remarks. Jack needs cheering up and you know how he thinks you have an infectious smile and laughter. So wear that new mauve dress that hugs your rump and shows off your cleavage and those legs. Jack says you're a knockout in that dress."

"Does he?"

"Damn straight and you know it."

"And you know I like Jack, but if he needs cheering up, why don't you wear something mauve colored? Isn't he always going on about how you're a vision in anything you wear?"

"Neida!"

"What?"

"Look girl, I am not in the mood for any of your nonsense tonight so don't give me any!"

Neida blinked, surprised at Betty's anger. "You're

not in the mood for my nonsense? Don't get your thong in a twist. If it means that much to you, I'll come to dinner tomorrow."

"No, Neida. Jack's depressed tonight. So you need to come tonight. So get your ass here tonight and you'd better arrive wearing that damned mauve dress or else."

She could hear frustration under Betty's anger. Jack must really be depressed. "No need to bite my head off, Bett," she told her. "I'll be there and I'll bring the damned mauve dress with me."

"Don't bring it. Wear it!"

"Fine, you royal pain in the ass. I'll wear it."

"Great!" Having gotten her way, Betty sounded pleased. "I'll see you at six-thirty."

"I'll be there." Neida hung up and turned her attention back to the chapter she'd been reading before Betty's call. The further she got into the love scene, the hornier she became. By the time she finished the scene, she needed a cool shower. She decided to save the rest of the book for Sunday when she could read it without interruptions which would allow her to more fully appreciate and enjoy the love scenes.

She poured her favorite bath salts and oils into very warm water. Sliding into the tub, she enjoyed a long, soothing soak before she dressed. Studying her reflection, she decided the mauve dress worked well with her skin tone. After a brief hesitation, she kicked off the two-inch heels and slipped on the three-inch shoes *he'd* sent. Wearing them made her feel sexy as hell. Satisfied she looked her best, she left her apartment for Betty's and Jack's house.

Betty let out a wolf whistle when she answered her

front door. "Now that's what I'm talking about. You look sexy as hell, girl. Those shoes and that bag are worth every penny he paid for them."

Neida grinned. "Yeah?"

"Oh hell yeah, girl!"

"I wasn't sure I should wear them."

"You'll be glad you did."

"You think Jack will like them?"

Betty winked at her. "Of course he will. Well, come in and let's get the evening started." She reached out, grabbed Neida's hand, and practically snatched her into the house. Betty closed the door and gave her a quick once over. "Wow. You're ready to impress the hell out of him and make him rock hard."

Neida frowned as she placed her handbag on the hall table. "Hey, don't go overboard. You do know that Jack's already very happily married don't you?"

Betty laughed. "If I have anything to say about it, you're going to soon have a Jack of your own with the initials BE."

"Don't start that again, Bett."

"Fine. Have it your way. Be a wet blanket. See if I care."

"It'll be a cold day in hell before you get your nose out of my business."

"That's what friends are for, Neida."

She nodded. "I know and believe me, I wouldn't have you any other way."

Betty tilted her head. "So we're still best friends forever?"

"Always, girl."

"Good. Remember that if you don't like my surprise."

"Surprise? What surprise?"

"Come and see." Betty swept her down the hall towards the living room. Soft jazz drifted down the hall.

She smiled at Betty. "You and Jack in the slow dancing mood?"

"I have to finish dinner. Do me a favor and dance with him."

Neida arched a brow. "That's not dance music, Bett. That's slow grind music."

"Don't I know it? I picked and programmed the stereo system very carefully."

"Well I'm not slow grinding with Jack."

"Damn right you're not. His slow grinds are all mine."

Neida grinned at her. "Have you been sampling the cooking sherry again?"

"Never mind your smart remarks." At the living room door, Betty gave her a gentle shove into the room. "Surprise!"

Surprise indeed. The sole occupant of the room was not Jack, as Neida expected, but the tall, sexy hunk she'd first seen at Becky's.

The dark suit he wore emphasized his wide shoulders. His white shirt was open at the neck leaving her longing to undo the rest of the buttons to expose his chest.

Neida stood staring at him with wide eyes and a racing heartbeat. Seeing him again felt like destiny. Surely he felt it too.

"Oneida Armstrong, this is Braden Elkhorn."

BE. Braden Elkhorn. *Thank you, God!*

"Braden, this is Neida. As you can see, she's a

stunningly gorgeous black woman with curves in all the right places."

Neida's cheeks burned. "Bett!"

"Oh yes." He nodded. "A blind man could see that."

Betty's smile widened. "Neida, Braden's Cherokee."

Neida turned to gape at Betty, who gave her a Don't-mess-with-me-cause-I-don't-take-any-prisoners look. "Neida, keep Braden company while Jack and I put the finishing touches on dinner." Grinning like the cat that ate the last tasty canary, Betty danced out the room humming happily.

Neida swallowed several times, trying to think of something witty or sexy to say before she gave herself a mental shake. *This is your chance to wow him, Neida. Do not blow this.*

His smile quickly spread from his lips up to his eyes as he crossed the room to her. "I'm delighted to meet you, Oneida." His warm, well-modulated voice danced over her skin with all the allure of a silken caress. He glanced briefly down at her feet before meeting her gaze again.

"Everyone calls me Neida."

"Do they? Are you aware of what Oneida means?"

"Something along the lines of eagerly awaited or sought one."

He nodded. "Yes, it does, Oneida."

She'd never particularly liked her name, but he made it sound like a secret, sensual caress. She felt hot and almost dizzy with excitement. For a long moment she felt tongue-tied. Then she imagined him kissing her breathless under a full moon. With that erotic image playing havoc with her senses, she spoke without thinking. "I can't tell you how glad I am to see you again."

"Ahhh." He sounded pleased. "I'm delighted to hear that."

Her cheeks burned as she realized she'd spoken aloud. "I...didn't mean...oh God."

"It sounded heartfelt. I hope you did mean it because I'm equally delighted to see you again."

"You are?"

"Absolutely. I'm a normal man and you're a woman of rare and exquisite beauty, as you must know."

"I'm very glad you think so."

"How could I not?" He extended his hand.

She forced herself to meet his gaze as she placed her hand in his. She tingled all over when his fingers closed around hers.

He lifted her hand and pressed his warm lips to her fingers. "You're wearing the shoes. They look exquisite on you—just as I knew they would."

Although her cheeks burned, she forced herself to meet his gaze. "I carried the bag as well. I left it in the hall."

"Did you know I'd sent them?"

"I hoped you had."

"Did the thought please you?"

Thrilled was more like it. She nodded, wondering how he'd gauged her shoe size so accurately. "Yes and they're both so beautiful."

"As are you."

Oh hell yes! She smiled.

He pressed his lips against her fingers again before

he released her hand. "Can I assume you like the shoes?"

Although they were an inch higher than the heels she normally wore, they made her legs look great. "It would be difficult not to. They're soft and supple…exquisite."

"Like their owner."

Hell to the yes! "Which one? Soft? Supple? Exquisite?"

He brushed his fingers against her cheek. "All of the above and so much more."

She moistened her lip. "I don't usually accept gifts from strangers, but—"

"Oh we're not going to be strangers for much longer." He trailed his fingers down the side of her neck, pushing her long dark hair, which fell past her shoulders aside. He turned to gesture to the sofa. "Let's talk."

Chapter Four

She walked to the sofa and sank down onto it.

He sat beside her, sitting close enough to excite her but not so close that his thigh touched hers. "Your friend told me you're not married or seeing anyone."

What would he say or think if she told him she'd been waiting for him? "I'm not."

"And you're a teacher?"

"Yes. I teach science and math at the middle school level."

"Ah. You're clearly the perfect woman; beautiful, intelligent, and intriguing."

She smiled, pleased.

"Do you have brothers or sisters?"

"I'm an only child. My father died last year so it's just me and my mother now."

"I'm sorry. My father is dead as well."

"And your mother?"

"She's still living." He raked a hand through his hair. "Do you have any plans for summer vacation?"

"I usually spend the first two weeks sleeping late. After that, I play it by ear."

"No firm plans for a trip or two?"

She shook her head. "I hate having my student loans hanging over my head so I'm forgoing vacations for a few more years so I can pay them off sooner."

"Practical *and* beautiful. That's a lethal and irresistible combination. "

She flashed him a quick smile. "So you're Cherokee?"

"I might look Cherokee, but it's only skin deep."

"What do you mean?"

He shrugged. "Both my parents were Cherokee, but I'm afraid they raised my brothers and I totally mainstreamed. I'm so Americanized that I only know a few Cherokee phases."

"You don't speak Tsalagi?"

"I have a passing ability to speak two other languages besides English, but Tsalagi isn't one of them."

"Which two languages?"

"Spanish and after a fashion — French."

"You're tri-lingual? I'm impressed."

"Don't be. I can easily read both languages." He arched a brow. "However, even though I spent at least part of my summers in New Orleans before, during, and after I learned French, I speak and sing Spanish more fluently. My butchered French has a decided Cajun flare to it. So maybe I should say I speak one other language and read two besides English, shâ chére."

She frowned. She hadn't made much effort to maintain her college-level French but remembered enough to know he'd just used a term of endearment. And sounded sexy as hell doing it. Who cared if it were butchered or not? "Shâ chére?"

"Look it up," he suggested.

"How can I if it's butchered?"

He laughed. "Oh it's butchered all right, but women seem to like hearing my butchered French. Do you think you might?"

"I'm a woman."

"Yes. I've noticed that about you."

She smiled.

"Oh damn, you have beautiful smile. If you like,

I'm sure I can learn to butcher Spanish for you as well."

"For me?"

"For you, querida."

Darling? Already? *Be still my heart.* She felt almost happy enough to float away. "But what if I wanted to hear something sweet in Tsalagi?"

"I'll learn."

"You will?"

"Yes. I will. While I'm doing that, I hope knowing I don't speak Tsalagi doesn't lessen my allure for you."

She had a feeling nothing on earth could lessen the allure of a man who could sweet or dirty talk her in three languages. "No."

He smiled. "I'm very glad to hear that, Oneida since I'll probably butcher that as well."

"The ability to butcher a language can be an irresistible attraction—in the right man…mon ami'."

"Mon ami'? Oh no. Friendship isn't going to satisfy me."

Me either, mon cher. "It's a starting point, Braden. Where do you live?"

"In California."

Oh hell! "You're here on business?"

He nodded.

"How long are you going to be here?"

"I design software. I can basically do my job anywhere there's a computer. How long I stay in Philly this go round depends."

"On what?"

He shrugged. "On a number of factors."

Something about the way he looked at her, led her to believe she was or could be one of those factors. "What brought you here tonight?"

"You haven't used my name once. In case you've forgotten—"

"I haven't."

"It's Braden. Braden Elkhorn and I'm here to see you," he told her.

Oh hell yeah! "I know this is Betty's doing, but how did she manage your presence here?"

"Once I knew you'd be here it would have taken an act of God to keep me away."

Oh my. My. The night kept getting better and better.

He rose and extended his hand. "Dance with me."

She looked up at him. Oh damn he was a big, sexy man. "This isn't dance music. It's grind music."

His smile turned into a charming grin. "Then grind with me?"

The thought of her mother's reaction to her quick acceptance of such an offer sent a thrill of excitement through her. "I'd be delighted to," she said and eagerly placed her hand in his.

He drew her to her feet and away from the sofa. Pausing in the middle of the living room, he brushed his lips against her fingertips before he drew her close. When her body touched his, he slipped an arm around her waist.

She placed her hands against his shoulders, staring up at him with her lips parted and the tip of her tongue extended. She felt hot all over and consumed with need for him.

He bent his head until she felt his breath against her ear. "Are you old enough to tease and please me, Oneida? Because that's what you're doing."

"Yes."

"You look very young." He nibbled at her ear.

She shivered. "I'm 26."
He sighed.
"That's over 21," she said quickly.
He lifted his head to look down into her eyes. "Yes, but a little on the young side for me. I'm 40 years old."
"I don't have a particular preference for older men, but…"
"But?"
"But I like you and that wouldn't change even if you were sixty," she said.
"I'm flattered. Now tell me, querida, do you know what I want?"

His ability to arouse her most deep seated sexual passions in a way no other man ever had excited her. She supposed it was too much to expect him to romance her a little before he bedded her. Nevertheless, his lack of finesse disappointed her. She lowered her lids to conceal her expression. "I received the chemise. I know what you want."

"And are you going to give it to me?"
"Probably," she admitted.
"Good." He slowly guided her around the room.

She relaxed, pressing her cheek against his shoulder and closing her eyes. So he wasn't romantic. No one was perfect, but he sure came as close as possible — at least physically.

While they swayed together, he'd kept his hands on her waist.

Several minutes into their second dance, she became aware of his cock against her body. She sucked in a breath at its length and girth.

He nibbled at her ear while he slid his hands down her back below her waist to massage her ass cheeks before palming them.

Neida trembled, curling her hands into fists against his shoulders.

He traced the tip of his tongue around the top of her ear.

A rush of moisture flooded her thong. She slid her hands up his chest to link around his neck as she mindlessly pressed herself against his cock.

He sank his teeth in her earlobe. "I'm burning for you."

Yes!

"Are you going to give me what I need from you?"

"Head's up, you two. I'm ready to serve dinner!"

Betty's warning voice sounding in the hall snapped Neida out of her sexual haze. He was definitely going to get what he wanted, but not on the same night they met. And not in Betty and Jack's home. She pushed against his shoulders.

He swore softly. Although he released her, he locked his gaze on hers.

Neida took a deep breath and forced herself to look away from him. She turned to face the door.

Betty spoke again from the hall. "Come into the dining room when you two are ready," she called. "Jack and I will be waiting."

The hairs on the back of Neida's neck tingled moments before Braden placed his hands on her shoulders. He leaned down to touch his lips against her ear.

She trembled. The touch of his mouth filled her with longing. "They're waiting for us."

"Let them wait."

That thought process lead to sheer, unadulterated

lust. "We should join Betty and Jack." Before she lost her resolve not to part her legs for him the first night they met.

"Why don't we do that another time? Right now, I want you to leave with me."

That's what she'd prayed and hoped for — that he'd want to sleep with her. She was tempted, but realized she wanted more than his lust. If she left with him, that would be all she got. One night of lust. And now that she'd met him, she knew one night with him would leave her longing for a multitude more. If she could contain her desire so that it didn't overcome her commonsense, she might manage to maneuver him into a fling that extended over several weeks.

She shook her head and walked towards the door.

He followed her, placing a hand across the entrance.

Don't cave, Neida. She moistened her lips and turned to face him. "That's not a good idea."

"Why not?" he asked.

One look at his face convinced her he wasn't interested in the anything more than sex. She saw no evidence that he felt any of the emotional connection she did. "Meeting you has overwhelmed me and I —"

"Overwhelmed you?"

She nodded.

"I'm close to 6' 6." Do you mean my height?"

"No! I like that you're so tall."

"Then what about me overwhelms you?"

"Everything."

"Everything? Am I wasting both our times?"

"Oh no. I meant it when I said I was happy to see you, but I'm just a little overwhelmed."

"Happy, but overwhelmed?"

"Yes, but in a good way."

"Damn. You're too young." He turned away.

She reached out to catch his hand. "I may be young, but I'm a legal adult who knows what I want."

He withdrew his hand from hers but turned back to face her. "So do I but surrendering to that desire might not be good for either one of us."

"We can explore the possibilities together — later."

"There's no time like now."

"Later," she insisted.

He brushed the back of his hand against her cheek. "I'm getting the feeling you're reluctant to be alone with me because you know what I want."

"I knew what you wanted when you sent the chemise."

"But?"

"There's no real but except that I've never had a one-night stand."

"I view that as a good thing."

And I'm not going to start with you. I want more than one night. She smiled. "I'm glad to hear that."

"So you've never had a one-night stand and—"

"I'm not quite sure how to behave with a man like you."

"A man like me? I'm no different from other men, but you're different from other women I've met."

"Different in a good way?"

"You intrigue me but you're younger than I thought. Forgive me for asking, but are you a virgin?"

"No. Did you want or expect me to be?"

To her relief, he quickly shook his head. "The days when I had any interest in deflowering a virgin are in my distant past. However, virgin or not, I can see you're not used to fending off the sexual advances of older men."

She clenched her right hand at her side. *You're blowing it, Neida.* "I don't want to fend off you or your advances."

He arched a brow. "I think maybe a part of you does."

"I know what I want and fending you off isn't on my do-to list."

"It probably should be."

"Why?"

He shrugged. "Even if you're not feeling as conflicted as am I, there's no denying the fact that I'm too damned old to try to seduce you."

She placed a hand on his arm. "You're not too old and I want to be seduced. I just don't want it to happen within hours of our finally meeting."

"Of course you don't." He shook his head. "I'm not usually so lacking in finesse. There's something about you that completely disarms me."

"Does that need to be a bad thing?"

"Given the circumstances — yes."

"What circumstances?" She cast a quick look at his left hand. "You're not married. Are you?"

He shook his head.

"Are you engaged or close to it?"

"No. There's no one even remotely special in my life or I wouldn't be here with you."

"Then what circumstances are you referring to?"

"None that you need to concern yourself with other than the fact that I've behaved very badly with you and I'm sorry, Oneida."

"Please call me Neida and please understand that I don't want an apology," she told him.

He stared at her mouth for so long she leaned against him, raising her parted lips.

He sucked in a breath and raised his gaze to hers. "You deserve one. I had no right to send you such intimate apparel or to behave like a horny old pervert with you."

This is not going well. "Please don't mistake my momentary confusion for reluctance. I'm an adult who—"

He shook his head. "Who deserves to be treated with far more respect than I've shown you."

You're in danger of losing his interest. Get a grip. "You're misunderstanding me. I admit there was a moment when I wanted more, but—"

"You wanted more than what?"

She stroked her hand down his arm. "One night with you."

His jaw clenched. "That's all I have to offer."

She'd settle for one damn night when hell froze the fuck over! Not that she was about to admit that. She centered her gaze on his left shoulder. "Then I guess I'll have to settle for that."

He slipped a finger under her chin.

She reluctantly looked into his eyes but couldn't decipher his expression.

"You're a beautiful, sexy woman. You don't have to settle for anything from any man." He brushed his fingers against her cheek.

She turned her head and touched her lips to his fingertips. "I can't be the only one this feels right to," she whispered.

He inhaled sharply and slowly stepped away from her. "Let's go have dinner with your friend."

Looking into his determined gaze, she sighed. Despite her pleas and attempt to make things right with him, she'd blown it. She needed to summon the remnants of her pride and somehow get through the coming meal. Later, after she'd licked what felt like a dozen open wounds, she'd regroup and come up with a plan to lure him into an extended fling. She nodded and left the room.

* * *

Nice going, Elkhorn. She'll be crying in a few more minutes. He followed her from the room. In the hallway, he caught her hand and turned her to face him.

Her lips trembled and she kept her lids lowered. She looked sexy and yet so vulnerable, he longed to take her in his arms and promise her he'd make everything wrong in her life right. *Damn, Elkhorn. Get a grip.*

He cupped a palm over her cheek. "Neida?"

She raised her lids.

Her beautiful dark eyes glistened with tears.

"Please. Don't cry," he whispered.

She moistened her lips and laid her hands against his chest.

Her touch ignited a level of desire he'd only experienced with one other woman. But not even with Kania had his need for intimacy been so immediate and overpowering. Feeling as overwhelmed as she'd declared herself to be, he yielded to what felt like a primal need and bent his head. The moment he touched his mouth to her full, sweet lips, he felt a surge of need so powerful, he had to struggle to suppress a shudder.

She made a soft sound, her lips parting under his.

The warmth of her lips and the touch of her tongue against his snapped his remaining control. He slipped his arms around her and drew her closer. Feeling her voluptuous body pressed against his inflamed his senses.

He peppered her mouth with countless, nibbling kisses until he needed more. Then he settled his mouth over hers and kissed her with a hunger he made no effort to conceal or control.

She responded with an eager acceptance and enjoyment that sent his cock hardening against his thigh. Consumed with the necessity of feeling her wet pussy greedily closing around and holding his cock hostage, he turned her so she stood with her back to the wall.

He held her there with the weight of his body, giving her a moment to protest. Staring down into her dark gaze, he brushed his fingertips against her neck and breasts.

Instead of protesting, she slipped her fingers into his hair. Urging his mouth down to hers, she sucked at his tongue.

Oh shit! He slipped his hands down her body, loving the feel of her weight before sliding them up her dress. Trailing the tips of his fingers along the back of her thighs, he palmed her ass. Her thong left her ass cheeks readily accessible.

Damn, she had a perfect ass — big, warm, and round. The thought of feeling her bare cheeks on his naked thighs as he pushed his aching cock up into her pussy sent a jolt of pure need through him. Hungry to fuck her, he ground his fully erect cock against her.

She trembled and dragged her mouth from his.

Oh no you don't. Trailing his lips across her cheek, he devoured her mouth, thrusting his tongue between her lips.

She slid her hands up his chest. Moments later, he felt her fingers in his hair and her warm lips eagerly moving under his again. *Yes, querida. Get me even harder and then let me spend the night loving and adoring you. Hell, one night was not going to be enough.*

After several heated kisses that left him burning for her, he dragged his mouth from hers to nibble at her ear.

She stroked her hands down his back.

He longed to bare her breasts and suck her nipple between his lips as he thrust his aching cock as deep in her pussy as he could get it. "Oh God, I need to fuck you," he groaned.

She inhaled quickly, curling her fingers in his hair.

Taking that as a sign of encouragement, he worked his palms into her thong. Palming her bare ass cheeks, he pulled her against his cock.

"Ah!" She shuddered then suddenly shoved against his shoulders. "No," she gasped. "Not here."

"Would it help if I used a Spanish word for fuck? Joder?"

She caught her breath. "I love that you can talk dirty to me in other languages, but the ability isn't going to help your case right now. We can't."

"We can. Right here. Right now," he told her, resisting her efforts to push him away. Almost beyond the ability to think of anything except sex with her, he reached between their lower bodies to unzip his pants and free his cock. Then he pushed her thong down her thighs. He stroked her slit, rubbing his thumb against her clit.

Her hips jerked. "Oh God! Braden—"

"We'll talk later," he told her. "Right now I need to be inside you." Palming his cock, he slowly rubbed the head of his shaft along her slit. He pressed his thumb against her clit.

She moaned.

He inhaled slowly, sliding the head of his shaft along her slit. She was already wet and ready for him. And he had to have her. Immediately. He pressed the head of his shaft against her clit.

"Oh God!" she whispered. "You're going to make me come."

"That's the plan, querida." He pushed his hips forward, closing his eyes to fully savor the first exquisite sensation of feeling his cock slip between her outer lips to lodge just inside the wet, welcoming warmth of her pussy. Paradise.

"Braden!" She shoved against his shoulders and wiggled her hips in an effort to stop him from pushing any further into her. "No!"

The panic in her voice broke through his sexual stupor. Realizing he was seconds away from forcing himself on her, he froze. He took a slow, deep breath and lifted his head to stare down at her. "Please don't ask me to stop."

"I'm not asking, Braden."

Thank God. He bent his head and kissed her lips.

She turned her head away. "I'm not asking. I'm demanding you stop, Braden." She shoved against his shoulders again. "Please…" she whispered. "I don't do unsafe sex. I need you to pull out of me. Now. Right now, Braden."

Holding himself still with several inches of his cock inside her, he closed his eyes and leaned his forehead against hers. "I can't."

She slid her hands down his body to push against his hips. "It's not a request, Braden!"

No! She said no. He allowed her to shove him away. As his cock was pushed from her body, he felt as if all the air had been sucked out of his lungs. He turned to lean against the wall. He kept his eyes closed while he listened to the sounds of her struggling to pull up her thong. If he opened his eyes and actually saw her pussy…

Wrestling his desire under control, he pushed his cock back into his briefs and slid his zipper up. Then he raked his hands through his hair before he turned to look at her.

She averted her gaze.

Damn, Elkhorn, you are one smooth bastard. Not. "I'm sorry," he said, aware that an apology was totally inadequate for what he'd almost done. "I lost my head, but I didn't mean to—"

"I don't want an apology."

"What the hell do you want?" *Damn, Elkhorn, your lack of finesse is becoming embarrassing.* He inhaled slowly in an attempt to cool his ardor and control his frustrated desire.

"For you not to expect sex the first time we meet."

Damn. Why the hell couldn't he have fallen into lust with a woman prepared to hop into bed with him the moment they were alone? He inclined his head.

"We should go into the dining room before Betty comes looking for us."

He stared at her. The only thing he wanted to eat was her pussy. Since his control was tenuous at best and his mood lousy, he shook his head. "Make my apologies, will you?"

"Your apologies? You're overreacting, Braden."

So what the hell else was new? He pushed himself away from the wall and walked down the hall to the front door.

She followed him. "Wait. Where are you going?"

He pulled the door open before he glanced over his shoulder. "To get laid!" Ignoring the dismayed look on her beautiful face, he left the house, closing the door behind him. Once in his vehicle, he sat with his hands clenched on the steering wheel for several moments before he swore, started the engine, and drove away.

Chapter Five

Neida stood in the hall staring at the closed entrance door until she became aware of Betty slipping an arm around her shoulders. "Neida? What happened, hon?"

She sucked in an aching breath and turned to press her cheek against Betty's. "He…oh Bett, he's going to fuck someone else!"

"Damn the stupid bastard!" Betty rubbed her cheek against hers. "Come into the living room and tell me everything and then we'll figure out what our next step is."

She pulled away from Betty. "There is no next step. Because I objected to him fucking me without protection in your hallway, he left and said he was going to get laid!"

Betty's eyes sparked with rage. "That's your cock and if he knows what's good for him, he'd better keep it in his damned pants and out of strange women!"

Neida reluctantly allowed Betty to lead her down the hall to the living room.

Betty poured them both a drink and then sat beside her on the sofa. "Now. Tell me everything and we'll come up with a new plan to reel his big ass in."

* * *

Braden was annoyed to find Raven seated in the living room of their suite when he returned. He was dressed in jeans and a tee shirt with his notebook on his lap. Clearly he had no plans for the evening, which would give him all evening to concentrate on the coming cross examination. Damn it.

Raven sat his computer on an end table. "It didn't

go well?"

Braden removed his jacket and sank down onto the sofa. "No," he said shortly.

Raven sighed, raking a hand through his hair. "Do you want to talk about it?"

"No, I don't want to talk about it."

"It went that badly?"

"Yes."

"Sorry to hear that, but let's not have any I-don't-want-to-talk-about-it shit, Bray. We're both a little too old to start keeping secrets from each other."

He shot to his feet and glared at Raven, who remained seated. "Who the hell is keeping secrets?"

"Apparently—you."

"Why the hell would I want to discuss how my evening went with you?"

Raven shrugged. "Because we don't keep secrets and I asked you how it went."

"I told you how it went—badly."

"As you very well know, I work best with a lot of details."

"If I told you anymore, you'd encourage me to be selfish and find a reason to try to excuse the inexcusable!"

"What?"

"You excel at encouraging me to do what I want rather than what I should."

"What the fuck? Are you saying I'm a bad influence?"

"In a word? Yes!" he said and stalked across the living room and into his bedroom. He slammed the door shut. After a cold shower he might feel more rational and less prone to blow up at the slightest provocation.

He stripped and took a cold, five minute shower. Back in his bedroom, he put on a pair of briefs and a tee shirt and jeans before he returned to the living room.

Raven, still seated on the loveseat, glanced up but didn't speak.

But he knew Raven well enough to know he was annoyed — with good reason. He raked a hand through his hair. "I didn't mean that."

Raven nodded. "Yes. You did."

He sighed. "Okay, I did mean it, but it wasn't true."

"You're damned right it wasn't true." Raven rose and stalked across the room to place a hand on his shoulder. "You give me one good reason why I should discourage you from pursuing a relationship with the only woman you've shown any real interest in since Kania? Why the hell should I encourage you to walk away from her in favor of pursuing a relationship with some woman of whom Mom will approve, but who will leave you emotionally and sexually cold?"

"Can't you understand that she's too damned young and inexperienced for me?" He turned away.

Raven clasped a hand on the back of his neck. "She's an adult capable of making her own decisions, Bray."

He turned back to face Raven. "She deserves more than a man who's so consumed with lust for her he—"

Raven tightened his hand against the back of his neck. "Then give her more than your lust!"

"I can't!"

"You won't. There's a big difference between the two, Bray."

"Look, I'm really not in the mood for the same tired

argument, Raven. Someone in this family should date and marry a Native woman."

"I know that's what you and Mom want. Hell, intellectually, it's what we all probably wanted and expected. And in a perfect world, it's what would happen. But this world is far from perfect. Neka is the only one of us who hasn't always preferred women with dark skin. So how likely was it that one of us would fall for a Native woman?"

"In my case? Very likely."

"Braden! Come on! Even Neka has finally realized that a beautiful woman with lush curves and dark skin is the only way to go. I don't think I need to remind you that you're not getting any younger and that you've already given up one woman you love."

"Who the hell mentioned love?"

"Fine. Lust. Whatever the hell you feel for her, it's far more than you've felt for any other woman in a long time. You have a right to be with a woman who moves you as she does. Let's not forget that Mom defied her parents to run away and marry Dad because he was the love of her life. Do you really think she wants anything less for you?"

"No, but you're assuming a lot."

"Am I really, Braden? I've never seen you lose it over any woman no matter how beautiful. Hell, you didn't even lose it over Kani—and you swore you were in love with her. So why did you lose control with your charming young lady?"

He shook his head. "Don't imagine things, Raven."

"As you damn well know, I'm not given to imagining things. We both know Mom knows you prefer black women. She wouldn't want you to marry a woman you don't love just because she was Native American."

"Raven—"

"At least give yourself a chance to get to know your wyanet, Bray."

Given that the Elkhorn men reserved the use of the word wyanet as an endearment for the special woman in their lives, Raven's use of the term in reference to a woman he'd only met once should have sparked a protest. "I think I've pretty much blown the option to get to know her better."

"How?"

He sighed. "You're right about my lack of control with her."

"What happened tonight, Bray?"

"I came within seconds of raping her!" He swallowed hard. "Hell, you might as well say I did rape her since I penetrated her without consent."

Raven sucked in a breath. "Don't use that word, Bray."

"Why not?"

"Because I'm sure it's not appropriate!" Raven snapped. "Let's sit down and discuss this rationally."

"There's no point—"

"Bray! Please! You can't walk in and tell me you raped her and then expect me to just drop it. We have to talk about it."

"Fine, but talk won't change anything."

"Humor me."

They moved to sit on either end of the sofa. Braden didn't attempt to gloss over his behavior.

Raven listened to him without interruption.

When Raven didn't speak after he fell silent,

Braden arched a brow. "Well?"

"Get a grip. I'd hardly call what you describe rape and I seriously doubt if she would either. There's a big difference between sexual cajoling and forcible intercourse. What happened between you two was sexual cajoling at most."

"You reach that conclusion based on what?"

"She's an intelligent woman. Yes?"

"Yes."

"Well, an intelligent woman in her friend's home who felt she was being attacked would certainly have screamed to signal a need for help. Remember, I met the hubby too. He's nearly a match for you size wise. If she'd felt the need for help, she'd have called out and he'd have been on your ass pronto."

"She was probably shocked—"

"Shocked hell. She's a teacher. Young or not, there's probably not that much she hasn't seen or heard. What did she do when you released her? Did she scream abuse at you? Accuse you of rape? Slap you?"

"No."

"Did she jamb her knee into the family jewels?"

"I told you what she did."

"Which was to suggest you go into dinner? When you left instead, she was upset, not because she felt you'd forced yourself on her, but because she didn't want you to leave."

"You don't know that."

"I know you didn't rape or even attempt to rape her. Do I think you should have stopped at her first no? Hell yes. Do I think she considers what happened between you rape or near rape? Hell no or she would have been glad to see the back of your big, dumb ass."

"Then how do you explain—"

"Did you use a condom?"

He stared at Raven. "Did I use…no."

"The hell you say! Why not?"

"I didn't go there intending to fuck her so I didn't have one."

Raven slapped him on the back. "Any intelligent woman would object to a man she's not in an exclusive relationship with sticking his naked cock in her. Don't go anywhere near her again until you have protection. And the next time, romance her a little before you try to fuck her."

He raked both hands through his hair, aware of a feeling of incredible relief coursing through him. "You think that was her only objection?"

Raven shrugged. "She might also have had a slight objection to being fucked in her friend's house—standing up yet. Make sure you're alone the next time your dick wants to play. And even if you intend to sleep with someone else, don't tell her."

"Since I'm here talking to you only an hour after leaving her, I think you can deduce that I didn't sleep with anyone else."

"Did you intend to?"

He would have if he'd been thinking with anything other than his cock—the same cock that longed to dive deep inside her. "No."

"Ah, so not only does she have your heart, she has the full attention of your dick as well."

Braden felt the back of his neck burning. "I'm in lust with, not in love with her."

"Really?"

"Yes. Really. I haven't had a fuck in three months and I'm horny as hell. And another thing, Raven, I don't need or want advice on how to handle my love life from you or anyone else."

Raven arched a brow. "Of course you don't. I mean, look how well you've handled the situation with her so far."

Braden stared at him.

Raven stared back and then laughed.

Braden joined in.

* * *

After a meal that neither one of them enjoyed, Betty kissed Jack and she and Neida went into the living room to talk. "Oh my God, Neida. You made such an impression on him that he wanted a quickie in the hall?"

Neida nodded.

Betty stopped pacing in front of the sofa to sit beside her. "I've had time to think. So why didn't you give him one?"

Neida stomach muscles churned. She'd asked herself that repeatedly during dinner. "In your hallway?"

"We're talking about a hallway not a shrine or a church."

"He didn't have a condom on."

"Okay, that is a no-no." Betty gripped her hand, smiling. "Oh Neida. Girl, you are the bomb!"

"What?"

"He seemed so smooth and in control when Jack and I went to his hotel suite to talk to him. But a few moments alone with you was enough to peel away the thin veneer of civilization and bring out the savage beast in him!"

"He's not savage nor is he a beast."

"You can say that after the way he behaved? He actually expected a wall banger! Be honest. Did you want to give him one?"

"Bett!"

"I'll take that as a yes."

"Bett!"

Betty bit her lip and then burst into laughter.

After a few moments of feigned outrage, Neida laughed too. When they sobered, Betty narrowed her gaze. "Give him a few days or maybe until the school year ends and then go see him."

"That's almost two weeks away," she protested.

"And?"

"And he can sleep with an awful lot of women by then."

"He won't."

"Do I believe you because it's probably true or because I want to believe it?"

"It's true."

"So where would I contact him?"

"At the hotel suite he's sharing with his brother."

"He has a brother?"

"He has three of them. Jack and I met Raven, who is as handsome as your big, lusty brave. Raven is also very charming. Now, let's give you a drink for courage before you go home for a long soak. Once there, don't waste time lying sleepless and wondering who's sharing his bed."

"Some lucky hussy."

"He was bluffing you, Neida. He's not with anyone else."

"I wish I believed that."

"Believe it. If you'd seen the look in his eyes when I told him I came to set up a meeting with you, you'd know he's yours for the taking."

"Don't I wish?"

"You don't have to wish, Neida. Trust me. He may give you a run for your money and make you suffer a few sleepless nights, but his big ass is yours if you want it."

"Yeah? What about his cock?"

Betty blinked at her. "Why Neida, what would your mom say if she could hear you saying such things?"

"Are you planning to tell her?"

"No."

"Then how's she going to know?"

Betty smiled. "Now you're talking."

Two hours later, Neida arrived home to find a gigantic bouquet of flowers. The accompanying card bore three words: *Forgive me. Braden.*

Neida sat on her sofa staring at the flowers. What was he apologizing for? Did he regret trying to have unprotected sex with her? Or was he asking forgiveness for having slept with another woman after he left her?

Get real, Neida. He's free to sleep with whomever he likes without having to apologize to you. He doesn't owe you anything. Well, maybe he hadn't at the beginning of the night, but once he penetrated her...Recalling the exquisite feel of his cock sliding into her pussy sent a shiver through her.

She resisted the urge to drive to his hotel. If he hadn't contacted her by the beginning of summer vacation, she'd go see him.

* * *

The next morning, he sent her a huge box of assorted chocolates. The card bore his initials only. She took the chocolates to Betty and Jack's house. After lunch, Neida and Betty kicked off their shoes and sat on opposite ends of the reclining sofa with the chocolates on the middle cushion between them. They giggled like teenagers as they savored and lingered over each bite of the decadent chocolates.

"What did I tell you, Neida? He's yours for the taking."

"Either that or he has something to atone for."

"These are absolutely to die for." Betty took another bite of chocolate and sighed. "You're a hard case. What does it take to convince you he has the big time hots for you?"

"I know he has the hots for me. I just want him to feel a little more than that."

"Sex him up good enough and nature and his feelings will take it over and sweep him off his big size thirteen's and right into your arms." Betty took another bit of chocolate. "Speaking of big feet and other big things…does he have anything else big you want to discuss? Like the size of his cock?"

Recalling the feel of having the big head of his shaft lodged inside her, she moistened her lips. "Bett—"

"You know what they say about big feet and big cocks. It's deliciously too true in Jack's case. It is true in his?"

"I doubt if he's ever had any complaints."

Betty released a lusty sigh. "Gorgeous, rich, single, and big dicked. Oh Neida, he's everything you deserve and hell will freeze over before we let him get away."

"You're jumping the gun, Bett. I mean—"

"No, I'm not but that's enough talk about cock size from you. What in the world would your mother say if she could hear you?"

Neida smiled, her thoughts on Braden Elkhorn—and his cock.

"Are you staying for dinner, Neida?"

"Thanks but I want to go home and finish the book I'm reading." And imagine Braden fucking her as she read the love scenes. Now that she had intimate knowledge of how thick he was, her fantasies would be more accurate and even steamier. She left the chocolates with Betty, despite her protests. "I can't afford to eat any more of them but you can."

"He intended them for you, Neida."

"I've eaten as many of them as I dare. I'm sure he won't mind your enjoying them. So do."

Braden Elkhorn's behavior during the next nine days confused her. He sent her large bouquets of flowers, exotic fruit baskets, a gift certificate for two to a local spa and bottles of white and red wine. But he made no effort to contact her or ask her out. Just as she decided she'd have to make the next move, he called her one night, three days before her school year ended for the summer. "Hi Neida."

"Braden!" Thank you, God!

"I'm on my way back to Philly and I wondered if you'd have breakfast with me tomorrow morning."

"Back to Philly?"

"I spent a week in Tulsa and a few days home. I'll be back in Philly late tonight. I can't think of a better way to start the morning than having breakfast with you."

She could—having sex with him. "I have to work tomorrow."

"I know but I thought we could have a quick breakfast at Becky's. What time shall I pick you up?"

"Seven o'clock. I have to be to work at 7:45 so it'll probably have to be just coffee."

"Becky's opens at six," he countered. "I'll pick you up a little after six. That will give us at least an hour together."

"Okay."

"Have you forgiven me for my behavior the last time we saw each other?"

"Yes—as long as you don't maneuver me against one of Becky's walls and insist on a quickie."

"What do you have against a good, hard wall banger?"

Her cheeks burned. "I don't do them."

"You should try it. With the right person, it can be off the scale."

"I'm not fond of quickies. I want a man prepared to take his time with me."

"I can do that."

I'll just bet you can. "No quickies against the wall."

He laughed. "Resisting the impulse will be difficult but I'll manage."

"That's a start."

"I've missed you like hell and I'm so eager to see you again, I can almost taste it."

She smiled. "You almost sound like a drug addict."

"I feel like one with you."

The admission surprised and pleased her. "The feeling is mutual, Braden. Have a safe flight and I'll see you tomorrow morning."

"Good night, sha cheré."

"Good night, Braden. Dream of me tonight."

"I've done little else since we met. I doubt tonight will be any different."

Smiling, she hung up the phone. Surely a man who felt drugged with desire for her was hers for the taking. Hers for the taking. She had a feeling she was in for a long, hot, sensual summer. In bed she lay fantasizing about him for hours before finally drifting off to sleep.

Chapter Six

He arrived the next morning with a single red rose. "For you, querida."

"Thank you. It's beautiful."

"Not nearly as beautiful as you are."

She smiled and accepted it. "Do you know what a single red rose symbolizes?"

"Passion…eternal devotion…love… or so I've been told. And I think we both know I have an abundant passion for you." He bent his head and kissed the corner of her mouth.

She sucked in a breath and stepped back. "I think we both know it's a shared passion, Braden."

He lifted her fingers to his lips and kissed the tips. "I like the way you say my name, but then I like everything about you, lovely, sexy, querida."

And she liked being called darling by him in any language. She moistened her lips. "We'd better go."

"Did my behavior last time cost me your trust?"

"No!" She placed a hand on his arm. "You weren't the only one aroused."

"Then you don't feel I was too…"

"Too what?"

"Too forceful?"

"Too force…no! I liked that you were so…hot for me."

"If you were aroused too and you didn't object to my level of…insistence, then what was your objection?"

Her cheeks burned but she maintained his gaze. "I don't have unprotected sex and we weren't alone."

He sighed and caressed her cheek. "It won't

happen again, Neida."

Why did her name sound so sexy and exotic on his lips? "Which one? The attempt at unprotected sex or—"

He locked his gaze on her breasts. "I'll leave you to discover that for yourself."

"I might like that," she teased.

"I'm counting on that."

They stared at each other in silence for several moments before he bent his head.

Feeling his warm lips against her ear, she shook her head. "Braden, we don't have time—"

"Yes we do," he whispered and turned his head until she felt his lips brushing against hers.

Unable to resist the allure of his mouth so close, she leaned forward with her lips parted.

He kissed her slowly, teasing her mouth with an increasing heat. His hands slid down her back to her ass.

She arched into him, pressing her breasts against his chest.

He clutched her ass and pulled her closer. "Oh damn querida. You've totally bewitched me so that I can't think of anything or anyone but you."

She turned her head, searching for his mouth. When he kissed her again, she clung to him. Just the touch of his lips on hers set her blood burning and her body on fire. Pressing her against the wall, he sucked her tongue between his lips and slipped his hands up her dress to caress her bare ass cheeks.

Her pussy pulsed and flooded. As they exchanged several heated kisses, she felt his cock hardening against her.

If she didn't immediately stop him, she knew she

was only moments away from feeling his hard cock pushing into her flooded pussy. Recalling how good having the head of his naked shaft briefly inside her felt, she was tempted to let him push his entire length inside her—raw.

But such thoughts would give her far more trouble than she was prepared to handle. Tearing her lips away from his, she pressed her hands against his shoulders. "Braden!"

Resisting her efforts to push him away, he sucked at her neck and slipped his fingers into her thong to rub his thumb against her clit.

She experienced a jolt of desire so strong she was hard pressed not to part her legs and encourage him to thrust his bare cock deep inside her. "Braden!"

He sucked harder at her neck and slipped his fingers into her pussy.

Oh God! She longed to melt. "No, Braden! No!"

After a moment of continued resistance, he finally allowed her to push him away.

She gasped, placing a hand over her neck. "What the hell is wrong with you that you can't seem to take no for an answer?"

He leaned against the wall beside her, staring straight ahead. "I can take it—when it's meant."

"When it's meant? You arrogant bastard! If I say it, I expect you to respect it. If you think I'm going to spend all the time we're alone fighting you off—"

He turned his head to look at her. "We don't have time to waste playing games, Neida."

"What?"

"Let's not squander the time we have together pretending you're going to actually want to fight me off."

She stared at him, feeling her face burn.

He inhaled slowly, closed his eyes briefly, and then met her gaze. "But as you said, we'd better go." He offered her his arm.

"You expect me to go with you as if nothing's happened?"

He narrowed his gaze. "I expect you to act like the adult you claim to be and acknowledge that when two people who are sexually attracted to each other are alone, sometimes things get out of hand."

"Just because I'm attracted to you doesn't mean I expect you to push me against any available wall and stick either your finger or your cock into me the moment we're alone!"

He leaned down to stare into her eyes. "I'm older and far more experienced than you'll ever be. I happen to know that's exactly what you want and expect. I know you cherish the thought of the power you have to make me lose complete control when I'm alone with you. So don't give me any shit trying to prove otherwise, Neida."

She shoved at his shoulders, furious at his refusal to take her word at face value. "You're as conceited as you are arrogant, Braden," she snapped, making no effort to dissipate the tension angry tension building between them.

"If I am it's because that's what you want me to be."

"The hell it is!"

"And in case you haven't yet figured it out, let me be blunt." He leaned closer to speak with his lips against her ear. "I'm prepared to be whatever you want me to be, querida."

Hearing the endearment, her anger dissipated. She curled her hands into fists to keep from slipping her arms around him. "I don't care what you think you know about me, Braden, I'm not having sex with you this morning."

He lifted his head to look down at her. "Not even a quickie?"

"No!" She snapped and then inexplicably, she laughed.

He laughed too. With the remaining tension between them dissolved, he engulfed her in a brief bear hug. "Then we'd better go have breakfast while I'm still feeling strong enough to resist you, my sexy temptress." Inhaling slowly, he released her and offered her his arm.

She slipped her arm through him.

Twenty minutes later they sat facing each other at Becky's. She picked at an egg white vegetable omelet while he sipped a cup of black coffee.

"Braden?"

"Yes?"

"I know I have no right to ask, but I have to know."

"Then ask and if I can, I'll answer."

"Who did you sleep with the night you stormed out of Betty and Jack's house?"

He put down his cup. "I went back to my hotel alone."

She broke off a piece of toast. "You didn't call anyone?"

"No. I slept alone that night and every night since then. Do you believe me?"

"Yes."

"Good. Now, can we celebrate the start of your summer vacation by having dinner Friday night?"

"Yes."

"Where would you like to go?"

To bed with you all night long. "I'll be a little too wound up to enjoy going out." She picked up her coffee cup. "Would you like to come to my apartment for dinner instead? I can cook—"

"Tell me what you'd like for dinner and I'll find a restaurant that does it well and bring wine so we can both enjoy the evening."

"I can cook."

"I'm sure you'll demonstrate that for me some time, but having to cook for me isn't a great way to start a vacation."

She sipped her coffee. "So you want to see me after Friday night?"

He responded after a long pause. "I'm not looking for a one-night stand."

Something in his words and gaze gave her pause. "But?"

"Who said there was a but?"

"My intuition."

"I'm the eldest child. I'm forty and I need to think about marriage very soon."

Clearly he wasn't thinking about it with her or she wouldn't have left the but hanging in the air unspoken between them. From her research on the number of people who spoke Tsalagi and identified themselves as Cherokee, she feared what was coming. "Are you seeing someone you plan to marry?"

"No, but I need to think about helping preserve our heritage."

Why did hearing what she'd suspected send a stab of disappointment through her? "So you want more than one night, but nothing serious because you plan to marry a Native American woman?"

His jaw clenched. "Yes."

"I see."

He sighed. "I know how bad that sounds and I'm sorry."

She shook her head and put down her coffee cup. "Your wanting to help preserve your heritage is perfectly understandable." *But why the hell can't you do that by learning to speak Tsalagi, embracing your heritage, and being my man?*

"But?"

"But nothing." She shrugged. "It's not as if I accepted breakfast or dinner thinking you were going to fall in love with me."

He ran a hand through his hair. "That would have been very easy for me under other circumstances."

Hearing him admit that he could envision himself falling in love with her sent a wave of pain knotting in the pit of her stomach. She swallowed hard and looked away from him.

He reached across the table to touch her hand. "I'm sorry."

She drew her hand away from his. "You've been honest and I couldn't ask for any more than that."

"I don't want to hurt you."

Given her feelings of dejection at his admissions, heartbreak seemed unavoidable. "I'm not hurt." Yet.

"Is our date still on for Friday?"

Any woman with half an ounce of pride would have kicked his ass to the curb. She sighed and met his gaze. It was time to face facts. She wanted him as much as he wanted her, but damned if she intended to have any "accidents" that had life-long consequences for her and the man she eventually married. "Yes — as long as you remember that I have no desire to become accidentally pregnant by a man who plans to marry another woman."

His jaw clenched. "Meaning what?"

She leaned forward and spoke in a low, cool voice. "Meaning don't you ever try to have unprotected sex with me again! Save that for the woman you plan to marry."

"I'm forty years old with no kids. I don't go around having unprotected sex."

"Really? Well, you've tried twice with me."

"Neither time was planned."

"That wouldn't have been much comfort had I ended up pregnant and alone, Braden." She sat back so she could see his face. Staring at him, she waited for his assurance that he wouldn't have left her pregnant and alone.

He stared at her in silence.

So now you know the deal, Neida. This is strictly about sex for him. Deal with it and make damn sure you never put yourself in a position that will allow him to leave you pregnant and alone. She had a feeling he would provide ample financial support but probably no or very minimal emotional support. She glanced at her watch. "We'd better go."

"Fine." He signaled for the bill and they left.

Outside Becky's she turned to look at him. "It's a beautiful day. I think I'll walk to work."

"Great idea. I'll walk with you." He fell into step

beside her.

She stopped and turned to face him. "I'd rather you didn't."

"Why not?"

"Because I don't want your company. Now I have to go. Thanks for breakfast." She turned away.

He caught her hand and turned her to face him. "I need you to understand that if one of my brothers was married or even dating a Native—"

She pulled her hand away from him. "I said I understand your position and I do."

"Then why do you look so hurt?"

Because as improbable as it was, she was already in love with him and about to have her heart broken. "I understand all I want or need to about you. Good luck."

His grip on her hand tightened. "I know it's selfish and unforgivable of me, but..." He touched her cheek. "You intrigue me and I ache to be your lover."

So he wanted and expected her to allow him to use her to satisfy his lust before he married another woman. Clearly he viewed her as just another willing pussy. She blinked rapidly to keep her eyes tear free. "I need to cancel our date Friday."

"Neida—"

She tugged at her hand.

He tightened his grip again, almost hurting her. "I know I have no right to ask this of you, but I promise I'll treat you well. And while we're together, I won't stray."

She tugged at her hand. "Tell that to the women you fuck until you settle down with your Cherokee maid."

"Look, I'll pay off your student loans."

She sucked in a breath and stared at him. "So you think you can buy your way into my bed as if I'm a prostitute?"

"No! I didn't mean it that way and I think you know that. I know hearing this is difficult for you. It's difficult for me to say and to see the look on your face and in your eyes…"

He paused, inhaling and exhaling slowly. "A better, more moral man would leave you alone, but I can't. I hunger to be your lover."

He wanted her to be satisfied with his lust while he gave his love and his name to some other lucky woman. Her instinctive need to take him anyway she could get him, shamed her. She tugged at her hand. "I'm not interested in being your prostitute, Braden, but I'm sure you'll find tons of other women who are — most of them without any financial reward."

"You're the one I want and need. You, querida. Just you."

"Well, you're not offering me anything I need. Now you're hurting my hand. Please release it, Braden."

He complied.

She rubbed it. "Please don't call me and don't send me any more presents."

"Please don't do this."

She couldn't allow herself to be swayed by the emotion she imagined she heard in his voice. Yet she couldn't ignore it. If she definitively kicked his ass to the curb, she might regret it when it was too late. "I need time to think. So just please leave me alone for a bit, Braden."

"I'm forty years old. I don't have any more damned time to waste playing games with you!"

So he considered romancing her before he fucked her a waste of his time? "Don't expect me to feel responsible because you've spent your life fucking every whore in sight and now feel your age pressing in on you!"

He sucked in an angry breath. "Fuck you!" he said and stormed away.

Shocked into silence, she stood staring while he got into his car and drove off before she turned and walked towards work. She managed to keep tears at bay, but when she arrived at work, Betty took one look at her face and followed her into her classroom.

"What's wrong, Neida?"

"I can't talk about it here."

"Let me guess. It's that damned Braden. What the hell has he done now?"

She shook her head and swallowed hard, hearing his contemptuous *fuck you* echoing in her mind. This time she knew he would be bedding another woman.

"No matter how bad things seem, we'll get through whatever comes together. Okay?"

She gulped in a quick breath.

"We'll walk and talk at lunch?"

She nodded.

Betty squeezed her hand and left her alone in her classroom.

* * *

After driving around for an hour, Braden returned to the extended stay suite hotel. He tried to work, but kept seeing the hurt and disappointed look in Neida's eyes when he told her he only wanted a sexual relationship with her.

After nearly three hours of pacing, he called Raven who he knew was probably in meetings. "I need to talk to you."

"When?"

"As soon as possible. What's your schedule like today?"

"I have several meetings scheduled but I can allow Jacob to handle those—"

"No. I can wait to talk."

"If you could, you wouldn't have called, Bray. Jacob is as capable as I am or he wouldn't be my right hand. He's up to speed and can easily step in and handle the meetings. I'll be back at the suite in forty minutes or do you want to meet somewhere for an early lunch?"

He wasn't hungry but he couldn't expect Raven to starve. "What do you want? I'll order room service."

"Steak, medium. I'll be there soon, Bray."

Braden hung up. He called room service, resisted the urge to lose himself in several drinks, and continued pacing. Raven arrived several minutes after room service. He lifted the top off the tray and looked up at Braden. "One steak. You had breakfast?"

"I'm not hungry. Eat and we'll talk."

Raven removed his jacket and replaced the cover. "It'll keep." He sat on the sofa. "I'm here to listen, Bray."

He moved over to the balcony doors and stared out at the adjacent high rises. "I made a real mess of things, Ray." He paused, took several deep breaths and told Raven of his conversation that morning with Neida, including his parting shot.

"Why did you feel the need to tell her you only wanted sex, Bray?"

He turned to stare at Raven. "You expected me to lie to her or let her think there was a chance of our forming a real relationship?"

"Why did you let her think you wouldn't have been there for her if she'd ended up pregnant?"

"What difference does that make, Ray?"

"To me? None but I'm sure hearing you say you wouldn't have left her alone and pregnant would have meant a lot to her."

"It would only have given her false hope."

"Well God forbid you should leave her with any hope, Bray!"

He narrowed his gaze. "You're not exactly helping here."

"How many women did Mom introduce you to while the two of you were in Tulsa?"

"She introduced me to two women while I was there but what has that got to do with anything?"

"I assume neither made any real impression or you wouldn't be so concerned about how your date with wyanet ended."

Each woman, in her early thirties and attractive, spoke Tsalagi and would make a suitable wife. Even though neither had moved him emotionally, he'd decided that once he got Neida out of his system, he'd return to Tulsa to romance them both. He'd propose to whichever one managed to make him want more than a one-night stand with her. But there was no point in admitting that to Raven, who would then feel obligated to try to dissuade him.

"Why the hell do you keep calling her wyanet,

Raven?"

"Are you still determined to marry for the wrong reason?"

"I don't need to tell you the facts about the number of Cherokees who can actually speak Tsalagi or who actively work to keep our heritage alive. We all have to do our part, Raven."

"I'm as interested as you in keeping our culture alive, but I'll be damned if I'll marry for any reason other than love! And if you're determined to marry a woman just because of her heritage, then I was wrong and you were right."

"About what?"

"Seeing Wya—Neida."

"What do you mean?"

"I think you should cut your losses and leave her alone now before she really gets hurt."

He stared at Raven. "Leave her alone?"

"Yes. Leave her alone, Bray. You were right when you said she deserved more than you were prepared to give her. Leave her alone to meet a man ready to love and marry her because of how she makes him feel instead of having a meaningless affair with one who's just interested in a last taste of brown sugar before he marries someone he doesn't love."

The blood rushed up the back of his neck and he clenched his right hand into a fist as he glared at Raven. "If you're trying to get me angry enough to knock you on your know-it-all-ass, I'm nearly there."

Raven narrowed his gaze and rose. He crossed the room to return Braden's stare. "Really? Well, I suggest you make sure you don't actually get *there* because I assure you that I have no damned intentions of being knocked on my know-it-all-ass for the sole sin of telling the truth."

Braden clasped his hand on the back of Raven's neck. "I'm not in the mood to be fucked with!"

Raven shoved his hand away and stepped back. "And I'm not in the mood to be threatened! Marry who you want for your very noble reasons but leave her the hell alone before you break her heart. Breaking the heart of one woman who loved you should be enough. There's no need to make a habit of it." Raven stormed across the room to snatch up his jacket. He put it on and crossed the room to the entrance door.

Raven's veiled reference to Kania infuriated Braden. "Where the hell are you going?"

Raven turned with his hand on the doorknob. "Since you're clearly not in a reasonable mood and we both have tempers, I'm going back to work before one of us gets his ass kicked! And guess what? It sure as hell ain't gonna be my ass getting kicked, Braden!" He pulled the door opened and slammed it shut behind him.

Braden swung his clenched fist up from his side. He brought it within a few inches of the window before he sucked in a breath and dropped it back to his side. *Get a damned grip, Elkhorn.*

Ten minutes later while he still stood staring out the window, the entrance door opened. He turned.

Raven closed the door and leaned against it. "I'm sorry, Bray. You called me because you needed to talk. I had no right to try and tell you how to live your life. I'll support whatever choices you makes because I know you always try to do the right thing."

Braden turned back to face the balcony in silence.

Raven's dig about his breaking Kania's heart still pissed him off. Probably because he knew it was true.

Raven crossed the room and placed a hand on his shoulder. "If you still need to talk, this time I'm prepared to listen without offering unwanted advice."

He shook Raven's hand off his shoulder and turned to face him. "You've made your opinions crystal clear. And you know what? Fuck you and your advice!"

Raven arched a brow. "So you're going to go on seeing her?"

"That's none of your damned business."

"I only asked because I just got a call from Layton Grayhawk inviting us both to his home for dinner Friday night. Now that you no longer have a date with Neida—"

"Fuck you, Raven!" He resisted the urge to shove Raven out of his way, stepped around him, and left the suite.

His cell phone rang an hour later while he drove along the back roads of a Philadelphia suburb. He glanced at his cell phone's display screen and recognized Layton Grayhawk's cell number. Raven had probably called Layton and asked him to call Braden. He let the call go to voicemail. Although he and Layton were friends, he'd had enough unsolicited advice for the day. But there was something Layton could teach him he'd find useful—if he somehow managed to make things as right as possible with Neida.

Chapter Seven

"He's an ass, Neida."

"He's not an ass, Bett."

Betty, seated beside Neida on their favorite bench in the small park two blocks from school, turned to frown at her. "He tells you you're good enough to fuck but not good enough to marry and you still want to defend him?"

"That's not what he said or meant. He could have lied to get what he wanted but didn't. He's an honorable man."

"He's an ass and a horny one at that! How dare he think..." Betty gritted her teeth. "If he thinks for one second...why didn't you tell him to go to hell, Neida?"

"Because part of me wants to..." She sighed. "Oh Bett! I think you were right. He's the one."

"You think?"

She nodded. "Yes. I do. At first I thought it was just a sexual thing, but he admitted that he only wanted sex from me twice and I still want to give in to him. I now know he's going to marry someone else and I still want him."

"Don't do anything rash, Neida. Pack your bag and come spend a week with Jack and me down at the shore."

Each year Jack and Betty spent the first two weeks of summer vacation at his parents' shore house alone. Later in the summer, they invited their friends to join them. Neida shook her head. "I'm not going to ruin your plans because I've been foolish enough to fall for someone I shouldn't have. Thanks, but no."

"Come, Neida. Jack will understand—"

"He's not going to have to understand. I'll be fine. You two have your two weeks and I'll come spend a few days after that."

"What are you going to do?"

She shrugged. "Don't worry about me. I'll be fine." She'd probably spend more time crying than she should over a man she'd only seen a few times. Still, she would be fine in the end. She'd survived the end of her relationship with Mark and she'd survive her brief association with Braden Elkhorn.

* * *

Two nights later, Neida sat alone on her balcony, sipping a glass of the red wine Braden had sent her. She'd spent most of the previous two nights researching Spanish, Cajun French, and Tsalagi on the internet. Not that she'd ever need any of them now — unless she swallowed her pride and willingly accepted Braden's terms. But she wasn't about to spend the night alone feeling sorry for herself.

She'd never had any trouble attracting male attention. She'd go to her favorite jazz club. And in the morning, she'd formulate a new plan.

By the time she'd showered and dressed, her stomach growled. Hungry for food and male companionship, she left her apartment.

As she neared her car, the driver side door of a dark SUV opened and a tall, well-built man who resembled Braden got out.

She paused, her heart hammering in her chest. Had something happened to Braden?

The man's quick, reassuring smile help allay her fear for Braden's safety.

"Forgive me if I startled you." He extended his

hand. "I'm Raven Elkhorn, one of Bray's brothers."

"Bray?"

"Braden's nickname. Mine is Ray and you're Oneida Armstrong."

"Yes." She extended her hand.

"It's a pleasure to meet you." He engulfed her hand in both of his briefly before releasing it.

"What can I do for you, Mr. Elkhorn?"

"Please call me Ray and consider spending a few hours with me tonight."

"That's a charming offer but my plans for tonight don't include spending any of my valuable time with any male named Elkhorn." She flashed a brief smile and stepped around him.

He stepped in her path with a resigned look on his handsome face. "He fucked up that badly, huh?"

Unsure how much he knew of what had happened between her and Braden, she moistened her lips. "I'm not in the mood to waste my Friday night discussing your brother."

"Ouch! I hope you don't believe in guilt by association of blood. Because if you'll give me a chance to prove it, I'm sure I can convince you that I'm far more polished and worth knowing than Bray is. Not to mention more attractive."

She stared at him. "Are all the Elkhorn men as conceited and arrogant as you and Braden are?"

He arched a brow. "It's only conceit if the high opinion of one's self isn't justified. I assure you, it's as justified in my case as it is in Bray's. Now if you don't have any plans for your night you can't bear to break, I'd like a chance to get to know the woman who's rattled my older brother so badly."

She hesitated. "I think you should know that even though you two look so much alike, I don't find you interchangeable. "

He released a long breath. "Oh God, you have no idea how glad I am to hear that."

"Why?"

"As I'm sure you know he likes you far more than he thinks he should."

"So where is he?"

He shrugged. "It's not my night to watch him, querida."

His cavalier use of the word she treasured hearing from Braden annoyed her. "Fuck off," she told him and turned away.

He caught her hand and turned her back to face him.

She stared at him. "Are you and Braden the only two Elkhorns unable to take no for an answer or is it a family trait?"

He laughed and lifted her hand to brush his lips against her fingers. "I can see why Bray is so taken with you. You're attractive and feisty. The two are an irresistible combination in a woman. Now, can I interest you in spending a few hours with me at a friend's dinner party tonight? "

"You don't look as if you'd have any harder time finding a date than Braden would. That is where he is. Isn't it? With another woman?"

He shrugged. "I don't think so."

"But he has been with one since we last saw each other?"

"That's something you should ask him when you see him again."

"I'll take that as a yes."

He shook his head. "I'm a lawyer. I know how to say exactly what I mean. And I mean you should ask him when you see him again."

"If the answer was no, you'd say no."

He smiled. "Bray was right. You're as intelligent as you are pretty."

"So the answer is yes."

He shrugged. "He's single so as far as I know that means he's free to see or sleep with whomever he likes—just as you are."

"But the difference between the two of us is I haven't!"

"He'll be very glad to hear that."

"Fuck both of you!"

"I'd be okay with that, but I doubt if Bray would."

She blinked. Was he suggesting they routinely slept with the same woman? "I don't do brothers."

"Again, Bray would be very glad to hear that. Me? Not so much. And for the record, the only assumption you should make about my noncommittal answer in reference to who he might or might not have slept with is that I don't know. If I had to guess, I'd say no."

"Why if you don't know?"

"Lately, you can't say hello to him without his threatening to knock you on your ass. His damned fuse wouldn't be so much shorter than normal if he wasn't sexually frustrated. If I were you, I wouldn't worry about other women turning his head. You've already done that." He smiled at her. "Ready to go?"

He appeared as sure of himself as Braden was. And like Braden, she liked him. There was something she found irresistible about a big, handsome Native

American hunk who thought she was beautiful. If only his name was Braden, he'd be perfect.

Nevertheless, commonsense dictated that she refuse his invitation. Her heart had other ideas. When he opened the front passenger door of the SUV, she slipped inside. "Am I dressed appropriately for where we're going?" she asked when he climbed into the driver's seat and started the vehicle.

"You look lovely." He gave her a quick smile before he pulled out of her complex parking lot.

"Lovely enough to spend the evening where?"

"At the home of family friends, Layton and Tempest Grayhawk. They live on the outskirts of the city."

"They won't mind my coming?"

"They're looking forward to meeting you."

"Why?"

"Braden and Layton have been friends for at least twenty years."

She turned her head to study his profile. "Is he going to be there?"

"Braden? Probably."

"So you and he are in cahoots to get me there?"

"Yes."

She heard no regret in his voice. "Why didn't he ask me himself?"

"Because he thought you'd say no."

"And you were okay with tricking me?"

"There's going to be no harm done, querida. If you feel a pressing need to scratch his eyes out when you see him, I'll be ready to drive you home."

"And what if I want to scratch yours out as well?"

"I trust you'll resist the impulse—or it's doubtful

we'll make it back in one piece."

She tossed back her head and laughed.

He laughed too and reached out to briefly brush his hand against her cheek.

"Just so there's no misunderstanding, I have absolutely no interest in you, Raven."

"Call me Ray and as I've said a number of times tonight, I'm very glad to hear it."

"Are there any more like you at home?"

"There are two more. Neka, who is two years younger than Bray and three years older than me, is very happily married. Shane is four years younger than me. Why do you ask?"

"Because I want to know how many more Elkhorns I'll be expected to take shit from."

He laughed and then sobered abruptly. "Shane is busy breaking hearts and my interests lie elsewhere. So the only shit up for grabs from us will come from Bray."

"I'm sorry."

"About what?"

"That things aren't going well for you romance-wise."

"How did you reach that conclusion?" he asked after a brief silence.

"You said your interests lay elsewhere. If there was no problem, you would have said you were already taken."

"Beautiful as well as intelligent. Small wonder Bray is so enchanted."

"Is he really?"

"Hell yeah. I'll have to watch myself with you."

"Is she married?"

"Yes," he spoke after a long pause. "As a matter of fact she is, but not for much longer."

"And when she isn't?"

"There will still be other complications that will probably keep us apart."

"So you're saying you're probably not going to marry for love either?"

"Barring a miracle? No but it won't be for the same reason that Bray won't."

"Let me guess. Elkhorn men don't do love."

"Oh but we do. As I said, Neka is very happily married and I hope that Shane will be one day as well."

"But—"

"But enough about me. I'm a big boy. I can take care of myself and I'd prefer you didn't mention this part of our conversation to Bray."

"You've just admitted to tricking me and now you're asking for a favor?"

"Yes. Cocky of me, isn't it?"

She laughed. "Yes. That seems to run in the family."

"So I've been told. I'm sure you're still pissed with him, but at the moment Bray has enough on his emotional plate without having to worry about my love life."

"Okay."

"Thanks," he said and they lapsed into a comfortable silence.

When he stopped the SUV in the oval in front of a house that could only be called a mansion, her heart raced. Among the many vehicles parked there was the dark sedan Braden had driven the last time she saw him.

She moistened her lips and hesitated when Raven alighted and came around to open the passenger side door.

He smiled at her. "Anytime you want to leave, I'll be ready to take you home."

"Is she here?"

"No. She's not in the partying mood."

"Not even to see you, Raven?"

"She's pregnant and in California."

She watched his jaw clench. "Are you the fath—"

"No! I'm not!" He closed his eyes briefly and then quickly shook his head and looked at her. "Forgive me. Talking about her isn't one of my favorite past times but that's no excuse for snapping at you."

Looking into his dark gaze, she saw the same level of implacability in his eyes that she'd seen in Braden's. "I don't understand. Why are you and Braden the only two brothers who can't marry for love?"

"He and I might look alike but we're very different. He's far nobler than I have any desire to be. I don't foresee marrying period because I don't intend to marry a woman I don't love. But I promise you, querida, that I'll do all I can to ensure he doesn't marry a woman he'll never love when he can have you."

"If you're implying that he's in love with me, don't bother."

"Are you so sure that he's not?"

"I'm positive he's not. There was nothing lover-like about him when he snapped that he didn't have any more time to waste playing games with me before he told me to fuck off the last time we saw each other!"

"Love talk if ever I heard any. Besides, he's told me to fuck off more times than I can count and I know he loves me," he said, placed his hands on her waist and urged her to get out of the SUV.

She shook her head. "You're impossible."

"It's part of my charm."

"In your own mind."

He laughed and then surprised her by putting his arms around her and pulling her close. "Don't give up on him just yet." He kissed her cheek, released her, and offered his arm.

She slipped her hand through his and they walked up the wide steps and into the house.

A handsome Native American male with short dark hair and an elegantly dressed African-American female met them at the door.

The woman smiled. "It's good to see you again, Ray." Her smile widened as she looked at Neida. "Introduce us."

Raven touched her elbow. "Layton and Tempest, this lovely lady is Oneida Armstrong. Querida, our host and hostess, Layton and Tempest Grayhawk."

She smiled and extended her hand. "I'm delighted to meet you both."

"Lovely indeed," Tempest smiled as they shook hands.

Layton clasped both hands around hers. "Braden is one of my oldest and dearest friends. It's a pleasure to meet you, Oneida."

A tall handsome male with long, brown hair and dark eyes came out into the foyer. Ray introduced him as Bancroft Grayhawk. When they shook hands, Neida experienced a strange sensation—almost as if he were probing her thoughts.

Startled, she compressed her lips and pulled her

hand from his.

Tempest Grayhawk smiled at her before speaking to Raven. "There's a buffet spread in the dining room, Ray. If you two are hungry, help yourselves and then come join us in the living room."

"Okay." Raven put an arm around her shoulders and walked her down the hall. "Let's go see what your bad boy is up to and then we'll eat."

She nudged him with her shoulder. "Why did you allow them to think there's something between me and Braden?"

He bent his head and brushed his lips against her ear. "Because there is."

Mindful of the Grayhawks behind them she hissed her answer. "No there isn't."

"Then what are you doing here taking shit from me, querida?"

Damn him. She elbowed him. "Don't call me that."

He stopped and turned her to face him.

She felt her cheeks heat up as the Grayhawks walked past them. What must they think of her?

Raven brushed his hand against her cheek. "It's early days yet, but if you prefer, I'll call you wyanet."

"Wyanet? Legendary beauty?"

"That's the general definition of the word. However, we use it as an endearment reserved for the special women in our lives. We all refer to Neka's wife as wyanet."

"It's appropriate in her case but not mine."

"I wouldn't be too sure of that if I were you."

"I like him a lot. Please don't give me false hope."

"He likes you a lot."

"So much so that he's prepared to marry someone

else."

"That's his plan."

"But?"

He shrugged. "But you're a beautiful woman who's captured his attention in a way no other woman has that I'm aware of and we're very close. I happen to think you have it in your power to change his plans — as long as you're prepared to be patient with him and take a little shit now and then."

She shook her head. "I'm going to take him at his word. He only wants a fling with me and a brief one at that because he's worried about his age. He carries on about it like he was sixty instead of forty."

"Let's face it, querida, he is getting a little long in the tooth."

"I happen to think he's the perfect age."

He smiled. "Really? Which do you prefer first; food or the perfectly aged bad boy?"

"I'd like to see him first."

"He'd like to see you too." He put his arm around her and they continued down the hallway to the room the Grayhawks had entered. Neida paused in the entrance and looked around.

The room was filled with people but she spotted Braden seated on a sofa between two women. One was a beautiful Native American. The other was beautiful and full-figured, African American female. As she watched, the Native American woman slipped her arm through his. The other woman leaned over to kiss him on the corner of his mouth.

Neida tensed and turned away just as Braden looked up and at her.

"They're both just friends," Raven said against her

ear.

She shook her head and pushed past him. She walked quickly down the hall. As she reached the door, a hand closed over her bare arm. The touch sent a tingle through her and she knew it was Braden instead of Raven who had followed her.

She turned to face him.

"Querida. Finally." He smiled and bent his head slowly.

She had ample time to avoid his mouth — had she wanted to. She didn't.

He cupped a hand against the side of her neck and touched his mouth to hers.

She trembled but resisted the urge to lean into him and part her lips. "Who have you been kissing besides the woman in the living room?"

"I didn't kiss her. She kissed me."

"And just who is she?"

"Her name is Rayna Redwolf. She's the niece of friends of mine. We have no sexual interest in each other."

She pushed at his shoulders. "Then why doesn't she keep her lips off yours?"

He nipped at her ear. "Rayna has an affectionate nature. It meant nothing beyond that to either one of us."

"And the other one?"

"Lelia Grayhawk, Layton's baby sister. Believe me, there's nothing between us. If I even looked at her with anything approaching sexual interest, I'd have to deal with all her damned brothers. And there are nine of them. Besides, as pretty and sweet as she is, she's not my type. She's far too thin and her skin is far too light for my taste.

"You know I like plus-size women with dark skin, large breasts, and big, round asses."

"There are a lot of pretty women here tonight."

"True, but none as lovely or as alluring as you are, querida."

"How long have you been here, Braden?"

"Why do you ask?"

"Because this place has a lot of walls."

"True, but I've been saving all my wall banging for you, my lovely querida."

She laughed and then sobbed.

"No." He slipped his arms around her and rubbed his cheek against hers. "There's no need to cry. I'm horny as hell and I've been tempted, but I haven't slept with anyone since we met."

A wave of relief and hope washed over her. She looked up at him. "Has your game plan changed, Braden?"

He sighed. "No."

So he still expected her to settle for a brief fling. Damn her for wanting to. She closed her eyes, unable to meet the brutal honesty she saw in his gaze. It was time to make a decision. She could tell him to go to hell and walk away with her pride intact. And then spend the rest of her life regretting never having slept with him. Or she could admit that she was in love with him and give him what he wanted — knowing he was going to leave her broken hearted.

Tears streamed down her cheeks.

He bent his head and spoke against her ear. "I'm sorry."

So was she — that she wasn't strong enough to walk

away from him. She balled her hands into fists and pressed them against his chest. "So how much time are you prepared to waste playing games with me before you go find your Cherokee maiden?"

He kissed her cheek. "I had no right to say that. Please believe that I cherish every moment I can spend with you."

"How long is that going to be?"

"You want a date?"

She pulled away from him and met his gaze. "Yes."

His jaw clenched twice before he spoke. "I was hoping we could spend the summer together."

"And then? Do you already have her picked out?"

He raked a hand through his hair. "Do you really want to do this?"

"Yes! Do you know who you're going to be romancing once you're through with me?"

He sighed. "There are two likely prospects — assuming either is still single by then."

She thought of the two women he'd been seated between in the living room. "Which one do you love?"

"Neither one of them and if it's any comfort to you, that's not likely to change!"

"Why should I take comfort in knowing you'll be in a loveless marriage?"

"You might consider it my just desserts for hurting you."

So he knew he was going to leave her hurt and didn't care. She swallowed hard. "Have you slept with either of them?"

"No, I haven't."

She swiped the tears away from her damp cheeks. "Where's Raven?"

He narrowed his gaze. "Why?"

"I need a long soak and a really gut-wrenching cry and he promised he'd take me home when I was ready to go."

He slumped against the wall near the door and lowered his head. "Have you considered Raven? He's a better man than I am." He sighed and lifted his head to look at her. "He wouldn't hurt you."

She bit back the urge to tell him Raven's interests lay elsewhere. "If I had a sister, would you consider her?"

"No."

She believed him. "I'm not interested in Raven or your other brother. You're the one I want."

He extended a hand to her. "I want you too."

"Just not enough to change your game plan?"

"Please. Try to understand my position."

"I do understand." She stumbled forward into his embrace. "I just wish it didn't have to be at my expense."

He tightened his arms around her. "It will be at mine too."

She clung to him with tears streaming down her cheeks. "I need to go home. Please get Raven."

"I'll take you."

She shook her head and pulled away from him. "I'll see you tomorrow. I'm going to spend the night crying and coming to grips with the fact that I'm going to give you what you want—even though I know how little you think of me."

He stared at her, his Adam's apple bobbing for several moments before he pushed away from the wall and stalked down the hallway.

She walked out of the house and stood on the steps. "Querida?"

At the sound of Raven's voice, she turned and burrowed into him.

He slipped an arm around her and kissed her forehead. He held her for several minutes while she sobbed before he wiped her cheeks and led her to his SUV. Although he didn't speak, he frequently reached out to squeeze her hand during the drive back to her apartment.

At her door, he gave her a card with his numbers on it. "I'm involved in talks here, but if you need me for anything, call and I'll come as soon as I can."

She nodded, struggling to hold back tears.

He bent his head to kiss her cheek before he left.

Chapter Eight

"So how's that selfish bastard brother of yours?"

Braden, pacing the length of Layton Grayhawk's home office minutes after he'd watched Raven drive off with a sobbing Neida, stopped. Layton sat on the sofa along one wall with a drink on the table in front of him.

"Look, I know Shane is a little used to having things his own way, but where the hell do you get off calling him a selfish bastard? And what makes you think I want to talk about him after I've just told you she thinks I don't care about or respect her?"

Layton narrowed his gaze. "You're responsible for what she thinks, Bray. And who said I was talking about Shane?"

He frowned. He could hear the muted sounds of music from the dinner party going on down the hall. "Then who the hell are you talking about?"

"I was referring to Neka."

Braden felt the back of his neck burn. "What the hell is in that drink, Layton? Neka doesn't have a selfish bone in his entire body."

"The hell he doesn't. His selfish ass gets to marry for love—twice while you have to do your duty and forego marrying for love even once?"

Braden clenched his hand into a fist and stalked across the room to glare down at his friend. "Fuck off, Layton! Neka had every right to marry for love!"

"But you don't? Why the hell does that seem fair to you, Braden? And don't give me any shit about the responsibilities of being the eldest son. I know all about imposing those restrictions on yourself."

"Look, Layton—"

"No. You look." Layton rose, forcing him to take a few steps backward. "Let's not forget you're talking to a man who married a Cherokee woman who actually spoke Tsalagi. And the result? We were trapped in an unhappy marriage for years. Since she knew I never loved her, she never fully trusted me and constantly imagined I was cheating on her.

"I wasted years married to her. Years that I could have spent with Tempest—had I not been foolish enough to marry a woman I didn't love for what I thought at the time were good reasons."

Layton gripped the back of his neck. "Don't do that to yourself, Braden. Believe me when I tell you that you deserve to marry for love just as much as your brothers do. Don't feel as if you personally have to undertake the burden of keeping our culture alive."

"Each family has to take an active role in helping to preserve our culture. Neka's already married again. Neither Raven nor Shane is likely to undertake the responsibility. That leaves me."

"The hell it does! Yes, there are challenges facing us as a people. Yes, we should all feel an obligation to preserve our heritage. But don't sell us short, Braden. Don't forget that we are as resilient as we are proud. Our culture survived The Trail of Tears and countless other obstacles during our history. It's strong enough to survive your marrying for love."

"I don't recall mentioning love."

Layton slapped his cheek. "Don't forget who you're talking to and wake the fuck up and smell the coffee before you run the risk of ruining both of your lives. I have personal, painful experience of how miserable it is to be trapped in a marriage to one woman when you're in love with another. Don't go there, Braden. Not only will you make yourself miserable but you're also going to crush her. She's young, pretty, and obviously in love with you.

"And I'd be very surprised if you're not in love with her."

"You've already married a Native woman and you have more brothers than I do and a greater chance that one or more of them will marry into our culture."

"I have no intentions of expecting any of my brothers to marry for any reason other than love. Now are you really implying I don't understand?"

"That's exactly what I'm implying."

"Then your wyanet has you more rattled than I thought possible."

"I never said—"

Layton raised a hand. "Spare me any more shit about your lack of deep feelings for her. You didn't drag me away from the party because you view her as an easy lay."

"I never said she was as easy lay. I do have deep feelings for her, but one of us has to marry within our cultures."

Layton sighed. "Even if the choice results in less desirable circumstances for your kids?"

"What?"

"Brandon and Malita are going to fare much better growing up knowing that Tempest and I love them and each other," he said of his son and daughter. "Had I still been married to Alison, they would probably have grown up in a much cooler home environment. Even if you're prepared to ruin your life and break her heart, are you prepared to deprive your kids of the advantage of growing up in a warm, loving home nurtured by parents who love and adore each other?"

He laughed and shook his head. "That's not fair, you bastard."

"Neither is your plan to spend the summer fucking her and then leaving her to pick up the pieces of her life afterwards. How do you think she's going to feel trying to put her life back together when she thinks of you being there for a woman you don't love while leaving her to struggle alone? If you're still determined to marry another woman, do her a favor and leave her alone."

"She knows and understands my reasons."

"She's 26 and in love with you. Get a fucking grip on reality, Braden and admit that you're going to crush her! If that's what you want, go ahead and have at it. If it's not, leave her alone—unless you're prepared to treat her with the respect your father would have expected you to."

Layton's reference to his father infuriated him. His father had taught him that a man should honor the woman he loved, not shame her. He clenched his right hand into a fist. It was clear Layton knew his father would not have approved of his behavior. "I don't need you quoting my father to me and I've heard all of the moralizing shit from you I want to." He stormed across the room, opened the door, and slammed it shut behind him.

In the hallway outside the living room, he encountered Brandon Grayhawk, who had a nasty habit of gripping a person's hand and invading his thoughts. Ignoring the hand Brandon extended, he pushed past him. "Get out of my way and don't attempt to invade my thoughts, Grayhawk!"

Braden stalked towards the open entrance doors without responding. Outside, he found his younger brother Seneka leaning against the hood of his car. What the hell. This night kept getting worse. Who had called Seneka? Ray or Layton? And why the hell did either one of them think a man who'd been lucky enough to marry the only two women he'd ever love have advice worth shit to offer anyone?

Overcoming the nearly irrepressible urge he felt to lash out, he extended his hand instead. "Neka, what brings you here tonight?"

Seneka clasped his hand in both of his. "Ray's worried about you."

"He doesn't need to be."

"Are you sure, Bray?"

He withdrew his hand from Seneka's. "I've already had a lecture from Ray and Layton and frankly, I'm not in the mood for one from you." He pulled his alarm fob from his pocket and opened his car door.

To his surprise, Seneka gripped his shoulder and swung him around to face him. "Really? I seem to recall having to listen to unsolicited advice from you and Ray when things weren't going well between Autumn and me. Neither of you cared whether or not I wanted advice. And guess what, Bray? I don't give a fuck whether you want it or not either."

He jerked away. "Fine. Give me your moralizing spiel and then get out of my face and business."

"What the fuck is wrong with you, Braden? People who love you should just stand by and watch you self-destruct without trying to stop it?"

"I would have thought you'd have more important

things to occupy your time than my love life, Neka."

"You know what? You're right. I'm going home. When you pull your head out of the sand and admit you need the people who love you around when things aren't going well, call me. I'll come—just as you've always come when I needed you."

Braden watched him walk to his car before he sighed and followed him. "Neka."

He turned. "Yes?"

Braden shrugged and extended his hand. "I'm sorry."

Seneka clasped both hands around his. "It's all right, Bray."

"No. Go ahead. Give me your take."

"I have no desire to tell you what to do but you should follow the course that will end with you as happily married as I am. If that means pursuing a relationship with querida, do it. There's no reason why you should allow outside considerations to dictate who you marry. Marry who you love, not who you think you should. End of spiel. I'm going home to Autumn."

He hesitated, choosing his words carefully before he spoke. "I'm curious, Neka. Have you never felt even a passing obligation to consider marriage with a Native woman?"

"When I was younger, I think I assumed that's what would happen. But once I met Kelli, there was no question of marrying anyone else for any reason. I felt the same way after I met Autumn so I guess the answer is no, Bray. I've never felt any obligation to marry a woman I didn't love just because she was Native American. I wish you didn't either."

Seneka had clearly never had the same talk with

their late father that Braden had. But since he was the elder son, it was appropriate that their father had only had it with him. He sighed. "Give wyanet my love, Neka."

"I will. You know she sends hers."

Braden nodded. "I know."

They embraced before getting in their separate vehicles and leaving the Grayhawk property.

He was so horny he felt ready to burst. There were a number of women he knew who would gladly spend the night with him without wanting or expecting any type of commitment from him. But he was reluctant to sleep with any of them before he decided how he should proceed.

It was going to be a long night, he thought as he parked his car. A long night during which he needed to decide what — if anything — to do about his growing and incessant hunger for Neida.

* * *

Three days later, his decision finally made, Braden flew home without having made any contact with Neida. He spent all his waking hours either working, exercising, or sleeping with various women. But no matter how many hours he put in at the office, or how strenuously he worked out, or how many women he slept with, he couldn't vanquish thoughts of Neida. Each sexual encounter, even as it took the edge off his physical hunger left him longing to make love to her.

He lost track of the number of times he picked up the phone to call her or the endless nights he spent wishing she were lying in bed beside him instead of the woman actually there. Worse were the hours he spent tortured by the thought of another man touching her.

Kissing her. Being there when she needed a shoulder to cry on and making her feel cherished.

But he'd done the best he could: paid off her student loans and resisted his need to sleep with her when he was still determined to marry someone else. He knew the hurt she felt now would have been worse had he surrendered to the temptation to have a summer fling with her.

As he thought of the years ahead, he felt overwhelmed and afraid he'd never know what his parents and all his married friends shared — a happy marriage.

* * *

After suffering through more than two weeks of silence from Braden, Neida knew if she wanted to see him again, she would have to make the next move. When she finally summoned the nerve to call Raven, she found that Braden was back in California on the verge of leaving for Tulsa.

She pushed her untouched drink aside and met Raven's gaze across the table from her in the restaurant where they'd met for a drink. "Is that where they live?" she asked.

"They?"

"The two women he's considering marrying."

Ray frowned. "He told you about them?"

She nodded. "He was always almost brutally honest. He never lied or tried to deceive me into bed."

"Yes. They both live in Tulsa."

"And he's going to propose to one of them?"

"Probably — unless someone can get him to come to his senses. I sure as hell can't."

"He'll never marry me and I feel so ashamed of still

wanting him knowing that."

He reached across the table to cover her hand with his. "I'm not so sure of that, querida. I don't know if he told you but he's been in love before and lost her for the same reason. That hurt him but I've never seen him like he is now. I think if you're willing to risk getting hurt even more and you think he's worth the effort, you can change his mind."

"How? If a woman he loved couldn't change his mind?"

"I happen to think he loves you."

She caught her breath. "Did he tell you he did?"

"No, but as I told you before, he and I are very close. I've never seen him like this. I can't promise you won't end up hurt even more."

"But?"

"But if you want him badly enough, why not try to change his mind? At worse, you'll end up spending the rest of the summer with him. At best, you'll land his big, dumb ass permanently."

"You're asking me to humiliate myself."

"I'm asking you to give love a try. I think he loves you and I'm almost certain you love him."

She lowered her lids and remained silent.

"I'm flying home tomorrow for a few days. Why don't you come with me?"

Her lids flew up. "You two live together?"

"No. We live within forty minutes of each other. You can stay with me or I'll be happy to put you up in a hotel if you prefer."

"What if he's with another woman? He has been with them. Hasn't he?"

"That's something you should ask him." He held

up a hand. "And before you decide to point out that you'll take that as confirmation, let me remind you again that if it is true, he's single and entitled to sleep with whoever he likes." Raven lifted her hand to his lips. "If he has been with someone else, we both know it didn't mean anything."

"Oh do we?"

"Damn right we do, querida. You must have felt his anguish at walking away from you. You're not the only one hurting."

"But I'm the only one not trying to sleep him out of my system."

"You have to understand that he's a normal man with a man's needs. Most of the people we sleep with don't mean anything to us. Hell, I've never slept with a woman I actually loved."

She frowned. "Never?"

"There have been a few I liked and even fewer I was fond of, but never one I loved." He shook his head. "But this conversation isn't about me. It's about you and Bray. Will you come with me?"

Braden had definitely been with another woman — probably more than one. And she felt certain Raven knew that for certain. She sighed. While the thought saddened her, she wasn't going to lose sight of the fact that Braden didn't owe her any fidelity.

"Come with me before he goes to Tulsa and does something he'll find hard to extricate himself from. Once he proposes, it will take an act of God to keep him from going through with it. We need to keep him from doing that. Will you come with me?"

She doubted Braden would change his mind but she wanted at least a few weeks with him before he was off limits. "Yes."

"Thank you." He squeezed her hand. "I'll shield you and help you as much as I can. We all will. My brothers and I will lend you every support possible without breaking faith with him."

"Brothers?"

"You'll meet Shane in L.A. Seneka is outside in his car. Can I call him in to meet you?"

"I'd like that."

"Excuse me for a moment." He picked up his cell phone and made a brief call.

Minutes later a handsome male with dark hair and eyes joined them. Like Raven, bore a marked resemblance to Braden.

"Neka, this is Oneida Armstrong. Querida, this is my older brother Seneka."

Seneka Elkhorn clasped both his hands around the one she extended. "Querida, it's a pleasure to meet you. My wife, Autumn, sends her best wishes and asked me to tell you she'd love to meet you. Like you, she's a teacher."

She smiled, amazed that not long ago she had objected to Raven calling her querida. Now it seemed perfectly natural to hear the same word on Seneka Elkhorn's lips. Of course, it didn't have the same impact as it did when Braden used the word. Nevertheless, she liked hearing his brothers use it as well. When they did, she could pretend she really was special to Braden. "I'd like that."

He released her hand and glanced at Raven, who inclined his head. He turned back to face her. "I understand from Ray that you're probably feeling more than a little hurt. I know there's not much I can say to change that, but I would like to try to help you understand Braden better so you'll know why he feels he has to marry another woman—instead of the woman his heart aches for and whose heart aches for him."

She felt a lump of emotion rising in her throat. "You think I'm in love with him?"

"Are you?"

She lowered her lids but nodded. "But I don't think the feeling is mutual."

Each Elkhorn brother reached out to touch her hand. "He hasn't told me he loves you, but I know his feelings for you run so deep he's as unhappy as you must be.

"Our maternal and paternal grandparents struggled to hold onto their identities as Cherokee and shunned all things American. The only concession they were willing to make was speaking English. They spent their lives poor and never prospered. When they married, our parents took the opposite but just as extreme position.

"They never spoke Tsalagi to us so we grew up with English as our native tongue. They rarely spoke of our heritage and encouraged us to embrace all things American. And we did and we've all done well in our chosen professions. Bray designs software, Ray is a corporate attorney, I'm a CPA and Shane is talented enough to do whatever he sets his mind to. At the moment, he's a sports agent.

"When our grandparents died, our parents realized there was no one in our immediate family championing the Cherokee culture. By that time, we were all as American as you can get. When his health started to fail, our father expressed regret for the way they'd raised us. He feared once he and Mom were dead, we'd lose all connection with our heritage.

"Before he died, he had a talk with me and clearly one with Bray. He expressed deep regret for not encouraging us to embrace our culture and asked me to remember who and what I was and to promise to teach my children of their heritage. As the next oldest, he told me he was depending on me to do my part to support Bray's efforts to help keep our culture alive."

"Forgive me but I understand neither of your wives was Native."

He arched a brow. "That's because I never fell in love with a Native woman. As much as I loved and revered my father, there was no way I was going to allow his regrets to dictate who I married."

"Then why does Braden?"

"He's the oldest and enjoyed an even closer relationship with our parents than my other brothers and I did. Since none of the rest of us has shown an inclination to marry a Native woman, he feels our parents' regrets pressing in on him." He sighed. "In addition, he wants to do his part to help preserve our culture because he feels it's the right thing to do."

"So he's going to marry a Native woman no matter what anyone says?"

He shook his head. "That's what I thought—until I saw the effect meeting you had on him. I think we can still save him from his all too noble ambition—with your help. I know it's a lot to ask—but not if you love him and think he's worth a little effort."

"I already agreed to go to California, but I'm almost certainly going to regret it."

Seneka placed his hand over hers. "If it's any help, know that my brothers and I will be there with you every step of the way."

"And your mother? What can I expect from her?"

He released her hand and sat back in his seat. "She's doing her best to ensure he marries a Native woman. But please don't get the wrong idea about her. She loves him and when she realizes marrying a woman he doesn't love isn't going to make him happy, she'll come around—as she did with both my wives.

"In the short run, you might not get a warm and fuzzy feeling from her," he admitted.

"But you'll get it from us," Raven said, squeezing her hand.

"My brothers and I won't break faith with him, but we'll do anything short of that to help smooth the path to his heart for you," Seneka told her.

The lump returned, tightening her throat. Tears filled her eyes. "Thank you," she whispered.

"Autumn is pregnant and I don't have as much free time as I'd like, but if there's anything you need, call me. It doesn't matter if it's a shoulder to cry on, a lift, or money. Call me and I'll be there for you—as I'd expect Bray or Ray or Shay to be there for Autumn."

She blinked and the tears spilled down her cheeks. Braden might not love her, but he must have said or done something to make his brothers offer this level of support.

Seneka took a card out of his wallet and placed it near her purse on the table before lifting her free hand to his lips. "Call me if you need me, querida." He rose and left the restaurant.

Raven smiled at her. "I know you've heard the

expression that all's fair in love and war. Are you ready to go to war for the sake of love?"

She nodded.

"He's not going to make it easy because he thinks he's on a noble quest, but we'll be with you every step of the way. So can you be ready to fly out tomorrow?"

"Can you get a flight on such short notice?"

"One of Layton Grayhawk's brothers owns a plane. Another is a pilot. We don't have much time so Neka and I arranged with them to have Peyton fly us to California tomorrow afternoon on Randall's plane."

"Does Braden know I'm coming?"

"No."

"Are you going to tell him?"

"No," he said.

"Why not?"

He didn't respond.

Great. "You're afraid he won't be there?"

"Yes, but not because he doesn't want to see you, but because he's determined to be noble—even if it ruins his life. And we're determined to do what we can to prevent that."

"How long will I be there?"

"Pack for about eight days. If things go as planned, you'll be coming back with me in a week and he'll follow us or should I say he'll follow you in a day or two." He paused. "The stakes are high, querida, so I hope you're prepared to do what's necessary to reel him in."

She met the dark gaze so like Braden's and felt her cheeks burn. There was no doubt what he meant. She nodded without speaking.

"Never let it be said that I'm not a proponent for

sex safe, but going raw and without any birth control would increase your chances of doing that—especially if you're lucky enough to get pregnant."

She jerked her hand away. "Are you nuts? I have no intentions of ending up alone and pregnant while he goes off to marry another woman."

"You wouldn't be alone. Even if by some disaster things don't work out with Bray, I'd step up to the plate. Under no circumstances would you have to worry about being pregnant and alone."

She stared at him. "What?"

He shrugged. "I know we're not interchangeable, but if you like Bray's big, dumb ass, you should be able to learn to tolerate mine. If not me, there's always Shay."

"What?!"

"We're determined to rescue him from himself but we don't plan to do it at your expense. Shay and I have discussed it and if Bray can't be swayed and you end up pregnant, we're both prepared to marry you—if you'll have either one of us."

"Then one of you would be in a loveless marriage instead of him."

"Let us worry about that."

"You're all nuts. First he asked me if I'd considered you and now you offer yourself and Shane as a consolation prize. You're crazy as hell, Raven, but very sweet."

"He asked if you'd considered me? The thought didn't seem to bother him?"

"You sound surprised."

"I am and I'm serious. My brothers and I are all wealthy. Regardless of how things turn out, you'll come out of this debt free, querida. Neka, Shay, and I have already set up a hundred thousand dollar trust for you. If things work out with Bray, you can consider it a wedding present. If they don't, we'll each add an additional hundred thousand dollars. If there's a pregnancy, Bray will, of course, provide child support."

Did he really think any amount of money could persuade her to risk being a single mother? "I'm not interested in risking a pregnancy or your money."

"I understand how you feel about being a single mother, but the money isn't really important. It's just our way to say thank you for risking additional heartbreak."

"I don't need a financial incentive!"

"I'm very glad to hear it, but just so you know that if I thought you did, I wouldn't be here." He glanced at his watch. "I'll take you home so you can pack before we grab something to eat."

Chapter Nine

Braden, who had a date for the evening, had just stepped out of the shower and wrapped a towel wrapped around his waist when he realized the stereo in his living room was on. He frowned, glancing at his watch. 8:40. He knew Shane had picked Raven up at the airport two hours earlier.

One or both of them must have decided to make a nuisance of themselves by coming by uninvited. Damn brothers. Who the hell needed them? He walked through the house. As he neared the living room, the words of a song called *Statue of a Fool* registered. The singer lamented that a statue should be built so everyone could see a man who had let love slip through his hands.

Braden stopped and closed his eyes briefly. A vision of Neida imprinted itself on his eyelids. *Let love slip through his hands.* Damn them. Thoughts of her had tortured him for nearly every waking moment for the last three weeks. What the hell did they want from him?

He snapped his eyes opened and sucked in an angry breath. "I have a date and I don't have time for any shit from either one of you asses!" He stormed into the living room and came to an abrupt stop.

Both Raven and Shane rose from either end of one of his sofas. Neida, who had been seated between them, bit her lip and stared at him with wide, beautiful eyes.

Looking at her, he felt as filled with happiness and relief as Noah must have felt when the dove returned to the Ark with an olive leaf in its bill after the flood. Once their gazes locked, they might have been the only two people in the room. Hell, in the world. He was vaguely aware of Raven and Shane speaking but he didn't care what they were saying. They'd just given him the greatest gift possible—her presence.

He lifted a hand to wave them off as he walked across the room to caress her cheek.

Tears filled her eyes. "Braden!"

He closed his eyes and drew her into his arms. Bending his head, he pressed his face against her neck, inhaling slowly so he could savor her perfume. The wave of emotion he felt holding her again overwhelmed his senses. His heart beat such a wild rhythm he suspected she must have felt it pounding against her body. "Querida."

She stroked her fingers through his damp hair and slowly turned her head. The soft, warm lips he'd spent weeks longing for touched his.

Braden struggled to suppress a shudder and to control the desire that thundered through him. He turned his head so that his mouth caressed the corners of her sweet lips. "You shouldn't have come here."

"It's taken a few weeks to accept that nothing's changed for you. It's going to hurt when it's over, but I'll deal with that later. I want to spend the rest of the summer with you—on your terms," she whispered.

He felt torn. The most carnal part of his nature wanted to shout with glee. Another, finer part, hated that he was about to allow her to enter a relationship with him he knew would damage her sense of self-respect. She deserved far more than he was in a position to offer her. He had no right to trample her feelings solely to fulfill his lustful desires.

"I don't have the rest of the summer."

She sighed. "Then I'll take what I can get."

Damn! He inhaled slowly and released her. "Make yourself at home and give me a few minutes to dress."

"For your date?"

"Don't start any shit with me, Oneida!" He turned and left the room in time to see Raven and Shane about to step across the threshold of the open entrance door. Briefly locking gazes with one after another of them, he inclined his head slightly.

Both smiled and walked out, closing the front door behind them.

He continued to his bedroom where he quickly dressed and then called to cancel his date. When he returned to the living room he found Neida pacing.

"You shouldn't have come."

She bit her lip.

He extended a hand. "But I won't pretend I'm not delighted to see you again."

She crossed the room to press against him. Slipping her arms around him, she nipped at his ear. "Enough to cancel your date?"

"Already canceled."

She drew away from him. "I suppose you've been sleeping with everything in sight."

"You suppose right."

She looked away.

He slipped an arm around her. "None of them meant anything to me. How could they when you're the only woman who makes me burn with need?"

She curled her fingers in his hair. "I had to swallow my pride to follow you."

"I know, love. I know. I'll keep my promise not to stray while we're together." He kissed her forehead.

"Are you hungry? Have you had dinner?"

"Yes. We had Chinese on the way here. But you must be hungry since you had a date."

He met her gaze. "Neither one of us was interested in food."

She shoved him away. "There's such a thing as too much honestly, Braden. I'm not interested in hearing the details about your various lovers."

He caught her hand and pulled her back against him. "My apologies, querida. I know this is hard for you. It's hard for me too because I'm wild about you."

She lifted her head to look up at him but didn't speak.

"How long are you staying?"

"For a week."

He looked around. "I didn't see any luggage in the foyer. Where is it?"

She pulled out of his arms and stepped away from him. "I'm staying with Raven."

He caught her around her waist, pressing his lips against the back of her neck. "The hell you are!"

"You can't be jealous — not when you asked me if I'd considered him."

He cupped his hands over her breasts. "I adore you." He kissed her neck. "I have from the moment I saw you."

She arched her back and pressed her hands over his on her breasts. Then yawned.

Oh hell. With the time difference, it was nearly one in the morning for her. And if she were half as interested in him as he was in her, she hadn't been sleeping well. He kissed her neck again. "I'll show you my bedroom and you can shower and get some sleep while I get Raven to bring your luggage here. Okay?"

"I'm not sleepy. But even if I were, I can sleep later." She turned in his arms, yawning again.

"If you were to fall asleep on me, it would seriously damage my ego, big time."

She laughed and leaned into him.

"We have a date for tomorrow morning?"

She nodded. "Yes, Braden. Yes."

He took her hand in his and led her to his bedroom. As he stood watching as she looked around his bedroom, he tried not to fantasize about what it would be like to share a bedroom with her — permanently.

She turned to smile at him.

This would be one of the longest nights of his life.

Several hours later, he lay in his moonlit bedroom, watching her. She slept in one of his undershirts that ended mid-thigh. He longed to reach out to draw her into his arms. But decided that she was well worth waiting a few hours more for.

* * *

Neida woke alone in bed. She lay still for several moments, frowning before she remembered where she was. And that she probably only had a little more than a week to win Braden's heart. Her overnight case sat on the floor beside one of the chairs on either side of the French doors. So her luggage was here. A beautiful vase with a single red rose sat on each nightstand and the dresser top.

Smiling, she slipped out of bed and went into the master bathroom.

It was a modern bath with a large, sunken tub with jets, two large showers with frosted glass and separate sinks and with lighted vanities. She took a warm shower. After drying off, and giving attention to her make-up, with a warm toweling robe on, she returned to the master bedroom.

Ignoring her conscience that told her she had no right to snoop, she quickly checked the master suite. The adjourning walk-in closet was empty and his held only male clothes. Satisfied the suite held no evidence of his sharing it with a woman, she applied her favorite toiletries and slipped on the chemise he'd sent her. She added thigh-high hose and the expensive sandals. Then she pulled on one of his clean undershirts and left the bedroom.

Following the aroma of freshly brewed coffee, she made her way to the kitchen.

Dressed in light colored sweats, Braden turned from the island with a cup in his hand. Tilting his head, he leaned against the island, locking his gaze on my breasts. "Damn. You take my breath away."

Even though she fully intended to spend as much time in bed with him as possible, she suddenly felt shy. She crossed her arms over her breasts.

"You're ruining the view," he said, his voice deepening.

Her cheeks burned and her heart raced with excitement as she met his gaze. She sucked in a quick breath and dropped her hands to her sides. It was time he saw what he was about to get.

"Much better," he said, smiling. "Perfect, in fact."

She smiled at him. "I take it you're a breast man."

"And a leg man." He raised his gaze to hers. "I like women with lots of padding and curves and smooth dark skin. "

Neida nearly hyperventilated. Could this day get

any better? "In case you haven't noticed, I have dark skin and lots of curves."

"Beautiful, dark skin. Oh believe me, I've noticed all your charms, querida."

Then why the hell was he still standing so far away? "But?"

He glanced behind him at the counter where she saw several covered dishes. "Are you hungry?"

"Yes, Braden, but not for food so let's deal with the but hanging in the air."

"Do you know why I left Philadelphia without contacting you?"

Because you're a selfish, miserable bastard who doesn't care how much you hurt me. She shook her head.

"I didn't want to risk hurting you anymore than I already have. I want you more than you can imagine, but I'm still reluctant to do anything to hurt you."

"How many ways must I tell you that I'm an adult capable of making my own mistakes and decisions before you'll believe me, Braden?"

"To hurt you would be criminal."

"So is keeping me sexually frustrated. Unlike you, I haven't been sleeping around. All I've had is wishes and fantasies to relieve my sexual frustration."

He compressed his lips but didn't respond.

Don't let jealousy ruin what's about to happen. "Now I want the real thing—you."

He exhaled. "Then why are you so overdressed? Turn around and take off the shirt."

Heart pounding, she turned and slowly gripped the edges of his tee shirt to lift it over her head. Standing in just the chemise, hose, and heels, she glanced over her shoulder.

His gaze was locked on her rear end. "You have a very nice ass."

"It's rather large."

He nodded. "So I noticed. It's large and round — just as a real woman's ass should be." He abruptly raised his gaze to her lips. "At the risk of sounding like I have a one track mind, could we just get the first one out of the way?"

"The first what?"

"Fuck."

Oh hell yeah! She moistened her lips and slowly turned to face him.

He held out his hand, looking into her eyes.

She walked across the kitchen towards him.

He took her hand in his and brushed the fingers of his other hand against her cheek. "In case I haven't already told you, I'm so happy to have you here."

She leaned into him. "Show me. Please."

"You have such soft, dark, beautiful skin. Everything about you is sexy and beautiful." He slipped his other arm around her waist and drew her close. "I don't know how I managed to keep my hands off you last night."

His cologne heightened her awareness of him. The feel of his hard body against hers sent a jolt of raw need through her. The time for talking was past. She lifted her chin with her lips parted and her tongue extended.

He bent his head.

She closed her eyes.

He brushed his warm, insistent mouth against the corners of hers.

"Oh Braden. I want you."

"And I want you, love," he whispered before he drew her into his arms and kissed her.

She clung to him, eagerly returning the warm, deep kiss as he stroked his hands over her body.

Each teasing caress filled her with heat and the need to feel his thick cock sliding deep inside her.

She trembled, touching her tongue to his.

He settled his lips overs hers.

Yes. Oh God, yes!

He kissed her with a slow, deliberate passion that left her trembling with need.

She slipped her arms around his neck, pressing her breasts against his chest.

He made an incoherent sound as he continued to kiss her.

She moaned, her desire for him overwhelming her.

He slid his hands down her back to palm her cheeks.

Neida loved having her bare ass touched. She ground herself against his groin, trying to show him how much she wanted and needed him inside her.

He deepened his kiss, sweeping his tongue into her mouth while he pressed her against his lower body.

Feeling the delicious hardening of his cock, she rubbed her breasts against his chest, her pussy flooding.

He dragged his mouth from hers to stare down into her eyes. "I ache for you," he told her.

After being celibate for a year, she needed sex and she wanted it with this handsome, sexy male whose hard cock pulsed against her body. She reached up to slip her fingers in his hair and draw his head down to hers.

Rightly interpreting her silent response as an admission she wanted to be fucked, he unzipped the chemise and pushed it off her shoulders. He stared at her breasts for several silent moments before he quickly pushed the chemise down over her thighs to her feet.

Placing her hands on his shoulders, she stepped out of it, using her foot to kick it aside. Then she stood naked except for her hose and heels.

He stepped back to stare at her. "Damn. You have an exquisite body."

She moistened her lips. "Let's see yours, Braden."

Rather to her surprise, he undressed so slowly she got the feeling he was doing a sexy strip for her.

Her heart pounded as he bared his upper body, revealing broad shoulders, a big chest, and narrow hips. She was going to love feeling that chest crushing her breasts as he fucked her. No. As they fucked each other. She was well past the point where she could be content with anything less than full participation.

After giving her a few moments to admire his upper body, he kicked off his shoes and removed his pants. There was a noticeable bulge in the boxer briefs he wore.

She stared at his groin. Oh lord. His thick cock was going to feel wonderful powering into her body.

She swallowed slowly. "Condom?"

He reached down to pull one from his trouser pocket. Placing it on the island, he gripped her waist and lifted her onto the island top.

She sat with her legs shamelessly parted and her wet pussy on display.

He moved closer. Taking her left leg in his hand, he bent his head, kissing her toes.

Oh. Nice.

He nipped, kissed, and licked a path up her thigh to her slit.

She sank her teeth into her bottom lip as his tongue pressed against her clit.

"Oh Braden!"

He spent several delicious moments making her moan and buck her hips wildly by sucking and gently nibbling her clit.

When she felt ready to burst, he pressed a long, wet kiss against her slit before he trailed a moist, biting path down her other thigh to suck her toes.

She compressed her lips, inching her hips forward. "Braden...?"

"Yes, my love?"

"Please..."

He nibbled at her toes. "Please what, querida?"

"Please," she moaned. "You know what I want and need. Don't make me beg."

"Never, love." He linked her legs around his body and stepped between her thighs.

Heart pounding, she reached out to slip her hands inside and down the back of his boxer briefs. She caressed his tight ass cheeks.

"Touch me," he urged.

"I am touching you," she teased.

"Touch my dick," he said.

Gazing into his eyes, she slipped her hands around his body. She ran her fingertips over his pubic hair before she touched his cock. It felt warm and semi-erect, almost but not quite ready to invade and conquer her pussy. She closed one hand around his shaft and cupped the other under his balls.

"Oh yes, love." He inched his hips forward.

She gently squeezed his balls while pumping his cock.

He reached out to pinch her nipples. When they hardened, he began to caress her breasts in sync with her stroking of his cock.

Once he was fully erect, she stared down at him. Lord, he wasn't just thick, but long as well. Oh God, she was going to enjoy every moment of having his big cock inside her pussy. Impatient to feel him inside her, she leaned forward to sink her teeth into his earlobe. "Please, Braden."

"Oh I'm going to please you." He slid a hand down her body to her slit.

Her hips jerked at the feel of his fingers probing her.

"You're warm and slick and I'm hard. I think you're finally ready for me."

She squeezed his balls. "Oh God, I've been ready from the moment I saw you."

He stepped closer, rubbing his cock along the length of her pussy.

Suppressing the urge to push forward to impale herself on his bare cock, she reached beside her for the condom. "Take off your briefs," she said. "I want to feel your pubic hair."

"As you like, love."

While he pulled off his underwear, she tore open the foil packet. When he stepped back between her thighs, she handed him the condom.

"You do it," he said.

She stared at his cock, imagining what it would look like after he'd withdrawn from her after having fucked her raw and come deep in her pussy. It would be slick with cum and pussy juice and even more beautiful than it looked seeping precum.

Moistening her lips, she reluctantly rolled the rubber over part of his big dick. Pausing, she slid her fingers over the bare half of his shaft. What would it be like to feel his big, bare cock buried to the hilt inside her, jetting cum into her pussy instead of wasting in in the condom?

"If I didn't know better, querida, I'd think you wanted to go raw," he said.

She lowered her lids to conceal her expression and shook her head. "We can't, Braden."

"We can—if we both want it. I'm fairly certain you don't make a habit of it and neither do I."

"I've never done it," she said.

"Never done what?"

"Had sex without a condom."

He tipped up her chin. "Never? Not even as a reckless teenager?"

"I was never reckless enough to have unsafe sex. The only naked cock that has been inside me even briefly is yours."

"Oh damn. Now you know I want to slide inside you raw even more."

"But you're not going to," she said.

"I could sweet talk you into it," he threatened.

She nodded. "I know you can but if you have even an ounce of consideration for my feelings, you won't, Braden."

He inhaled quickly. "I have far more concern for you than you think I do."

She believed him and for one crazy moment, she

wanted to pull the condom off, toss it away, and impale her pussy on his bare cock.

He reached down and finished covering his cock before he positioned himself at her entrance. He then endeared himself to her by leaning down to kiss her. His mouth, warm and insistent, brushed against hers, sending a tingle through her.

Greedy for the intimacy she'd craved from the moment she saw him, she gripped his hips and pushed hers forward. The movement forced the head of his shaft between the lips of her slit.

"Oh shit!" He slid his hands down her back to cup her ass and pulled her closer, quickly impaling her on his entire thick cock.

She gasped and shuddered before bucking her hips against his and tightening her vaginal muscles around the thick, hard length firmly in possession of her pussy.

Chapter Ten

She expected a quick, hard fuck that ended before she came. Instead, he delighted her by keeping his movements slow but steady, giving them both time to enjoy each wonderful plundering stroke. His lips coerced hers apart and he sucked her tongue into his mouth as he guided his wonderful length in and out of her.

Hot with need and desire, she rocked her hips, moving with him, while her heart raced with joy and her pussy sent chills of ecstasy all through her body. Between addictive kisses, he slapped her ass cheeks and whispered to her in a voice deepened with desire.

"You're so beautiful. I've never met any woman who moved me more. My darling, I adore you and worship the ground you walk on."

Neida drank in every husky assurance, totally lost in him and the sense of delight having him so deep inside her gave her. Under his expert attention, her climax built rapidly. With her back arched and satisfaction just a few strokes away, she dug her nails in his ass and humped wildly on his cock.

"Oh Braden. Fuck me and make me come. Make me come. I'm so close."

He slipped a hand between their bodies and rubbed his thumb against her clit. "Come, my darling. Come."

A shudder shook her whole body and she experienced the most powerful climax she'd felt in years. As she came, she compressed her vaginal muscles around him.

"Holy shit!" Clutching her so close it hurt, he

rutted into her with deep, almost painful strokes until his big body shook.

Knowing he was coming thrilled her. She clutched him close as he shuddered in her arms.

Replete and confident she'd satisfied him, she slumped back against the island top.

Resting his weight on his arms, he bent over her to engage her in a series of kisses so hot and passionate, that she was a breath away from coming again when he finally turned his head so that his lips brushed against her cheek. "Oh damn, querida. That was the most incredible sex I've ever had."

She stroked her fingers through his hair. "Ever?"

"I don't stutter, Neida. I said and meant ever." He nipped her earlobe. "You're sweet, sexy and you had me from the day we met."

But for how long? Think positive, Neida. You just have to find a way to keep him from going to Tulsa and damning you both to a life filled with second bests.

She caressed his face, fighting the urge to whisper that she loved him.

He kissed her again before he eased his cock out of her.

She bit her lip to stifle a sound of protest and sat up.

He gripped her hips and lifted her off the island.

The moment her feet touched the floor, he engulfed her in a warm embrace. "God I missed you." He released her to gaze down into her eyes. "Walking away from you was the hardest thing I've ever done."

Really? Then I'll just have to make sure you don't have to do it again. She smiled and stretched on her toes to kiss the corner of his mouth. "What does a woman have to do to get something to eat around here?"

He laughed and slapped each ass cheek hard. "Go shower and I'll make some toast and pour the coffee."

"Toast and coffee? I don't keep the curves you claim to be so fond of by eating toast for breakfast—especially after the workout you just gave me."

"I am fond of your curves and of you, querida." He caressed her cheeks. "I don't eat breakfast myself, but I made several items for you to choose from. They're on the warming trays behind you." He kissed her again.

She slid her hands across his shoulders and reluctantly stepped away from him. "You keep that up and I'll decide I want more of you for breakfast."

"We can do that." He slapped her ass until each cheek stung.

She gasped, feeling her pussy flood.

He bent his head and bit each nipple.

"Ouch," she said and stumbled away from him.

He laughed and paddled her ass again before she rushed out of the room with each cheek feeling as if they were on fire.

As she made her way back to the master bedroom, she noticed flowers in the living room and upstairs and downstairs hallway for the first time. Eager to see him again, she showered quickly, dressed, did her face, and hurried back to the kitchen.

He was at the counter again. His hair was damp, and he wore jeans and a short-sleeved pull over that emphasized his superb upper body physique.

He turned to smile at her. "Damn. You look lovely."

She glanced down at the new cream and mauve cotton pants suit she wore. "I'm glad you like it."

He extended a hand. "I like you."

She crossed the kitchen to lean against him, tilting her head back to meet his warm, dark gaze. "I more than like you, Braden."

He slid his arm around her waist. "How much more?"

"Too much to disclose on an empty stomach," she said and waltzed away from him. "Where's the breakfast you promised me?"

"I thought you might enjoy breakfast out back." He slipped an arm around her shoulders and walked her out to the patio.

There were five tables with umbrellas. He must entertain a lot. Several covered dishes occupied the top of the serving sideboard that ran along one outside wall of the house.

He removed the covers and handed her a plate.

She chose an omelet, breakfast sausage, and French toast.

He carried her plate to the table, seated her, and then returned to pour her orange juice and coffee before sitting opposite her with a cup of coffee.

The omelet was delicious with bits of bacon and cheese, the sausage juicy and tender, the toast golden brown. While she ate, he sat sipping his coffee, his gaze locked on her.

"You're staring," she said, pushing her plate aside.

He shrugged. "I'm a normal, horny male and you're a beautiful woman. Of course I'm staring. I've made reservations for dinner out tonight. How would you like to spend the day?"

There was a pool beyond the patio. "I'm still feeling a little jetlag and I have a new swimming suit I'm eager to try out for you."

He arched a brow. "I'm sure it's a very flattering suit but nothing beats miles of warm, naked, dark brown curves."

"You swim in the nude?"

"This area is private and I don't have any nosey neighbors so I sometimes swim in the buff."

She moistened her lips. It was one thing to allow him to see her naked when they had sex. Swimming, when everything would jiggle, was another matter. On the verge of insisting on wearing her swimsuit, she met his gaze. Seeing the look of complete desire in his eyes, her protests died. No man who didn't love every inch of her body could possibly emote such desire when he looked at her.

Besides, while her breasts jiggled, his cock would hopefully be doing the same thing. Heat burned her cheeks at the thought of pool sex. "Sounds like a plan," she said. "Now can we discuss who you've been fucking since we last saw each other?"

He sighed. "I was trying to fuck you out of my system, but obviously, without any success whatsoever." He reached across the table to place a hand over hers. "I really do adore you, Neida."

Did she have what it would take to turn his adoration to love within a week? "These women in Tulsa…"

"What about them?"

"Which one are you leaning towards?"

He shook his head. "I don't have a preference. Neither will ever make me feel a quarter of what I feel for you."

She stared at him. What sane man would marry

another woman under those circumstances? "I wish you wanted me enough to not choose either one of them, Braden."

"I'll do what I have to do, but you shouldn't mistake that obligation as a sign that I'm not totally into you." He lifted her fingers to his mouth. "I couldn't possibly adore you anymore than I already do."

A fat lot of good that would do her if she wasn't successful in changing his mind. "The feeling is mutual, Braden."

He stared at her in silence.

"What?" She touched her face and ran her tongue over her teeth. "Is my nose shiny or something?"

He released her hand and sat back in his chair. "I'm trying to come up with the right words so you don't misunderstand what I'm about to say."

"Just say it."

"I'd like to do something for you."

"Something like what?"

"Financial."

She shook her head. "You've already paid off my students loans. That's enough."

"I have a lot of money and it would provide a measure of comfort to know I'd used some of it to make your life easier."

More likely it would assuage his conscience. "I don't want your money, Braden. I want you."

"You said you understood, Neida."

"I do—with my head. My heart's another matter. The two of us really want you."

"You know I want you too, but my plans haven't changed, Neida."

She withdrew her hand from his and picked up her

coffee cup. "Then we'll just have to make the most of this week." And she'd have to try not to fall even deeper in love with him.

"I know that's not what you want to hear, Neida and I'm sorry."

There was no doubting the sincerity in his voice or the look in his eyes that went beyond mere desire. "The house is filled with flowers. You have a credit with the florist you were trying to use up?"

"The single roses in the bedroom are from me. The rest are from Neka."

"That's sweet of him, but then—"

He rose and walked round the table to lean down to kiss her on the neck. "Our time together is too short to spend it talking about my brothers." He took her hand in his and lifted her to her feet.

She turned into his arms. "He's charming."

"So am I."

She rubbed her cheek against his. "Yes. You are." *And I love you.*

He hugged her. "I'd give anything to change the circumstances that will keep us apart."

So would I. But since she couldn't, there was no point in brooding. She kissed him and eased out of his arms.

He returned to his seat.

She sat down to finish her coffee. "Can I have a tour of the house?"

"Of course." He rose and walked around to her chair. "Me casa es su casa."

Didn't she wish?

He had a large two-story home with five bedrooms, three full baths and two powder rooms. The furnishings were modern and sparse. What was there was designed to save time and effort. The house was very nice but could have benefited from a woman's touch.

"Are you going to miss this house and living on the West Coast?" she asked when they returned to the patio after their tour. This time, they sprawled on lounge chairs, her in a swimsuit, him in swimming briefs.

He shook his head. "No. It's nice enough but I don't have any particular emotional attachment to it. I wasn't raised here and I've never shared it with anyone special and…" he trailed off and stared at her. "Actually, I take that back. And maybe I will keep it."

"Why?"

He caressed her cheek. "Spending a week here with you will probably make it nearly impossible to sell."

"Somehow I don't think your wife would appreciate your keeping it for that reason."

He shrugged. "Probably not, but since she'll be under no illusions about my feelings, I can't see what she'll have to complain about."

She stared at him. "You mean you're going to tell her—"

"I'll pay her the courtesy of being honest with her—as I have been with you."

Then, God willing, both of his likely prospects would have too much pride to marry a man intent on marrying for the sake of duty rather than love. She shook her head. "That's going to be one hell of a proposal."

He stared at her and then laughed. "I suppose it will lack a little romance."

"A little?"

"Okay. It will lack all romance."

"But you think you're so wonderful that one or both of them will jump at the chance to enter a loveless marriage with you? You must have a lot of money."

"I have enough to entice even a greedy woman into marriage, but you have a point. Maybe they'll both refuse."

"If they do? What then? You start over?"

"I hadn't given that any thought," he admitted.

"Because you're so sure no one could possibly refuse the chance to enter a loveless marriage with you?"

He arched a brow. "You think I overrate my charms?"

"Vastly."

"You might be right."

"If I am?"

"Then I might consider I'd done my best—and come looking for you."

"You flatter yourself if you think I'd be interested in being your consolation prize!" She got up.

He rose and caught her hand before she could turn away. "You know perfectly well my heart belongs to you. That would make it impossible for you to be anything but my first choice."

Neida leaned close to kiss his chin before stepping away from him. "I'm ready for a swim." She unzipped her bathing suit and looked at him.

He stepped close enough to push it off her shoulders, exposing her breasts. Bending his head, he kissed each nipple before pushing it over her belly and down her thighs.

She stepped out of it and kicked it away.

Keeping his gaze locked on her nude body, he quickly removed his swimming briefs before he took her into his arms.

Then his cell phone rang.

He swore softly and released her.

She blinked. "Don't answer it, Braden."

He shook his head. "It's my mother. I'd better make sure everything is okay. Give me a few moments." He picked up his cell phone from the table and walked a few feet away. "Hi, Mom…I'm fine…How are you?…Actually, I am a little busy, but I was going to call you to reschedule our lunch date…No, I'm not alone…We'll reschedule our lunch date after I return from Tulsa…Yes. I'm still going…We'll see…Bye, Mom." He put his cell phone down and turned to smile at her. "Now where were we?"

"About to take a swim," she said and slipped into the pool before he could put his arms around her again.

He dived into the pool and came up in front of her. He cupped his hands over her breasts. "Why swim when we can make love?"

"Because I want to swim," she said, turned on her back and floated away from him. If he thought he could discuss marrying another woman in front of her with his mother while not mentioning her and then expect to fuck her the next moment, he had another think coming. She knew the score but she wasn't about to have it shoved down her throat.

He annoyed her by giving up and swimming several laps of the pool.

She floated to the steps and climbed out onto the tiles.

He let out a lusty wolf whistle that restored her good humor.

Smiling, she wrapped a beach towel around her body and stretched out on the lounger.

He stalked across the pool tiles to the lounger. Kneeling beside it, he opened her robe and slid a big palm down from her breasts to cup between her thighs.

She closed her legs on his hand. "If you think the way back into my good graces is through my pussy, you're absolutely right." She spread her legs and reached a hand down to cup his cock. "Especially if you cover this beautiful bad boy and slide him deep inside me."

He pressed a quick kiss against her mouth. "I'll be right back," he said.

Still smiling, she watched him walk quickly into the house.

When he returned five minutes later, he had a condom over his fully erect shaft.

She patted the lounger between her legs. "Now that's what I like to see, a beautiful bad boy dressed and already to play."

He knelt beside her lounger. Sliding a palm up her inner thigh to her pussy, he slipped a finger inside her.

She closed her eyes, enjoying the dual sensations of his finger inside her and his mouth and teeth nipping at her toes. "Oh Braden. Braden."

Sliding a second finger inside her, he sucked her toes until her pussy gushed.

Then, while she moaned, he bent his head and kissed her pussy.

Her hips bucked. "Braden."

His tongue pressed against her clit several times,

sent countless shivers through her body.

"Oh Braden. Eat me. Please."

"Oh I'm going to, love." Tilting her hips, he dragged his tongue along her slit several times.

She moaned and shuddered. "Oh God. Eat me. Eat me."

Pushing his tongue into her, he ate her to a slow and exquisite climax that had her jerking her hips off the lounger.

He added two fingers and sucked her clit.

Wrapping her legs around him, she pressed his head closer as she came.

He licked her pussy lips, extending his tongue inside her before he rose to join her on the lounger, sliding between her legs.

She reached down to close her fingers around his cock and guide it into her body. When she felt the big head slip between her outer lips, she bit her lip. "Oh…"

He pushed his hips forward, powering his entire shaft inside her.

"Oh God!" She jerked her hips off the lounger and rocked them against his. "Oh…Braden…yes!"

"Yes," he echoed, slipping his palms under her body to cup her ass. He rolled them over so that she lay on top of him. "Fuck me, querida."

She slipped her tongue in his mouth and kissed him hungrily until he thrust his hips off the lounger, forcing his cock deep into her body.

She gasped, pushing against his shoulders. "Not so fast, handsome. This time I want to be in control." Lifting her upper body off his, she sat up and slowly raised her hips, allowing all but the head of his cock to slip from her body.

He slid his hands down her back to her waist and pulled her back onto his cock.

"Oh yes!" Trailing her hands down his body, she rode him slowly, enjoying the hard, deep motion of his shaft thrusting back up into her body. Each time it did, she felt a jolt of pleasure shake her body. Arching her back, she tossed back her head, clutched her hands on his shoulders, and rode him quickly, bucking her hips wildly.

His cock felt so good sliding deep into her pussy and setting it aflame. She wanted to prolong the pleasure building in her for as long as possible. He made that impossible when he reached up to pinch her nipples hard before he ran a palm down her body to rub his thumb against her clit.

The muscles in her belly tightened and she could no longer hold back the powerful climax induced by the wonderful motion of his big cock powering in and out of her pussy. Shuddering with pleasure, she collapsed on his chest. "Braden...Braden...oh Braden."

Curling his fingers in her hair, he drew her mouth down on his.

Gyrating, her hips with a slow heat, she compressed her vaginal muscles around his cock with a steady pressure until he tore his mouth from hers, clutched her ass in his hands, rutted his cock into her, and finally came.

After he stopped coming, she lay sprawled on his body with her face pressed against his damp shoulder. *Braden...Braden...I love you. I love you.*

He stroked his hands down her back to cup her ass, whispering something soft and indistinct.

"What? What did you say, Braden?"

"Damn, you're so sweet and making love to you is different and more powerful than it's ever been with anyone else. You're not like anyone else." He clutched her close. "I don't know how I'm going to live without you."

Heart racing, she lifted her head to look down at him. "You don't have to try to find out. I'm yours if you want me enough, Braden."

"There's no question that I want you enough. I ache for you. I think you know that, querida. Please help me do what I feel I have to do."

"Oh Braden. Please don't."

"I have to, love."

She sighed and lifted her hips, in preparation for climbing off him.

He pulled her back down onto his cock and kissed her, pushing his tongue into her mouth. He caressed her ass and hips.

She returned his kisses for several moments until she became aroused again. Then she tore her lips away from his. "We can't, Braden. Not without a fresh condom."

He allowed her to slip off his shaft before he pulled her back down into his arms. "Then just let me hold you."

"If you want; forever, Braden."

He held her close. "Oh God, querida, I wish."

"So do I, Braden."

"Are you going to be able to forgive me?"

She wanted to say no, but couldn't. "I'll need some time, but yes. I'll forgive you." *Because I love you.*

He cuddled her closer, pressing his lips against her hair. "Let me take care of you financially."

"No. You've already done as much as I'm going to allow you to. Let's not argue. I just want to fall asleep in your arms and have you hold me forever."

He kissed her hair and held her until she fell asleep.

Chapter Eleven

Hold her forever? God, how he wished he could. Forever with her would be paradise, but apparently, marital joy wasn't in the cards for him. He'd have to be content knowing Seneka was happily married. Hopefully, Raven and Shane would also be lucky enough to join Seneka in wedded bliss.

He kissed her forehead and gently eased her body to one side. Rising, he covered her with a toweling robe. Then he repositioned two of the freestanding umbrellas to shield her from the sun before he went inside. After a quick shower, he changed and returned to the patio where he sat watching her sleep until his cell phone rang.

Braden glanced at the screen and frowned. Arrow, T with a Tulsa phone number. There was no way in hell he was going to answer the call—even if Neida hadn't been there. He hadn't given her his number. An old-fashioned guy, he preferred to do the chasing in a relationship—unless the woman in pursuit was Neida. He turned off the ringer and allowed the call to go to voicemail.

Then he called his mother. "Hi, Mom."

"Braden, what a nice surprise."

"Tina Arrow just called me."

"That must have been a nice surprise for you."

"It was a surprise all right, but not a particularly pleasant one."

"Why not? I thought you liked her."

"I don't know her, Mom."

"All the more reason to spend some time talking to her before you go to Tulsa."

"I didn't give her my phone number because I didn't want her to have it, Mom and I'm not interested in talking to her until I go to Tulsa."

"So you're angry?"

Damn right he was. "We're on the same page, Mom, but I'm going to get there in my own way and in my own time. I'm not interested in having my time with my guest interrupted by anymore calls from Tulsa."

"You are angry."

He didn't respond.

"Is your time with your houseguest that important?"

"Yes. It is, Mom."

"What's she like?"

He knew what she wanted to know and wasn't in the mood to try to placate her. "She's African-American and full-figured. Just as I prefer my women, Mom."

"I see. Does she know of your plans to go to Tulsa?"

"Yes."

"And she's still willing to—"

"If you're about to suggest anything negative about her, Mom—please don't."

"I...won't. But you're still planning to go to Tulsa?"

"Yes."

She sighed. "I'll call them both and tell them not to disturb you."

So she'd given his number to both of them. Great. "Thank you, Mom," he said. Still annoyed, he ended the call before she could respond.

Moments later, his cell phone rang. He inhaled slowly before he answered it. "Yes, Mom?"

"I just wanted to say I'm sorry, Braden. I know I shouldn't have given either of them your number but I'm just so excited at the thought of one of my boys marrying a Native woman. I guess I was afraid if too much time passed, you'd change your mind."

Hearing the fear in her voice dissipated some of his anger. He sighed. It was a good thing one of them was excited at the thought. "I understand that, Mom, but I need you to allow me to handle my own personal life in my own way. Please don't interfere again."

"I...I won't, Braden."

He hated the disappointment he heard in her voice but he'd be damned if he'd waste any of his time with Neida talking to other women. And she needed to understand that. "Thank you."

"I love you, Braden. You know that?"

"Yes. I know, Mom and I love you too. I'll talk to you soon."

After ending the call, he called the office for an update. Then he spent some time working on his laptop before he glanced at his watch. Rising, he crossed the patio to kneel down beside the lounger where Neida slept.

Lifting the toweling robe, he feasted his gaze on her nude body. She had such lovely, smooth dark skin. Her large breasts with the wide aureoles beckoned his lips and tongue. Tearing his gaze from her breasts, he looked down her body. He loved her long legs, rounded belly, and big round ass.

His gaze was drawn back to her stomach. How sexy would it look slowly swelling as his baby grew inside her? The thought nearly made him hard. *That's not going to happen so don't torture yourself with such sweet fantasies.*

He raised his gaze, not allowing it to linger on her pussy. Her long dark hair fell across her cheek. He pushed it aside. She was so beautiful. It was strange how she managed to look both sexy and in need of protection.

What a life he would have if he could spend the rest of it making love to her and cherishing her. Going to sleep each night with her in his arms and waking with her beside him the next morning would be paradise. A paradise he wasn't destined to share.

He caressed her cheeks before he kissed her on the corner of her mouth.

Her eyes fluttered open. She smiled up at him. "Braden."

Damn he liked hearing the husky inflection in her voice when she said his name. But then he liked nearly everything about her. Actually, he more than liked everything about her. And that was the rub. If he just liked her, he wouldn't feel so torn.

"What time is it, Braden?"

"We have dinner reservations so it's time to get up and shower and dress."

"What?" She frowned and sat up, pulling the toweling robe up to cover her breasts. "Why did you allow me to sleep so long?"

"You were obviously tired."

"I was a little, but..." She linked her free arm around his neck. "I can sleep when I return home. I want to waste as little time sleeping as possible while we're together."

Thinking of the remaining time they had left, he nodded. "I know the feeling."

"Almost two days gone and only five left." She stroked her fingers through his hair. "I don't want to spend much of the remaining time left in the company of other people."

"Meaning?"

"Cancel dinner out and let's eat in."

"I rarely eat at home. There's not much here."

She leaned close to press her lips against his ear. "It's not food that I'm interested in eating, Braden."

The thought of her soft, warm lips wrapped around his cock sent a wave of lust crashing over him. He turned his head to look into her eyes. "That's a tempting offer, but I'm not interested in having you think all I want is sex."

"Even though that is all you want?"

He jerked away from her and rose. "That's what you think?"

"Yes, but I came prepared to deal with it."

He inhaled and exhaled slowly before he could trust himself not to snap at her. That was how it must look from her prospective—even though nothing could be further from the truth. "If that's all I wanted, I would have stayed in Philadelphia and pressed you until I got what I wanted. I left without doing that because I didn't want to hurt you and now you have the nerve to accuse me of just wanting sex?"

Silly bitch! "Do I need to remind you that you're the one who followed me?"

She looked away and lowered her lids. "No. I don't need a reminder that I tossed my pride away to follow you."

Oh shit! He hated the sound of dejection in her voice. He knelt beside her lounger again. "I'm sorry.

That remark was totally uncalled for."

"It doesn't matter."

But the pain in her voice said otherwise. Thank God he hadn't actually called her a bitch out loud. "It does matter. Hurting you any further is the last thing I want to do."

She shook her head and got off the lounger. "I'll go shower," she said.

He rose and crossed the patio to catch her hand. Resisting her efforts to pull away, he turned her to face him. "I'm not sure what I can say to convince you that I'm not just after sex with you. I—"

She pressed her fingers against his lips. "You don't have to say anything else, Braden. Everything you said was true. I know it's not just sex. Obviously you can have any woman you want."

"You're the only one I want, querida."

"Unfortunately, the feeling is mutual."

Her words stung like hell, but from her point of view, meeting and becoming attracted to him would have to be seen as unfortunate. He released her and watched her hurry into the house. He returned to the table and called Raven. "I need a favor, Ray."

"Name it."

"Come and get her and take her home."

"Does she want to go home?"

"The longer she stays, the more she'll be hurt. And I think I've hurt her enough. Come and get her."

"Where is she?"

"She went to shower and dress. How soon can you be here?"

"In half an hour."

"Let yourself in."

"Where will you be?"

"I'm leaving now. I'll be gone for a few hours. I expect her to be gone when I return."

"Does she know I'm coming?"

"No."

"Are you going to tell her?"

"You can do that when you arrive."

"Bray! You're just going to walk out without telling her?"

"Yes and if I want any advice from you, I'll ask for it. Until then, mind our own damned business." He slammed the phone down and went inside.

Suppressing the urge to go to the master suite, he retrieved his gym bag from the foyer closet, picked up his SUV keys, and left the house. Although he had a gym in his house, he decided to go to the club where he had a membership and sometimes took clients and visiting friends to workout.

Two hours at the gym should tire him enough to make sleep possible when he had to sleep alone that night.

After he drove off his property, he toyed with the idea of leaving a message on Neida's cell phone while she was still in the shower but changed his mind. Five minutes later, his cell phone rang. He activated his Bluetooth. "Yes?"

"Where are you, Bray?"

"I'm on the way to the gym. Where are you?"

"On my way to your house," Raven answered.

"Then why are you calling me?"

"To get you to change your mind. Do you really think walking away from her again without any warning is the way to go, Bray?"

"She thinks all I want is sex."

"And you think dumping her again—after you got it is the way to change her mind about that?"

Damn him! "I told you I didn't want any more advice, Raven!"

"And I'm telling you you're making a big mistake."

"I'm not Neka. I don't need your advice on how to handle my love life."

"Really? Newsflash, Bray, for all the teasing we give Neka about his lack of experience with women, he's the only one of us who's managed to successfully land every woman he's gone after."

Damn if he wasn't right. Braden swallowed some of his fury.

"Don't walk away from her again. Go back home before she realizes you were going to abandon her to me."

"What the fuck is wrong with you, Raven? You're behaving as if I were abandoning her in the middle of the desert. After all, you're the one who landed me in this present mess."

"You consider her a mess, Bray?"

"Fuck off, Raven and get your ass over to my house." He ended the call and clenched his hands on the steering wheel. One of these days he was going to knock Raven on his know-it-all ass.

* * *

Neida emerged from the shower with a new determination to wrestle her emotions back under control. Expecting anything more than sex from Braden would only make things more difficult for her and might even result in his pushing her away prematurely.

She dressed and stood in front of the mirror in the

dressing room adjourning the master bedroom. The cream-colored dress with the short shelves and scooped bodice showcased her breasts. The skirt ended just below her knees, allowing her to accent her legs without wearing a dress she considered too short.

Satisfied she looked her best, she put a cape over her dress before she spent several minutes brushing her hair. When she was satisfied with her efforts, she put it in a French braid. Removing the cape, she added the diamond earrings her parents had given her as a college graduation present, sprayed herself with her favorite perfume, slipped on her heels, picked up her matching clutch, and went into the living room.

To her surprise, Raven, instead of Braden, occupied the living room. "Raven." She smiled and crossed the room with her hand extended.

Smiling, he took both of hers hands in his. "Querida, you look lovelier every time I see you."

"I could say the same about you. You are one big, handsome hunk."

"I am. Aren't I?"

"And so very modest too."

They both laughed before she stretched up to kiss his cheek.

He slipped an arm around her waist.

Smiling, she glanced around. "Where's Braden?"

He bent his head to brush his lips against her cheek. "Braden? Braden who?"

She lifted her head to look up at him. "You know, Braden. He's taller and better looking than you."

He arched a brow. "Slightly taller? Yes. But better looking? Querida, I had no idea you had such poor eyesight. You must be practically legally blind if you think he's better looking."

She laughed again and leaned into him.

He kissed her neck.

She jerked back. "Raven!"

"Yes, querida?"

She pressed a hand to the spot on her neck he had kissed. "What are you doing here and where's Braden?"

"Right here."

She bit her lip and jerked away from Raven. How long had he stood in the doorway?

Raven smiled and deliberately put an arm around her shoulders. "As usual, Bray, your timing stinks. Neida and I were just about to get better acquainted."

The look on Braden's face assured her there was no mistaking Raven's meaning. She could almost feel the tension between the two brothers.

Braden stalked across the room to them. He removed Raven's arm from her shoulders and slapped his cheek. "In your dreams. In future, see that you keep your lips to yourself."

"If you're not careful, it'll be in your nightmares," Raven retorted and slapped Braden's cheek as hard as his had been slapped. "The next time I get a call like that, I'm keeping her."

Raven turned to smile at her. "I'll see you in four days. If you need me before then, call me."

She hesitated. What had happened while she was in the shower to bring Raven there? "Thanks."

"Walk me to the door?"

She glanced at Braden, who shrugged, but stepped in Raven's path.

Oh joy. After a moment of indecision, she slipped

her arm through Raven's. "Which way to the door?"

She watched the brothers exchange long, cool looks before Braden finally stepped aside.

She and Raven left the room.

At the front door, Raven turned to smile at her.

"Are you two all right?" she asked.

"Of course we are."

"Why are you here?"

"He was fearful of hurting you, so he asked me to come."

"And he left?"

"What should matter is that he's here now, querida."

She felt like slapping him. "Do you ever just answer a simple question?"

"What do you expect from a lawyer?" He kissed her cheek and left.

She returned to the living room.

Braden met her at the door.

"Have you changed your mind about our having dinner out?" she asked him.

"No."

"Then why aren't you dressed for dinner?"

"Give me half an hour to shower and change and then we'll talk—after dinner out."

Dinner out? Great. She nodded.

He was back in the promised half an hour wearing a dark suit with a white shirt and dark tie.

She stared at him. Tall men looked good in dark colors. He looked exquisite.

He offered her his arm. "Dinner awaits, darling."

Although he smiled, she felt the tension in him. It would be her job to get him to unwind so that he sounded as if she really were his darling.

She slipped her arm through his. "Braden?"

He kissed her cheek. "Let's go eat."

They dined under the stars at an exclusive restaurant. He resisted all her efforts to discuss what had led to Raven's presence until she sighed and gave up.

Following a meal neither one of them fully consumed, he rose and extended his hand. "I believe this is my dance."

She nodded and got to her feet. When his arms closed around her, she pressed her cheek against his shoulder.

He brushed his lips against her forehead and put his hands on her waist.

They shared several dances in silence before returning to their table.

"Have I told you how beautiful you are?"

She smiled. "Thank you."

He reached across the table to touch her hand. "In fact you're perfect in every way."

"Perfect?" She pointed to his drink. "What's in that glass?"

He shook his head. "Were you interested in getting to know Raven better?"

"Not in the way you're implying. My interest in him doesn't extend beyond his being your brother."

"Tell me about your lovers."

"What do you want to know about them?"

"How many were there?"

"Including you?"

He nodded.

"You make three. First came Mark and then Peter.

Peter—"

"Tell me about Mark."

"Why him?"

"Women always seem to cherish fond memories of their first love."

"I guess we do. We started dating in our junior year of high school. I was so afraid of ending up pregnant and not finishing school that I was a virgin until prom night."

"And then?"

"And then I wasn't."

"Did you enjoy your prom night with him?"

"If you mean did I enjoy our first time? No. He was sweet but eager and clumsy and it hurt like hell."

"But it felt better the next time?"

She felt her cheeks burn. She'd never discussed her sexual experiences with anyone but Betty. "No. It took a few times before I decided it might not be so bad." Once she had, she'd loved feeling his big, hard cock sliding in and out of her. "We dated all through college. After graduation, he accepted a job teaching overseas."

"Leaving you behind?"

Because he was ready to dump her he assumed everyone else was? "He pleaded with me to marry him and go with him."

"But?"

"As I told you before, I'm an only child. My poor mother wouldn't have had a moment's peace with me so far away. Besides, I wasn't as idealistic or as brave as he was. He's one of the best people I've ever met. He was on a mission to help where he thought he could do the most good. So I stayed and he went."

"Do you have any regrets?"

"Sometimes I wonder how my life would have been different if I had gone with him."

"Did you love him?"

She nodded. "With all the passion and angst of a first love."

"Where is he now?"

"He's still teaching English in far flung places. Still spending his salary on supplies and anything that will help his students have a better life instead of on himself. He's very giving of himself and what little money he has. I've always planned to commit to send him part of my salary as soon as I could. Now that my student loans are paid off I can send part of that money to him."

"What the hell? I didn't pay them off so you can send money to another man, Neida!"

"He makes so little and has even less by the time he spends it on supplies or clothes or medicines or God only knows what for his students. He's a good man who needs all the help he can get. There's no reason for you to begrudge him anything, Braden."

"And what's this paragon's full name?"

"Mark Wyman."

"And where does he teach?"

She told him and then frowned. "Why are you so interested? You're not planning to do anything to hurt him. Are you?"

"You mean like wring his neck or put one of my feet up his ass? No."

His attitude annoyed her. "You're assuming a lot. He's a big man—just like you. And he leads a much tougher life than you do."

"You think wealth has made me soft and your

paragon can kick my ass? Is that what you're implying? Because if it is, you shouldn't let the trappings of money fool you into thinking I'm soft. I'm perfectly capable of keeping what's mine and kicking the ass of any man who thinks differently — regardless of his size, age, or how tough he might be."

"I'm not implying anything, Braden. I just want to know why you're so interested in him."

He shrugged. "I have a passing interest in him because you clearly still have strong feelings for him."

"What makes you say that?"

"Your voice softened and you have the look of a woman talking about someone she loves when you discuss him."

"He was my first love and lover. He was always warm, sweet, considerate, and loving. At a time when I worried about my weight, he looked at me as if I were the only girl in the world worth knowing. He's always made me feel as if I were beautiful."

"You are beautiful."

She smiled. "I'm glad you think so too."

"How did you handle his departure?"

"Not well. I spent the first two weeks crying every time I thought of him and I thought of him a lot. Then I sobbed uncontrollably every time we talked. Finally, he said we should limit our contact so I could move on. Now we exchange emails a couple of times a year. We generally speak to each other during the holidays."

"Visits?"

"We haven't had any since he left because every time he saves enough to come home, one of his students need something and he spends the money on them." She smiled. "But he's coming home soon."

"Is he? And do you hope to see him when he does?"

"We dated for six years and ended our relationship as very close friends. I don't hope to see him when he comes home; I'm going to see him."

"And if this good, close friend of yours wants benefits during his visit?"

She shrugged. "I'll probably oblige."

"What the hell?"

"Why shouldn't I?" She met his gaze. "He'll always have a special place in my heart and it won't matter to you."

"Why the hell wouldn't it matter to me?"

"Because you'll probably be happily engaged by then."

"I probably will be engaged, but you know damn well it won't be happily, you silly little bitch."

The muscles in her stomach clenched and she stared at him. "I don't know what kind of women you've been associating with, but I'm old-fashioned enough not to expect a man who wants to sleep with me to call me names!" She rose and stormed off to the ladies' room.

Inside, she took several deep breaths and then went into the stall to lean her forehead against the door. She fought back the urge to cry. She'd known before she came that he didn't think much of her. So having proof of it shouldn't hurt so much. She knew many women didn't object to the word bitch, but she did and always would. To hear it from the lips of the man she loved hurt like hell.

Her luck with men she loved hadn't changed. Just once she'd like to meet a man who thought she was worth more than his principles. First Mark had to go to impoverished parts of the world to do his part for humanity. Now Braden had to marry a woman he didn't love to do his part to preserve his culture.

Chapter Twelve

After she'd freshened up and composed herself, she returned to their table.

He immediately rose to seat her. Once he'd pushed her chair in, he leaned down to speak with his lips against her cheek. "I'm sorry. That won't happen again."

He returned to his seat and sat looking at her with an inscrutable look in his dark eyes.

Another man might have offered an explanation. He didn't.

"I think I've spent enough quality time with you for one night. Can we leave?"

He compressed his lips and signaled for the bill.

They didn't speak at all on the forty-minute drive back to his house. In the foyer, she turned to find him leaning against the closed door, staring at her.

What was he thinking or feeling? The look in his eyes gave nothing away. And though he must have known she needed reassurance after his earlier disappearance and the argument at the restaurant, he said nothing. Just stared at her.

That's when she knew that following him had been a mistake. Despite his and his brothers' protestations, this was and always had been about sex for him. He was the proverbial tall, dark, handsome male who also happened to be rich. And used to getting what he wanted when he wanted it. And she'd been all too willing to oblige.

She had no one to blame but herself. She'd tossed aside the love of men like Mark and Pete, who'd wanted to marry her and chased after a man who'd told her up front he'd be marrying someone else but wanted a fling with her.

To her shame, she still wanted to give him what he wanted. She swallowed a lump of emotion and lowered her gaze. "Can I use a guest room?"

"Yes. There are four. Take your pick." He pushed himself away from the door and walked down the hall to the living room.

Neida stared after him, her eyes filling with tears. She sucked in a breath and they spilled down her cheeks. Wiping them away with the back of her hands, she went up to the master bedroom. She tossed her clothes into her suitcase and wheeled it to the bedroom furthest away from his.

Then she sat in the chair by the window and cried. The ringing of her cellphone startled her. She gulped back more tears and removed it from her clutch. Elkhorn, R.

She wiped her cheeks and answered the call. "Hello?"

"Are you all right?" Raven asked.

"Why wouldn't I be?"

"Braden asked me to call to see if you needed me. Do you, querida? I can be there in – minutes. Or if that's too long, Shane is at home and can be there in half that time."

Although Shane had been charming, her connection with Raven was stronger. The temptation to ask him to come was strong. She feared that if she did, there would be no going back. "I'm sure you have better things to do than drive around on my behalf all day."

"I generally mean what I say. I said I'd back you up

and I will. I'm on my way."

"No! I'm fine. We had a few words but it's not as if we're on the verge of killing each other. He's wherever he is and I'm in one of the guestrooms. There's no need for you to come at all."

"I'll see you soon," he said and ended the call.

She continued to sit by the window for twenty minutes or so. Then, feeling the need for a drink to boost her courage so she couldn't go to pieces when Raven arrived, she went down to the living room.

She stopped in the doorway. Braden sat in the moonlit room with a drink in his hand and a bottle on the coffee table in front of him. He didn't speak or rise. Just stared at her.

She moistened her lips. Was he in the habit of drinking his problems away? Maybe Raven coming was a good idea after all. "I wanted a drink," she said.

He nodded towards the bar along one wall, gulped down the contents of his glass, and picked up the bottle to pour another one.

Even as he kept his gaze on her, he seemed so far away. She stared at him, uncertain what to say or how to react to him. Maybe asking Shane to come was an even better idea.

She gave herself a mental shake. Get a grip. He's done nothing to make you think such thoughts. He didn't drink at dinner. If he wants to drink alone in his own house, that's his business.

Just as she started to back out of the room, deciding it might be best to leave him alone, the entrance door open. She turned, surprised at how quickly Raven had arrived. But it was Shane Elkhorn who walked in and closed the door.

She stood, watching his approach. Although all the Elkhorn men were handsome, Shane was stunningly so with a big, sculptured body, sensual dark eyes and a quick, warm smile that probably made all the women he turned it on weak-kneed. Like his older brothers, he was tall, probably as tall as Braden.

"Querida, it's always a pleasure to see you again," he said, for all the world as if they'd run into each other unexpectedly instead of his coming in answer to Braden's call.

When he reached her, he put an arm around her shoulders and gave her a quick hug.

She immediately felt surrounded by warmth. Blinking to hold back tears, she leaned against him.

With his arm still around her shoulders, he turned them around to look in the living room where Braden sat gulping down another drink. "Bray? Are you all right?"

Braden placed his empty glass on the table and rose. "I'm just Jim dandy, Chief." He walked across the room to stop in front of them. He glanced down at her. "I'll leave you two alone to get better acquainted."

"No!" She pulled away from Shane and turned to snatch at Braden's hand as he walked by them.

He pulled his hand free but turned to face her—silently.

She glanced briefly at Shane before giving Braden her full attention. "I appreciate his coming, but I didn't call either of your brothers, Braden. You did."

"You moved into a guestroom, Neida!"

"You walked out on me earlier and then called me a silly bitch! I don't like being called names by a man I…"

"A man you what?"

They stared at each other and she knew he wanted her to admit she loved him. But hell would freeze over before she humiliated herself by making much an admission to him. "I don't like being called names—period!"

"You're overreacting and I did apologize."

But hadn't gone out of his way to make her believe he meant it. "I don't consider bitch an endearment, Braden! I consider it an insult from a man who doesn't respect the woman he uses it on. You can't call me one and then expect me to want to sleep with you."

"Fine. Sleep with whoever the hell you like!" He stared at Shane, who stood silently at her side, before he stalked away.

Shane swore softly and followed him. "Braden!"

"What?" Braden swung around and the two brothers faced each other.

"What the hell is wrong with you, Bray? I know how you feel about her. You know damned well I'd never stab you in the back like that."

Neida rushed down the hall to stand beside them. She didn't want them angry at each other because of her. "Do you want me to leave, Braden?"

He tore his gaze away from Shane to look at her. "No."

The single word spoken with a depth of despair shook her.

"I don't ever want you to leave." He extended a hand to her.

She pressed against him closing her eyes.

"And I think that's my cue to leave." She felt Shane's lips brushing her hair.

She clutched his hand. "Thank you for caring enough to come," she whispered.

"Anytime, querida. Ray's on his way, but I'll tell him not to bother."

Moments later, the front door opened and closed. And they were alone.

He cupped his hands over her cheeks and lifted her face. "Look at me."

She opened her eyes.

"As you've probably guessed by now, I have a temper. Most of the time, I keep a firm grip on it. When my emotions are involved, I sometimes lose it. Please don't let my short fuse make you think I don't respect you. I do—that's why I left Philadelphia without trying to press you. I didn't want to hurt you or do anything to injure your pride or self-respect."

Too late to worry about that, but she appreciated the sentiment behind his words.

"You were so silent."

"I was afraid of making things worse, Neida."

"You strike me as a man who can handle himself with any woman."

"I can—unless the woman in question is important to me—as you are." He brushed his lips against her cheek.

She smelled the alcohol on his breath. "Do you have a problem with alcohol?"

He lifted his head to look down at her. "I never have but I'm sure I'll be driven to drink before this is all over."

She stared up at him and suddenly a wellspring broke and she laughed.

He laughed too and then engulfed her in his arms,

holding her so close, his embrace bordered on the painful. "Spend the night with me, querida. No sex. We don't have much time left and I just want to hold you and wake up beside you tomorrow."

She nodded, slipping her arms around his waist. "I want that too, Braden."

He walked her to the master suite before going to retrieve her suitcase from the guestroom.

They undressed and took separate showers. She took longer. When she emerged from her shower, his was empty. Slipping a toweling robe over her nude body, she sat at the vanity and brushed her hair quickly before braiding it.

Then heart racing, she dried off, slipped on a satin nightgown. When she returned to the master suite, moonlight filled it. Braden lay on the bed with the cover pushed down to his feet. His chest was bare but he wore a pair of pajama bottoms. Steeling herself against the ache to rush across the room and beg him to love her, she removed her robe and slipped onto the bed beside him.

She turned onto her side, sighing with contentment when he curled his big body against her back. Nice, she thought, closing her eyes as he slipped his hands over her breasts. Settling back against him, she drifted to sleep.

* * *

Neida woke the next morning longing for Braden. Before she opened her eyes and rolled towards his side of the bed, she knew she was alone. Reaching for the adjacent pillow which bore faint traces of his cologne, she pressed it against her face, inhaling slowly.

The aroma of freshly brewing coffee assailed her

senses. Slipping out of bed, she showered and went to Braden's dresser. She opened each drawer until she found his t-shirts. Removing the top one, she slipped it over her nude body and then left the room for the kitchen.

In the foyer, two vases of flowers stood on the table. Pausing by them, she plucked the card from each. The word *Querida* was on both envelopes.

One card bore the initials RE. The other SE. Raven and Shane. Handsome and thoughtful. They would make two women very happy one day. Smiling, she continued towards the kitchen.

Braden stood at the patio doors in the kitchen sipping from a cup of coffee. The boxer briefs he wore allowed her to fully appreciate his tight ass and long, muscular legs. She licked her lips, thinking of his ass muscles clenching and unclenching as he drove his hard cock in and out of her aching pussy.

He turned suddenly and smiled at her. "Morning, Querida. Did you sleep well?"

She nodded. "Yes, but now I'm hungry."

He glanced towards the counter where she could see several warning trays with covered dishes. "What would you like? We have—"

"You. I want you, Braden."

His smile widened as he crossed the room to her. "That can certainly be arranged." Placing his coffee cup on the counter, he stopped in front of her. "If you're sure."

She gave him a cool look and nodded curtly. In no mood to beg for his cock or to play games, when he stopped in front of her, she deliberately reached out and cupped her hand between his legs.

His nostrils flared as he leaned down to speak against her lips. "If I were you, I'd have breakfast first."

"Why?"

"Because I plan to fuck you all day," he said, nipping at her bottom lip.

A thrill of delight danced through her. "What woman in her first mind would want food when she could have you instead?" she asked, slipping her arms around his waist.

"You're the only woman I care about," he assured her. "Am I forgiven for last night?"

She looked up at him. "Unfortunately, I'm probably incapable of not forgiving you for anything short of rape or murder, my handsome Braden."

He stepped back until her arms dropped away from his body. Then he took her hand in his and led her back to the master bedroom. She followed eagerly. There, he removed his briefs before seating himself on the side of the bed. He drew her between his thighs and pulled his t-shirt over her head, exposing her naked body.

"Protection?"

"Haven't you ever wanted to feel my bare cock inside you?"

"Every time I look at you."

"Great. So?"

"So I'm horny, not crazy. And I have felt part of it—even if only briefly. Protection, Braden."

He reached in the top drawer of the nightstand and handed her the foil packet.

She accepted it and slowly reached down with her free hand to grip his shaft. Smiling into his eyes and rotating her hips, she gently pumped and massaged him until she felt his cock lengthening in her fingers.

When he started thrusting his shaft against her fingers, she released him to reach down to roll on the condom. Then she took one of his hands and trailed his fingers along her slit.

He stared at her breasts for a long time before he looked up at her. "Do you have any idea how utterly beautiful and alluring you are, Neida?"

She smiled down at him, stroking his hair. "Why don't you show me?"

"Oh God I adore you," he whispered, wrapped his arms around her and rolled them onto the bed.

Lying on her back with him between her thighs, she smiled up at him. "You are the most handsome man in the world."

"If you can say that after meeting, Shane, I'll have to question your eyesight."

She stroked her fingers through his hair. "Shane who?" She drew his lips down to hers. "For me, you're the only man in the world. Take me, Braden. I'm yours."

He touched his mouth to her. "Mine?"

"Yours," she promised, licking at his lips.

He kissed her and eased his cock into her.

"Oh," she shuddered and clung to him, closing her eyes.

He alternated between pressing burning kisses on her lips and neck and filling her ears with hot words of devotion and desire. She ached to have him fuck her into a quick, fiery orgasm. Instead, he made love to her with a sweet heat that kept her on the brink of ecstasy for what felt like a torturous eternity before he finally surged deep inside her. When he clutched her ass and ground his hips on hers, his pubic hair rubbed against her budded clit.

With the world exploding around her, she gasped and came.

He held himself still as she moaned her way through her climax. Then, he thrust his cock in and out of her with a rough need until he groaned and collapsed into her arms, his big body shuddering with his release.

She held him close until he stopped shaking and rolled over onto his back with her on top of him. Smiling, she rubbed her cheek against his damp shoulder. "Oh Braden there's no feeling in the world as wonderful as having you deep inside me."

"None," he whispered. "When I'm with you like this, I feel as if I have everything in life I'll ever want or need. You're everything I want and need, darling. Everything."

With the sweet words filling her ears and warming her heart, she fell asleep.

* * *

Braden woke just after 10 a.m. and laid watching Neida sleep until the urge to turn her onto her back and slide his naked cock in her pussy became very difficult to resist. He slipped out of bed. He called Shane and they spoke briefly before he went to the gym to work out some of the sexual tension that had built lying watching Neida sleep.

After an hour workout, he took a shower in one of the guest bedrooms before returning to his bedroom to dress. By the time he finished, he heard the entrance door opening and closing.

Descending the stairs, he saw Shane walking down

the hall with a thermal carrier in each hand. He followed him into the kitchen.

Shane turned to face him. "Everything okay?"

He nodded. "Yes. How much do I owe you?"

"My treat." He put the carriers on the island and leaned against the counter. "Are you in love with her?"

Braden didn't answer.

Shane crossed the room to place a hand on his shoulder. "Don't let her get away, Bray. If you do, you'll spend the rest of your life regretting it."

He shook Shane's hand off. "Don't you think I know that?"

"Ok, but what you might not know is who I'm dating."

Shane had always taken full advantage of his appearance and of the attraction many women held for Native American men—as had Braden and Raven. Neka had been the only exception—content to be a one-woman man. "And who is that?"

"Her name is Cherylyn Danvers."

"And?"

"Her mother's Caucasian but her father is Cherokee and she takes after him. She's tall and considering she's on the slender side, kind of sexy. She spends her summers in Tulsa teaching introductory Tsalagi courses."

About to remove the food Shane had picked up for him from one of his favorite restaurants from their containers, he turned to stare at him brother. Shane had always dated full-figured women with dark skin and unprocessed hair. After a moment, he shook his head. "No, Chief. Don't do that."

"Don't do what?"

"Don't think I'm going to allow you to sacrifice your future just so I can be with Neida."

"You know something, Bray? I'm all grown up. I'll date who the hell I want. I wish you'd do the same and not let another woman you adore get away from you."

"Shane! We all know you prefer black women."

"So do you and who can blame either of us? A full-figured black woman not afraid to let her natural beauty shine through without trying to cover it up, has no peer. But just because I love black women, doesn't mean I can't find other women interesting enough to bed. With enough time, I'll persuade her to come off her birth control and we'll go raw. Wish me luck, Bray. She returns from Tulsa in October. If I play my cards right, she might be pregnant with by the end of the year."

"Shane—"

"Give querida my regards."

He caught Shane's arm and swung him around. "There's no need for both of us to be in an unhappy marriage."

"Who the hell said anything about marrying her?"

"You said you wanted to get her pregnant."

"I do, but what's that got to do with marriage?"

"You know we weren't raised that way. Dad taught us to honor—"

"The women we love. I like her well enough to enjoy sex with her but I don't love her. If she gets pregnant, I'll take full financial responsibility for her and the baby. I'll be an involved father and do my absolute best to be the kind of father that dad was. Mom will have her almost full Native grandchild and you can marry for love."

"I'm not going to let you do that, Chief."

Shane jerked away. "I'd like to see you try to stop me, Bray." He turned and walked away.

Braden raked his hands through his hair and called Raven, who answered almost immediately. To his surprise, Raven didn't seem unduly upset when he told him of Shane's plans.

"I don't understand you, Raven. You rant and rave because you think I should pursue a lasting relationship with Neida, but have no problem with what Shane is planning."

"The big difference between the two of you is that he's not in love with anyone and if he does marry her, he won't feel a pressing need to stay married if the relationship goes south. If anyone is going to do his family duty, it should be someone who isn't in love."

"Then why the hell don't you do, it, Raven?"

"Because, like you, Braden, I happen to be in love already! And no, I don't want to discuss it or her."

The despair he heard in Raven's voice made him ache. "Oh hell, Ray. Why didn't you tell me? Who is she?"

"She's married and off limits. It'll take me awhile, but I'll be fine."

"What can I do to help, Ray?"

"You can honor my request to wait until I'm ready to talk about her. Right now, I can't. When I can I will, Bray."

Oh shit. The way things were going, Neka would have to be happy enough for all his brothers. He sighed. "I'll be here when you need to talk, Ray."

"You always have been. Thanks, Bray. Give querida my love."

"I will. Ray—"

"Just give me some time, Bray and then we'll talk."

Shit! He returned to the master bedroom feeling weighed down and more certain than ever that he had to stay the course. Even if he couldn't help Raven, he could stop Shane from making a decision he'd soon regret. That meant he had to be engaged within the next two months or so—before Shane made a mistake he'd have to spend the next 22 years paying for in the form of a child he might or might not love as deeply as he should.

Feeling in need of emotional comfort, instead of waking Neida for lunch, he stripped down to his boxer briefs and slipped into bed with her, pressing his body against the curve of her back. Mentally exhausted, he fell asleep.

Chapter Thirteen

Hunger pangs woke Neida. However, once she realized Braden slept beside her, her thoughts turned to sex.

Turning onto her side, she studied him. She sat up and touched his handsome face before stroking her fingers over his hair. She loved everything about him from his thick, dark brown hair to his long, thick cock he thrilled her with each time they had sex. All the parts in between were just as perfect.

From his wide shoulders to his unshaven chest down to his very well defined abs. She trailed her fingers down over his ribcage. He must work out regularly so that there was not an ounce of excess or unattractive weight on his big, male body.

She slid her palm down to his groin and then below to run her nails over his cock that lay along one thigh. Even flaccid, it was beautiful. She closed her fingers around it and gently massaged it.

Feeling a faint stirring in it, she caressed his balls before pumping his cock again.

His lids shot up and he stared up at her. "Neida. What are you doing?"

Embarrassed at having been caught touching him while he slept, her cheeks burned. "Nothing."

"Nothing? My cock is almost erect."

She lowered her lids and sat against the headboard, releasing him.

He sat up beside her. "You were saying?"

She shrugged and turned to meet his gaze. "I was marveling at how perfect your body is."

"Really?" He smiled. "You have my full attention,

querida. Marvel aloud."

She leaned over to touch her mouth to his. Sliding her lips across his cheek she whispered in his ear. "I love every inch of it."

"The feeling is mutual."

"You're a man with a big, hard body that makes me feel glad to be a woman." *Your woman.*

"No shit?" He sounded pleased.

She smiled. "No shit, Sherlock." She nipped his earlobe before licked a path down the side of his neck. "I love the width of your shoulders and the way you don't shave your chest. You have just the right amount of hair. Not too much and not too little. There's something really sexy about feeling your chest hair against my nipples when you're pinning me down and thrusting so deep inside me, I feel almost as if your cock is an extension of my body I can't be happy without." She bit at each nipple, taking a moment to savor the quick inhalations he made in response.

After several moments of rubbing her cheek against his chest, she licked and kissed a path down to his groin. She slid her fingers into the waistband of his underwear and pushed them down from his hips.

Breathing deeply, he lifted his hips from the bed.

She pushed the briefs down his body until he kicked them off, leaving him naked.

Oh hell, yeah. That's what I'm talking about. Laying her face against his pubic hair, she inhaled slowly. Then she turned her head and pressed her tongue against his urethra.

"Shit. Be careful," he warned.

Careful hell. There would be time to be careful when she was back in Philly. For their remaining time together, careful was not going to be in her vocabulary. Sliding down his body until she sprawled between his legs, she dragged her tongue along the underside of his shaft several times before she lovingly wrapped her fingers around his cock.

"Damn."

Hearing the husky sound, she smiled up at him. "Every part of your body is perfect. Especially this," she said. "It's the most perfect one in the world."

His only response was deeper breathing and a tensing of his body.

"I know it's given countless women endless nights of pleasure, but none of them could want or need to taste it as much as I do now, Braden." Lowering her gaze and head, she kissed the head. Taking a deep breath, she parted her lips.

"No!" He suddenly gripped her shoulders and prevented her from taking his cock between her lips.

Surprised, she glanced up at him. "Braden? What's wrong?"

"Nothing's wrong. I'd just rather you didn't."

She frowned. "Didn't what? Suck your cock?"

"Yes."

"But I want to." She attempted to slide her lips over him.

"No." He retained his grip on her shoulders until she slid her body up his and stared down into his eyes.

"What's wrong, Braden?"

"I told you I'd just rather you didn't."

"Why? Don't you enjoy it?"

"I enjoy it as much as the next man. I'd just rather you, in particular, didn't."

They stared at each other for several moments

before her mother's words to the effect that men didn't respect women who sucked their cocks crossed her mind. "Is it because you think only tramps or whores suck cock?"

"Exactly."

She sucked in a breath. "That's one way of looking at it. Another way is that it's a way for a woman to show her man how much she cares for him — as I care for you, Braden."

"Care for me?"

The intense, almost pleading look in his eyes left her in no doubt that he wanted to hear her say she love him. But somehow the word stuck in her throat. She nodded, hoping that would be enough.

He inhaled slowly but didn't speak.

"It's something I've been fantasying about since the moment I saw you. We have so little time left together. Please don't keep me from fulfilling my fantasy, Braden. I want to taste you and feel you sliding between my lips and into my mouth. Please."

His jaw clenched and he finally released her shoulders and rolled away.

"What are you doing?"

He glanced back over his shoulder. "Getting a condom."

She shook her head. "I want to suck and taste your cock, Braden. Not that."

"Are you sure? I might not be able to control my climax and you might end up with some cum in your mouth before I can pull out."

"Who said I wanted you to pull out?"

He stared at her. "What?"

Her cheeks burned but she didn't look away from

him. "I can't have your bare cock in my pussy but I want it in my mouth. I want to taste your cum and your cock."

"How many times have you done this?"

"Counting this time?"

He nodded.

"I don't go around sucking the cock of every man who winks at me, Braden. This will be my first time."

"Holy hell, Neida. Are you sure you don't want to save your first time for someone else?"

She would fall for another man and get married one day, but knew she'd never love anyone more than she did him. "I'm positive, Braden."

"Your first time should be special."

"It couldn't be any more special with anyone else, Braden. You're the one I want and need to taste."

"Oh God. I should warn you that I'm not going to last very long once I feel your mouth on my cock."

"I'll take any brevity involved as a sign of how much you enjoy my mouth and tongue."

"There won't be any pleasure in it for you."

"Sucking your cock is all the pleasure I need from the experience."

His jaw clenched and he lay back on the bed.

"Thank you," she whispered before kissing her way down his body. She spent a few moments rubbing her cheek against his pubic hair before closing her fingers around his semi-erect cock. She kissed and licked at the head of his shaft and his urethra before finally drawing it into her mouth.

"Oh shit!" He groaned and curled his fingers in her hair.

Cupping her free hand under his balls, she closed

her eyes and tentatively ran her tongue around the head. She spent some time getting used to the feel and texture of his cock before she started to pump it while she squeezed his balls.

His shaft lengthened and hardened. Almost immediately he groaned and pushed his cock up into her mouth. Within seconds, he was fucking her face with an urgency that took her breath away and both pleased and gave her pause.

She had several scary moments when he surged so deep in her mouth that her gag reflex triggered. Struggling not to panic and rip her mouth away, she dug her nails into his ass and sucked harder.

With his hands on the back of her head, he pushed his entire shaft in her mouth with a rapidity that frightened her. Moments later, a blast of cum shot from his cock into her mouth.

Panic set it and she tried to jerk her head back.

He resisted her efforts and a second and third blast cannonballed in her mouth so quickly, she felt as if she couldn't breathe. She was going to strangle under the barrage of what felt like never ending jets of cum.

Then, as she slid her hands around his body to push against his thighs, he suddenly pulled out of her mouth, grabbed the bedcover and continued ejaculating into it.

Relieved her ability to breath had returned, she fell back aside the bed, her gaze locked on his jerking hips while he finished coming. When he had, he slumped back against the bed, taking slow deep breaths.

He reached out his hand to pull her onto his body. He held her close and whispered something incoherent against her forehead.

"Did you like it?" she whispered.

"Oh hell yeah." He stroked his palm down her body and slapped her ass cheeks. "I know you didn't enjoy that."

She swallowed slowly, trying to decide what his cum tasted like. "I had a few scary moments, but I'm always going to cherish the memory, Braden."

He hugged her close.

They lay together for nearly half an hour before her stomach growled.

He caressed her ass. "I'm a thoughtless fuck. You must be starving. Lunch is in the kitchen and hopefully hasn't spoiled."

She rolled off of him and climbed out of bed. "I am hungry and this time I want food and not a big spewing cock drowning me in cum."

"Ungrateful wench." He sat up and slapped her ass. "That's the last time I let my sore cock anywhere near those voracious lips of yours. We'll have lunch after a quick shower."

Smiling, she sashayed into the bathroom.

To her surprise, he released a lusty wolf whistle but didn't follow her.

When she hurried to the kitchen fifteen minutes later, wearing another of his t-shirts over her bra and thong, she found him on the patio, bare chested but wearing jeans while he removed covers from various serving trays.

Rather to her surprise, her level of embarrassment was quite manageable. She joined him on the patio, her stomach rumbling.

He turned to smile at her, handing her a plate. "You can have your choice of three entrees."

She chose Chicken Kiev, roasted vegetables, and slender slices of French Toast. He had steak and potatoes. He carried both plates to the table and seated her. "What will you have to drink? Wine or—"

"It's a little too early for me. Seltzer water will be fine."

He returned with a tray with ice, two bottles of seltzer water, and coffee.

While they ate, she asked him if he'd ever been in love.

"Yes." He glanced down at his plate.

Hmm. Looked like she'd have to pull the information from him like a dentist pulling teeth. "So you loved her?"

"Yes."

"What happened? Why didn't you marry her?"

He sighed and finally looked up at her again. "Nothing was right. I'd always expected to be married by the time I was in my mid to late thirties. By the time we admitted we were in love, I'd already begun to feel an obligation to marry a Native woman. She felt an obligation to marry a civic-minded black man with a plan—like the single father who raised her. Between the two of us, we allowed ourselves to grow apart. Then she met what I'm told is a black woman's fantasy—a successful, single black male who didn't have any kids and wasn't gay.

"So naturally enough, she married him. And now she's pregnant."

"She fell out of love with you?"

"She must have done."

"Is she happily married?"

"I don't know but I hope so. I'd hate to think of her

being unhappy."

"You still love her." She bit her lip. That had sounded almost like an accusation.

He nodded. "I'm probably always going to love her, but I'm no longer in love with her."

But at least she'd had his love once—which was more than Neida could ever hope for. "What is she like?"

"Very much like you except she's older and not so deliciously shy yet sexy as you are."

"What's her name?"

"Kania."

"Was she pretty?"

"Yes—almost as lovely as you are, Neida."

She smiled, feeling her jealousy of the other woman fading. "Did she break your heart when she married another man?"

"At the time I thought it was broken but it turns out it was just badly bruised."

"Do you still see or keep in contact with her?"

"No. Her husband knows of our past relationship and wouldn't approve."

"Do you miss her?"

"We were friends for nearly fifteen years. Yes. I miss her." He leaned forward, placing his hand over hers. "But I'm really not interested in discussing other women. I want to focus all my time and energy on you."

She smiled. "I like the sound of that."

After the meal, he told her the cleaning women were coming in and wanted him out of their hair. They dressed and went for a drive that ended in an upscale shopping district. Despite her protests, he led her into a jewelry store filled with pieces so beautiful, she found it difficult not to exclaim every few seconds.

"What can I buy you?" he asked.

She shook her head. "Nothing. You've already paid off my student loans."

"That was then. This is now. We're not leaving until I've bought you at least one present. Either you can pick something you love or leave it to me and take a chance on my taste."

Her gaze was drawn to a beautiful diamond tennis bracelet.

Noticing her wishful gaze, he nodded to the jeweler. "We'd like to try this on."

The fit was perfect and despite her resolve not to allow him to buy her anything, she couldn't bear to take it off. She smiled at him, squeezing his hand. "Thanks."

He nodded. "You're welcome." He looked at the jeweler. "I think those diamond studs would go great with the bracelet."

"Excellent choice," the man responded and whipped them out of the showcase.

Although both Mark and Peter had loved her, neither had been wealthy. She found it exciting to be with a handsome, sexy male with the financial resources to buy her diamonds without mortgaging his future salary. She didn't protest when he bought the studs as well.

"Shall we buy a necklace to go with it?" Standing behind her, he asked the question with his lips inches from her ear.

She turned to face him. "Thank you. No."

"I can easily afford it and I want to."

Neida met his gaze. She might never meet another rich, handsome man eager to shower her with jewelry. She caved. "Thank you, Braden."

He smiled and turned to look at the jeweler. "We'd like to see some necklaces that match the earrings."

They chose one together that was so beautiful, she could barely stand taking it off for the jeweler to slip it into a box.

After they left the jeweler's, they had coffee at an outdoor café.

"Where would you like to have dinner?" he asked.

"Somewhere quiet and intimate."

"What type of food are you in the mood for?"

"American."

"I know just the place," he said. "We can go casual or dressy. Your choice. After dinner we can dance under the stars."

Dancing under the stars with him. What more could a woman ask for? "Sounds like a plan."

They spent a magical evening together. They slow danced on the restaurant's patio for over an hour after a leisurely meal. On the drive back to his house, he turned on the car stereo.

A sexy, mellow male duo sang about feeling a fire inside while holding a woman close.

She listened for a few moments before her eyes widened. "Braden! That's you singing."

"Actually, it's me and a friend of mine, Kristopher Macarik and a couple of band members."

"Band members? You sing lead in a band? What's it called?"

"Rolling Thunder and we take turns singing lead."

"Where can I buy your CDs?"

"None of us are professional singers. We all have day jobs and get together a few times a year to do private shows for fun. Sometimes we record our sessions. Most of the time we don't, but I'll be happy to give you a copy of the few CDs I have."

"I'd love them. Do you play an instrument?"

"I play guitar, a little sax and band members tell me I play the worst drums and fiddle imaginable."

"You're full of surprises, Braden. I would have liked to see you perform."

He hesitated before he responded. "We're doing a fais do do at a band member's house in a few weeks."

"A fais do do?"

"It's a Cajun country dance party."

"Oh."

"You're welcome to come as my guest if you like."

In a few weeks, he'd probably be engaged to another woman. Having one of his former lovers there would be very disrespectful and undoubtedly hurtful to his fiancée. "Thanks."

"But no thanks?"

"I can't imagine whoever you propose to would want me there. I know I wouldn't in her place."

"I'm sure Raven would be happy to have you as his guest."

"You can't think I'd be interested in seeing you there singing love songs to another woman, Braden."

"Any love songs I sang would be for you, querida. And I sing a mean Spanish love song, if I do say so myself."

"I'll bet you do but I think it would be best if I contented myself with any CDs you have to share."

They lapsed into an easy silence. She was surprised

when all he seemed to want was a cuddle when they slipped into bed together.

Lying on his back with her on top of him, they traded warm kisses and undemanding caresses until she fell asleep.

* * *

In the morning, she was delighted to find Braden still in bed beside her. She turned from her back to her side to smile at him. "Braden! What a nice surprise."

He bent his head to nibble at her ear. "I'm starving."

She ran her fingers through his hair, enjoying the morning stubble on his face brushing against her neck. "You don't eat breakfast," she reminded him.

He rolled her on her back and slid between her legs. "It's not food I'm interested in."

"Unfortunately for you, I am interested in food." She shoved at his shoulders until he rolled on his back. She slipped out of bed and went into the master bathroom.

He gave her five minutes before he followed her and turned her to face him as she was about to step into the shower. "You know what they say, *querida*, feed your man when he's hungry and you don't have to worry about another woman doing it for you."

She narrowed her gaze. "Oh yeah? Well, if you happen to know another woman you want, have at her!" She stepped into the shower and closed the door in his face.

There was a brief silence before she heard his laughter as he left the room.

She smiled and turned the water on. *Damn girl, you're starting to believe his love lies about wanting only you.* After showering, she dressed and followed her nostrils to the kitchen and the smell of brewing coffee.

Braden sat on the island: shaved, naked, and fully aroused. He held up a condom. "Come feed me, querida."

She looked at his cock, long, thick, and calling to her pussy. *Oh hell yeah. Baby, here I come.* She pulled her dress off, exposing her naked body before she crossed the room to stand between his legs. "Has anyone ever told you that sex on kitchen surfaces isn't very sanitary?"

He drew her close enough so that she could feel his cock against her belly. "Has anyone ever told you that you're wasting time talking that could be better spent making love?"

Extending the tip of her tongue between her lips, she trailed her fingertips down his chest to his groin. "You have a point," she said, reaching for the condom that he'd put on the island beside him.

After tearing the foil packet open, she leaned in to kiss him as they reached between their bodies to roll the condom over his cock together. With his shaft covered, he reached up to roll her nipples between his fingers.

She moaned against his lips as he slipped off the island, turned her around, and lifted her up onto it. Then he took her left leg in his hands and kissed her toes. "You make me burn like no other woman ever has," he whispered, sliding his lips up her leg and inner thigh.

Neida's stomach muscles clenched and her pussy flooded. "Oh Braden. I need you inside me now."

"Soon, darling, soon." He licked her slit and

pressed his tongue to her clit before kissing his way down her other thigh and leg.

"Oh hell Braden!" She bucked her hips in response.

Easing a finger inside her, he finger fucked her pussy while he nibbled at her toes.

She bit her lip. "Now, Braden."

He slid another finger into her and pumped them in and out of her.

"Oh Braden!" She pushed his fingers out of her. "Please."

He stepped close enough so he could drag the head of his shaft along the outside of dripping pussy.

"Mmm." She stroked her hands across his shoulders. "Very nice, handsome, but I need more."

"How much more?"

"I need your big, hard cock nuts deep inside me. Now."

Leaning forward to gaze into her eyes, he spoke in a voice thick with desire. "I don't want to rush. I want to savor every moment with you."

"Oh honey. You mean that."

"Oh yes, querida. I mean it." He touched his lips to hers. "When I say I cherish and adore you, I mean it." He nibbled his way from her mouth to her neck and down to her breasts. "I worship you and every inch of your beautiful, sexy body."

Neida cupped her hands over his head as he laved her right nipple with his tongue. With it hard, he burned a path of hot kisses to her other breast.

Feeling his warm, eager lips close over her nipple she curled her fingers in his hair and urged his head closer.

While sucking her nipple, he reached down to slip

his fingers inside her.

"Oh Braden. Braden. Please give me what I need."

"I need it too, querida," he told her. "I need it and I need you." Removing his fingers, he positioned his cock at her entrance.

"I'm yours, Braden."

He kissed her and eased his shaft slowly inside her.

She closed her eyes and moaned at the delicious feeling of his hard length inching into her body.

When he was fully seated in her, he cupped her face between his hands. "Look at me."

She opened her eyes. "Braden?"

He stroked his hands down the sides of her neck. "You mean more to me than any other woman ever has."

"Any? Including Kania?"

"Yes. Including her." He slid his hands down to cup her ass and pulled her closer. "I adore you, Neida. I need you. I worship you."

She bit her lip, her heart racing as he started to slide his cock in and out of her with a long, steady heat that sent fire and need surging through her. Delicious eddies danced up and down her spine. Within moments, she was lost in riot of wonderful sensations strengthened by the depth of her love for him.

"Oh Braden. Braden." She gripped his shoulders, gasping against his ear. "Oh Braden, I lo…" She sank her teeth into her bottom lip to silence the confession she ached to make.

He suddenly stilled his movements and drew back to stare at her; almost as if he knew she'd almost admitted something he wanted to hear. "What? What did you say?"

"Nothing." She humped herself on his cock, hungry for him to move inside her again.

He gripped her hips and held them still. "What were you about to say?" he asked in an insistent voice.

She blinked up at him and moistened her lips before she spoke. "I was just thinking of asking you to keep fucking me," she said.

His gaze narrowed. "We're not fucking, Neida. We're making love. There's a big difference between the two."

His sudden anger annoyed her. Why should he expect her to admit to loving him when he'd be romancing two other women in less than a week? Did he think she was prepared to totally abandon the tattered remnants of her pride for the sake of a fuck that meant nothing to him?

"I know that."

"Then why do you call it fucking instead of what it is?"

Because it was only making love for her. She touched his cheek. "Please, Braden. Are you going to spend our remaining time together making me beg for what you say we both want?"

"No." He released her hips.

She surged forward, impaling herself on his cock.

He shuddered and burned his lips against hers.

She ached for a quick release and could feel the tension in him. She wanted to be fucked—hard and fast.

He had other ideas. He caressed her and kissed her mouth, neck, and breasts until she felt as if an inferno raged inside her.

Mindless with the need to come, she dug her nails

into his shoulders and humped wildly on him until a dam of pleasure burst and she came, sobbing his name against his ear. "Braden, Braden...oh Braden..."

He cradled her in his arms and whispered softly to her until her shudders subsided. Then he shortened his strokes and powered his cock rapidly in and out her until his big body shook and he clutched her so close he hurt her.

She pushed against his shoulders. "You're bruising me, honey."

He inhaled slowly before he released her and stepped back.

Feeling his cock slipping out of her sent a jolt of regret through her. She opened her eyes and they stared at each other in silence for what felt like several minutes.

"Oh God, Neida. I need you," he whispered. Closing his eyes, he leaned his forehead against hers.

Hearing the raw emotion in his voice, she decided that maybe she hadn't been the only one making love. She turned her head and kissed his hair. "I've been yours for the taking from the moment I saw you, Braden. That hasn't changed. There's only one thing stopping us from being together—you."

He pulled away from her. "Don't please. I have to stick to my game plan."

She stared at him. Why did he expect her to make it easier for him to dump her for another woman? *Because he's going to do it no matter how much you beg and you love him.* She sighed and then nodded. "I'd better go freshen up."

He lifted her off the counter and set her on her feet.

Chapter Fourteen

Braden watched her leave the kitchen. His chest felt tight and his heart ached. How the hell could he possibly give her up and never see her again in just a few days? He leaned back against the island, closing his eyes. *God, please. Help me be strong enough to do the right thing. I can't let Shay ruin his life for me. Help me not to need her so much.*

He inhaled and exhaled deeply several times before his heartbeat resumed its normal rhythm. Get a grip on your emotions, Elkhorn. Even if things were different, she's still too damn young for you. By the time she's fifty and still beautiful and desirable, you'll be ready to collect social security! Stop wasting time worrying about impossibilities. Be thankful for the time you've had and have left with her. A permanent relationship with her is absolutely out of the question.

He took a cool shower in one of the guest bathrooms and quickly dressed. He was seated on the patio drinking a second cup of coffee when she joined him. Pushing his chair back, he extended his hand while patting his lap with his free one.

She stopped on the other side of the table with a surprised look on her face. "You can't want me to sit on your lap."

"Why not?"

"I'm a full-figured woman."

He nodded. "That's one of the sexiest things about you." He patted his lap again.

She walked around the table and gingerly sat on his lap.

He pulled her closer, wrapping his arms around

her and pressing his lips against her neck. "But then everything about you is totally delicious."

"Speaking of delicious, you might not eat breakfast but I do. And I'm starving."

He kissed her neck and released her.

"Don't get up." She turned to press a quick kiss against his mouth before she rose and walked over to the sideboard.

He watched her choose items from the sideboard before sitting across from him at the table. "Orange juice or coffee?" he asked.

"Orange juice," she said.

After pouring her a glass, he sat sipping his coffee, watching her eat. How the hell was he supposed to be content with another woman after loving her? How could he bear knowing another man was sharing her bed? He would have to cherish every moment of the last days with her since the memories would need to last him a lifetime.

* * *

The next three days seemed to fly by. She and Braden spent their days taking long drives after breakfast. They had lunch and dinner out. They spent most of their nights making love into the early morning.

Having him lying on top of her, buried deep in her pussy, filling her ears with words of need, passion, and devotion made her ache for the future they would never share. More than once, she fell asleep with tears streaming down her cheeks.

Neida woke alone in bed on their last full day together. She showered quickly, dressed, and hurried out onto the patio. There she found a bare-chested, jean-clad Braden pacing.

As she was about to join him, her cell phone rang. Braden turned to look at her.

She smiled at him and noting Raven's number, lifted the phone to her ear. "Hello."

"Morning, querida. I hope I'm not interrupting anything."

"No. I'm just heading out to the patio to have breakfast."

"I wanted to remind you our flight tomorrow leaves at 2 p. m. Shay or I will be there to pick you at 10."

Which meant she had just over twenty-four hours left with Braden. Her eyes misted.

"Querida?"

She blinked. "Ok. I'll be ready. I'll pack today."

"On the off chance that he asks you to stay, say no."

"What? Why would I do that?"

"To make him realize he'll have to make a choice. Make him come after you. Don't stay and make it easy for him to have his cake and eat it too."

Her cheeks burned. She turned her back to Braden who stood on the patio staring at her so intently she wondered if he could read lips. "Are you implying I've been too easy?"

"Absolutely not. You've given him a taste. Now you have to be prepared to walk away from him — no matter how he tries to get you to stay. He'll probably ask you to stay until he's ready to go to Tulsa. No matter how you're tempted, don't."

"Why not? If he wants me to stay?"

"He's my brother and all four of us are close, Bray

and I are closer. I know him better than anyone else. Please trust me when I tell you that you can't stay under his terms—unless you're prepared to become his mistress. Are you?"

"Yes—when hell freezes over!"

"That's what I thought. Don't let him talk you into staying. Make him follow you. Okay?"

"I—"

"Don't cave, querida."

"Fine. I won't."

"I know this is hard for you, honey, but hang in there and you might be able to rescue him from a life devoid of love. I'll see you tomorrow, but if you need either me or Shay before then, you call. We've both left the day open. One of us will come ASAP."

She nodded, a lump lodging in her throat.

"Querida?"

"I'll see you then." She ended the call, took a long breath and then pressed her forehead against her arm.

"Neida?"

She turned to see Braden walking towards her.

He paused on the threshold. "Is everything okay?"

"That was Raven. Our flight leaves at 2 p.m. tomorrow. He wants me to be ready to leave here by 10 tomorrow morning."

He glanced at his watch and then at her.

"I think I'll go pack now." She turned away.

He caught her hand. "Neida?"

She looked at him, blinking back tears. "Yes?"

"What's the rush? Let me call Randall and Peyton Grayhawk to see if I can make arrangements to have Peyton come take you home in a few days."

"It's silly to waste money like that when I can go

tomorrow for the price of a regular airline ticket."

He linked his fingers through hers. "Let me worry about the cost."

"Thanks for being willing to spend the money, but I'd better go back with Raven."

"Why?"

"Why?"

"Yes." He drew her forward until he could put his arm around her waist. "Why?"

"I have plans, Braden."

"Don't hand me that shit, Neida! What plans do you have that can't wait a few days?"

She lowered her lids. "They can't wait."

He put a hand under her chin and lifted her head. "Why not?"

"I don't want to ruin our last day together, Braden."

His gaze narrowed. "It's him. Isn't it?"

"Him?" She moistened her lips. The way he spat the word him out, she knew he was referring to Mark. Had he been outside the bedroom listening when Mark had called just before she showered?

"Your perfect Mark."

"He's in Philly now," she admitted. "He's been there for the last three days trying to reach me. He's only going to be there for another few days. If I don't go home tomorrow I'll miss him."

"Then miss him."

She pulled away. "I don't want to miss him. It's been nearly five years since we've seen each other."

He gripped her arms. "You can see him the next time he comes."

"I'm going to see him this time, Braden."

"No, you're not."

She stared at him. "Yes. I am. If you think I'm going to disappoint a man who's never put another woman above me for one who only wants me to stay with him until he can go romance another woman, you're grossly overrating your charms, Braden."

He released her and stepped back to stare at her. "Are you telling me he's more important to you than I am?"

"I'm telling you I'm not going to treat him like you're about to treat me, Braden!"

"You know I wouldn't hurt you if I had a choice!"

"I don't see anyone with a gun to your head, Braden. I'm not just going to pretend he's important to me. I'm going to show him. His parents moved to Montana three years ago. He came to Philly for one reason — to see me. I'm not going to disappoint him. I'm flying home tomorrow, Braden."

"You'd rather spend time with him than me?"

"I could ask you the same thing about your women in Tulsa, but what would be the point? Your mind is made up and so is mine. There's no reason for us to spend our last day together arguing over people the other one will never know."

"Neida—"

"Please, Braden. You must know that I want to stay with you, but I'm not willing to suggest to him that the effort he made to see me was wasted. I'm probably not going to see you after tomorrow. Hopefully, he'll always be my friend."

"Then he should understand!"

"Given what you plan to do, so should you! I'm going to need all my friends after tomorrow, Braden. I can't afford to alienate one over a fling."

"A fling?"

"I'm probably always going to cherish fond memories of this week with you, but when you strip away the pretense and the pretty words of need and adoration, you're left with a fling."

"What the hell pretenses are you talking about? Who the fuck is pretending, Neida?"

"Me! That I mean more to you than I ever could."

"Oh fuck! There's just no getting along with you, is there?"

She stared at him. In a moment he'd be calling her a silly little bitch or worse. And this time she wouldn't forgive him. Not that it would matter to him. "Just once, I'd like to fall for a man who can put me first. Just once. First Mark had more important things he had to do with his life than spend it with me. Now you. But he at least wanted me enough to want me to accompany him — as his wife. But you just expect me to be okay with knowing how unimportant I am to you."

He released her. "I've had it up to my neck trying to convince you of something you refuse to believe. Go right ahead and do whatever you feel you have to."

"I will — just as you're going to do."

"So this is tit for tat, Neida?"

"No. It's me not willing to belittle the effort he made to see me. Put yourself in my place, Braden. If you had to choose between a woman who had never put another man before you and one who had, which would you pick?"

He turned and walked back onto the patio. He sat down and picked up his coffee cup, staring straight ahead.

She stood where she was, uncertain what to do. She could see his jaw clenching and unclenching. Should she call Raven and ask him to pick her up a day early? If she left to pack, would she find Braden gone when she returned?

Almost as if he'd read her mind, Braden put his cup down and turned to look at her. "I'll be here when you finish packing. Please join me then, Neida."

A wall of relief nearly overwhelmed her. She nodded and went to the master bedroom.

When she returned to the patio forty minutes later, he was dressed in dark pants and a white pull over. He rose. "What would you like for breakfast?"

"I don't have much appetite. Just coffee for me."

He pushed her seat in and poured her coffee before he resumed his seat. "What would you like to do today?"

"I'm feeling selfish. I don't want to share any of today with you with anyone else. Let's stay in."

He nodded. "We need to have a talk."

"What about?" She sipped her coffee.

"Your financial future."

"No. You've already paid off my loans and your brothers have already offered me money. This isn't about money for me."

"My brothers and I know that, but your arrangement with them has nothing to do with this conversation. I have a lot of money. I make a lot of money. There's no reason why you shouldn't allow me to make your life a little easier."

"You've already done that when you paid off my student loans. I'm not taking anything from your brothers or you."

He spread his hands. "We're not going to spend the rest of our time arguing."

"No," she agreed.

He pushed his seat back and extended a hand. "Are you sure you want to try that again?"

He smiled. "Positive."

She rose and walked around the table to sit on his lap.

He wrapped his arms around her.

She leaned back against him. "This is nice but if I sit on you for much longer, your knees will be permanently numb."

He laughed. "Let me worry about my knees." He lifted a hand to turn her face towards him and kissed her, pressing his tongue against her lips and into her mouth.

She closed her eyes, returning his kiss with a greedy warmth that made her pussy flood.

He cupped his hands over her breasts, rubbing the heels of his hands against her nipples.

She trembled with need she struggled to suppress. When he slipped his hand down her belly to cup between her legs, she dragged her mouth away from his. "We can't, Braden."

"Why not?"

She bit her lip. It was silly to find it difficult to mention her period to a man whose cock she had sucked, but somehow the words wouldn't come. She looked at him in silence.

He arched a brow and finally removed his hand from between her legs. "I see. Damn, but your timing stinks."

"It's not like I have a choice on the timing. Besides,

you should be happy." She rose and walked back to her seat.

"Why should I be happy?"

"It means our precautions were adequate and you won't have to worry about trying to be a long distance father to a child you never wanted."

He shook his head. "What is it with you, Neida? Why do you persist in deliberately misunderstanding me? What the hell makes you think I'd feel that way about any child of mine—especially if you were the mother?"

"Well, I'm glad if you're not. I grew up in a loving household with parents who loved each other and me. I wouldn't want any less for my kids."

"Just so you know, Neida, I wouldn't have been a long-distance father. Nor would I have left you to deal with a pregnancy alone."

But she'd still have been a single mother. She smiled. "Thanks for letting me know that, Braden."

"In spite of your somewhat less than flattering opinion of me, I've never had to lie to a woman to get what I want. That's not a brag, Neida. It's a fact. When I tell you I adore you, that's also a fact."

"The feeling is mutual, Braden."

"What about Mr. Perfect?"

"Oh Braden. There's no need to sneer like that when you mention him."

"Jealousy, honey. Pure and simple. I know you won't have the same reverence in your voice five years from now when you talk about me."

She arched a brow. "You're assuming, of course, that I'll even remember you to talk about then."

He laughed. "Oh my beautiful Neida, you wound

me."

She smiled and picked up her cup.

To her surprise, they spent an enjoyable and relatively awkward free day together. They swam and lounged around the pool for most of the day but didn't talk much. He had dinner and lunch delivered from one of his favorite restaurants. The food was delicious but neither of them ate much.

After dinner, they spent most of the night slow dancing under the stars out by the pool. He put on a karaoke version of one of the Rolling Thunder CD's and sang to her. She'd never heard any of the songs before. One in particular called *The Keys To My Heart* touched her.

With her eyes closed, his arms cradling her close, and his deep voice singing in her ear, it was easy to pretend that she did own the keys to his heart and that she was the love of his life.

They danced late into the night before slipping into bed together. Lying with her cheek pressed against his shoulder, holding tears at bay was difficult. Sleep was elusive. She longed for reassurance that their week together had been as special for him as it had for her. But although he held her, he said nothing.

She spent most of the night drifting in and out of fitful bouts of sleep. Each time she startled awake, she was aware that he was awake as well. Just as she managed to fall into a deeper sleep, she felt warm lips brushing hers.

Her lids fluttered and lifted.

Light filled the room. Braden, fully dressed and shaved, sat on the side of the bed. "Morning."

She smiled and yawned. "Morning." She yawned

again. "I feel like I've just closed my eyes. What time it is?"

"It's just after 6. I know you're tired and I am too, but since we have less than 4 hours left together, I was hoping you'd opt to get up early and sleep on the plane."

She nodded.

"Good. I'll get breakfast ready while you shower and dress." He rose.

She got out of bed and walked towards the bathroom.

"Neida?"

She glanced over her shoulder. "Yes?"

"Make it a quick shower?"

"I will."

"And you're beautiful from the moment you wake up, so don't linger over your hair and make-up."

"What?"

"We have so little time left, Neida and you're gorgeous with or without makeup."

"And you're handsome and smooth."

"And sincere."

She smiled and walked into the bathroom to shower quickly. After dressing, she looked around the bedroom to make sure she'd packed everything. Then she stood, trying to commit the room to memory since she would never see it again. But the more time she spent in the bedroom, the less time she'd have with Braden.

He embraced her when she joined him on the patio. "Would you like to go for a short drive after you eat?"

She shook her head. "No. Let's lounge around the pool until it's time to head for the airport."

"Are you sure I can't convince you to stay for a few more days? I talked to the Grayhawks and Peyton can fly out in three days to fly you home."

"Mark would be gone by the time I got home, Braden."

"That's the point: to keep you two apart."

"Oh Braden!"

"Why so shocked? You came here in the hope of keeping me from going to Tulsa. Didn't you?"

"Yes," she admitted. "But I failed—and so will you." She kissed his cheek. "So let's just enjoy our few hours together."

He nodded and released her.

After breakfast, they shared a lounger by the pool. Despite her best efforts to stay awake, she fell asleep. She woke alone on the lounger with Braden kneeling beside her. "Raven and Shane are in the living room."

She sucked in a breath and blinked hard to keep tears at bay.

He kissed her, rose, and reached down to offer her a hand.

She stood up, adjusted her clothes, and looked at her watch. 9:45. "I'll just make a quick trip to the powder room."

He nodded.

When she'd freshened up and walked into the living room, all three brothers stood up. Both Raven and Shane greeted her with a kiss on the cheek.

"Are you ready, querida?" Raven asked.

She glanced at Braden.

He gave her one of those silent stares she hated.

"Yes."

Raven looked at Braden. "Are you riding with us,

Bray?"

"I think it's time I went into the office and did some work."

"So you're not coming?"

"No."

Raven picked up her cases. "We'll wait in the car, querida."

Neida watched him and Shane leave the room before she turned to look at him. "Braden?"

"I'm not big on public displays of affection," he said. "I hope you have a safe flight."

And that was it? He didn't even care enough to go to the airport with her? Fine. She turned and walked out of the living room and down the hall towards the entrance door. It was open and she walked through it.

Raven and Shane sat in the front seat of a dark SUV with the doors open. Raven got out of the passenger seat with a hand extended.

"Neida!"

She turned.

Braden left the house and closed the door.

Her heartbeat quickened. "Are you coming after all?"

He nodded. "Yes." He closed the distance between them and put his arm around her shoulders.

The next four hours passed in a blur. One moment she was seated in Braden's passenger seat headed for the airport, the next he was brushing his lips against hers, whispering good-bye and stepping back to allow Raven to put his arm around her. Then they boarded the plane and it was over. Over.

Chapter Fifteen

Just after twelve that night, Braden stood in the doorway of his kitchen, staring at the island where he and Neida had made love twice. He then walked out to the patio and finally to his bedroom. Every room, even the ones she hadn't spent much time in, seemed stamped with her presence.

How had she managed to make such an indelible impression both on him and his house in such a short time? He closed his eyes and leaned against his bedroom door. Raven had called him three hours earlier to say he'd seen her safely home. What was she doing now? Was she alone? Or with *him*?

A rage built in his gut and he curled his lip back from his teeth at the thought of another man touching her. Caressing her. Kissing her warm lips. Sliding inside her and wallowing in a pleasure like none he'd ever felt with any other woman—not even Kania.

He took a slow, deep breath. He'd loved Kania and he'd gotten over her. It would probably hurt like hell for far too long, but he'd get over Neida too. He stripped, took a quick shower, padded through the empty house to the living room for a drink and then went back to his bedroom. There, despite his exhaustion, he lay sleepless until the early hours of the morning.

The next morning, he struggled hard to resist the urge to call her in the hope of keeping her from sleeping with her ex. He suppressed it and went to work instead. Each moment he spent alone, he thought of her and ached with the certainty that his heart had been shattered beyond repair.

Hang on, Elkhorn. In five days you'll be in Tulsa and on your way to an engagement that will force you to abandon thoughts of her. Or damn yourself and the unlucky woman who ends up as your wife to a miserable marriage. Just hang on. It hurts like hell but you can do this. You can do this. You will do this.

He rolled onto his stomach, closing his eyes. *Oh God, Neida. Neida.*

* * *

"You're in love with him."

Seated on the sofa in her moonlit living room with Mark's hand cupping her breasts and his lips pressed against her neck, Neida kept her eyes open. If she closed them, she might forget herself and whisper Braden's name.

Despite the years they'd spent apart, she and Mark still shared a closeness that made trying to deceive him difficult at best. "Yes," she whispered. "But I love you too."

He sighed, kissed her ear and rose.

She stared up at him. He was as tall as Braden with smooth dark skin, brown eyes, and a warm smile that lit up his handsome face. The moment they'd seen each other again, the years had melted away and she'd rushed into his arms, raising her lips for a long kiss.

Although no longer in love with him, she was still attracted to him. Sleeping with him so soon after being with Braden would feel almost like infidelity, but it wouldn't be unpleasant.

"You'd rather go into the bedroom?"

"Yes," he said. "I would."

Steeling herself, she rose and slipped her arm through his.

He stepped away from her.

She frowned. "What's wrong, Mark?"

"I'd like to go into the bedroom and make love to you all night."

"But?"

He brushed the back of his hand against her cheek, much like Braden often did. "But I have a feeling he'd be in there with us and I'm really not that interested in knowing him well enough to sleep with him."

Neida laughed and then leaned against him, sobbing.

He held her until her sobs subsided. Then he sat on the sofa, urging her down beside him. "Tell me about him," he invited.

"What do you want to know?"

"Everything."

She talked about Braden, answering the many questions he posed until there seemed nothing left to say.

Then they went into her bedroom, undressed, and slipped into bed together. She fell asleep sprawled across his big body with the sound of his warm voice singing one of her favorite love songs to her, *Pledging My Love*.

In the morning she woke to find a letter on the nightstand near her bed.

She glanced around the room they'd spent two nights sharing and knew he'd left without giving her a chance to say good-bye.

Rolling onto her side, she sat up and picked up the envelope.

Hey sweet girl,

What can I say? It was great to see you again. I

know you wanted to see me off at the airport, but my heart wasn't up to the challenge of saying good-bye to you like that a second time. Forgive me for taking the cowardly way out.

I'm hoping for a miracle that will allow you to be happy with Braden. If not, don't despair. You'll find love with the right man at the right time. Love will be all the sweeter for having been delayed.

Until then, know that as long as I'm alive, there's always going to be one man in the world who'll love you until the day he dies. If things change and you feel a sudden urge to rough it, I'd love to marry you and spend the rest of my life with you by my side making a difference for people who need so much and have so little.

If not, take my advice and go back to L.A. and fight for him. Although I'd be a little sad, I'd love to have you write and tell me you two are getting married. Go fight for him and win him and show him why you're really the only woman in the world worth marrying.

I'll email when I get back home safely and talk to you in a few months.

Loving You Always,

Mark

Neida bit her lip as angry tears rolled down her cheeks. What was wrong with her that she fell for men like Mark and Braden who both insisted on putting causes above her while running away from a man like Pete who had wanted to love and adore her? And what the hell did he mean she was the only woman in the world worth marrying? Didn't he intend to marry one day?

She balled his letter up and then quickly attempted

to smooth it out and hold it against her heart. "I want you to be happy with someone else." Because she had a sinking feeling she was always going to be in love with Braden.

* * *

Two days later, Braden stood in the terminal saying good-bye to Shane who had driven him to the airport for his flight to Tulsa.

"Are you sure you want to do this, Bray?"

Braden nodded curtly. Torturous thoughts of Neida in the arms of the man she spoke so warmly of had ensured he got little rest. He wasn't in the mood to argue with Shane. "Thanks for the lift. I'll see you when I get back," he said.

Shane nodded before he walked away.

Boarding for his flight to Tulsa was announced. *Time to pay the piper, Elkhorn.* Braden picked up his carry-on bag and strolled forward.

* * *

"I think Mark's right. You should go back to L.A. Neida. If it's a question of money, you know Jack and I will be happy to make you a present of the fare."

Lying on a chaise on her balcony trying to appreciate the warm starlit, summer night a day later, Neida closed her eyes. "It's not a question of money," she said into the phone.

"Are you sure?"

"I'm positive, Bett. Not only are my student loan payments history but when I unpacked, I found two prepaid credit cards in my luggage in the CD's Braden gave me. One was from Braden, the other from his brothers. Between the four of them, I now have a three hundred thousand dollar nest egg."

"Then go back, Neida."

"It's too late. He flew to Tulsa yesterday. He's probably already wining and dining his future wife. And even if he isn't, chasing him didn't do me much good the last time."

"Then come spend a few days down here with us," Betty said.

"Thanks but I am lousy company. I'll come down before the summer is over but right now I think I just want to be alone."

"Oh Neida. Honey, call me if you need me."

"I will. Thanks, Bett." She ended the call and put her cell phone on the lounger beside her.

Mentally and physically exhausted, she fell asleep. Her ringing cell phone woke her later.

Yawning, she opened her eyes and picked it up from the lounger. "Hello?"

"Querida."

"Braden!" She sat up, her heart beat quickening.

"Hi, love."

"Braden...I didn't—"

"Are you alone?"

Not that it was any of his business. "Yes. Are you?"

"I know it's late and unexpected but I was hoping I could come up and see you."

"Come up and see me?" She frowned. "From Tulsa?"

"No. From your lobby."

She pressed a hand against her pounding heart. "My lobby? You're in my lobby? Now?"

"How else could I come up and see you from it? Yes, Neida. I'm in your lobby now."

"Oh Braden. What happened in Tulsa? Did things

go badly with both of them? Are they already seeing someone else?"

"I have no idea. I didn't go to Tulsa. Can I come up?"

"Yes." She ended the call, got off the lounger, and went to release the lobby door so he could gain entrance to the elevator banks. Then she stood at the door waiting until her apartment doorbell rang.

After a cursory glance out the peep-hole to make sure it was him, she unlocked the door and flung her arms around his neck.

He engulfed her in a tight embrace.

They clung to each other for at least a minute before she pulled out of his arms and stepped back.

He walked inside and closed the door.

She longed to rush back into his arms but decided she needed to know why he was there first. "What happened?"

"I got to the airport, they announced my flight was boarding and I couldn't get on the plane."

Don't get too excited, Neida. "Why not?"

"I wanted to see you one last time before I officially became entangled with anyone else."

So he still planned to go. Oh hell! "So you want to drag things out between us to ensure maximum damage to my heart?"

His jaw clenched. "Yours isn't the only heart involved, Neida."

"Mine is the only one I'm interested in protecting from any more damage. Any to your heart would be self-inflicted and entirely voluntary, Braden."

"So to hell with me?"

"It's your choice."

"Fine. You must know I have no desire to hurt you."

"That doesn't mean I'm not going to end up with a broken heart."

"I thought you'd be happy to see me."

Damn him and his self-assurance. She gave him one of the cool stares he was so fond of giving her.

He raked a hand through his hair. "Do you want me to leave?"

She would if she had an ounce left of the sense she'd been born with. "No, Braden. I don't want you to leave." *Ever.*

"I know I'm being selfish but I couldn't go without seeing you again."

She bit her lip to stifle the urge to beg him to stay with her. "I am happy to see you."

He glanced around. "Is the paragon still here?"

She balled a hand into a fist and hit his shoulder. "His name is Mark and he's on his way home."

He lifted her hand from his shoulder to kiss her fingers. "And while he was here, did the two of you...?"

"Sleep with each other? Wouldn't you like to know?"

"Yes. I would."

"How have you spent your time since we saw each other?"

"None of my time has been spent in anyone else's bed. Can you say the same thing, Neida?"

With the affirmative trembling on her lips, she paused. Maybe it was time she stopped allowing him to be so sure of her. And she actually would have slept with Mark had he not backed off. "Can I get you something to drink, Braden?"

He caught her hand. "You can answer my question."

"Yes, I can—but I'm not going to."

"So you did sleep with him."

His accusatorial tone annoyed the hell out of her. "You say that as if I owe you some explanation or loyalty. Let's not forget that when you left Philly, you readily admitted that you'd slept with other women."

"So why don't you readily admit to sleeping with him?"

"Because it's none of your business who I did or didn't sleep with after you told me you were going to get engaged to another woman! Now did you come to argue or can we move on?"

He stared at her with a cool look in his eyes.

Damn if she'd let him make her feel ashamed of having control of her own sexual destiny—just as he did. She stared back. "How long will you be in Philly?"

"Two weeks."

"And then?"

"And then I'm going to Tulsa."

Maybe. Maybe not. "Where are you staying?"

He stroked a finger down her cheek. "With you—of course."

"What?"

"Okay. If you don't like that idea, come stay with me while I'm here."

"Aren't you and Raven sharing a suite?"

"We usually do, but I kicked his ass out. He's staying in one of Randall and Benai Grayhawk's guest-houses. That leaves me free to share the suite with you."

"Oh Braden! You shouldn't have forced him out."

"Not to worry, querida. He was happy to be kicked out. Why don't you come share the suite with me? The amenities include three bedrooms, 2 full deluxe baths, a balcony with a view of the city skyline, and maybe most importantly…"

"Most importantly what?"

"It sports a huge kitchen with an absolutely exquisite island."

They stared at each other and then they both laughed.

The remaining tension between them dissipated.

She leaned against him. "Oh Braden. Welcome back to Philly."

He kissed her hair. "So? Will you come, querida?"

She linked her arms around his neck. "Okay, but only for a day or two. My kitchen doesn't have an island and I've become exceedingly fond of them."

He slapped her ass. "I know the feeling. There are two restaurants in the building in case you haven't eaten. Go pack your bags and we'll begin to make the most of the next two weeks."

Damn right and if she couldn't hold onto him this time, she'd have to accept that they weren't meant to be together. "Okay."

As she turned away, he caught her hand and turned her into his arms.

When she lifted her head, he bent his.

She closed her eyes and parted her lips.

He brushed his mouth against hers several times before he licked her lips. Then, burning the taste of his mouth onto hers, he slid his palms down her body to cup her ass as he pressed his tongue against her lips.

Neida's pussy gushed and her heart raced. She leaned forward, sucking his tongue into her mouth. Grinding herself against his groin, she returned his kisses with a greedy need that made her burn for him.

Lost in a haze of desire, she lost track of all commonsense and time. One moment they stood near the door, kissing and caressing each other, fully dressed. The next, he had her pressed against the wall near the door with her top pushed above her bare breasts and the bottoms pushed below her ass.

His warm lips sucked at her right nipple as he stroked his erect shaft along her slit. Then, without warning, she felt the big, warm head of his naked cock slide between her lips and deep up into her pussy.

She gasped and her eyes flew open. "Braden!"

He lifted his head from her breasts to stare down at her before he eased all but the head of his length out of her. "It's too late to protest now," he said, his voice deepened with passion. "There's no way I'm pulling out of the sweetest, tightest pussy that feels as if it were made especially to cradle and delight me." Then he thrust his hips forward, sending his cock balls deep inside her.

With her pussy on fire, her ability to reason vanished. Closing her hands on his ass cheeks, she rubbed her breasts against him and fucked him back with a need and heat that matched his. "Oh Braden. Braden, fuck me like only you can."

"That's the plan, love, to fuck you until you're walking bowl-legged for hours after I pull out of you."

"Oh damn! Do it. Do it, please!"

Moments later, they clung together, moving with a wild, sensual rhythm that sparked emotions she'd never felt with either of her other lovers.

Tearing his lips away from hers, he burned a path across her cheek to her ear. "Oh damn love, you are so sweet. You make me burn with need like no other woman has. I ache for you."

"Show me," she whispered. "Show me I'm the only woman you want."

"Want and need, my love. For me there's only you, Neida. Only you."

With her ears filled with words of desire and her pussy stretched over him, she rutted herself on his cock until it exploded inside her. She couldn't feel him coming, but she felt a trickle of his cum slide down her thigh.

Knowing his seed filled her pussy triggered her orgasm.

He eased his cock out of her and they tumbled, first to their knees and then onto their sides, facing each other.

He rolled onto his back, pulling her body on top of his.

With her sexual needs satisfied, partial sanity returned. "Oh Braden. How could you without protection?"

He stroked his palm down her back to her ass. "I had to—at least once. Besides, you made no attempt to stop me."

So it was her fault her wanted to behave irresponsibly? "I don't recall getting much of an opportunity," she pointed out and sat up.

He reached out to pull her back down to him. "I haven't had unprotected sex since college and you're on birth control." He kissed her hair. "Even if by some miracle, you ended up pregnant, we'd be in it together one hundred percent."

"How could it be one hundred percent when you'd be engaged to another woman?"

"You can't think I'd marry anyone else if you were pregnant. Can you?"

She recalled Raven urging her to have unprotected sex with Braden before her trip to L.A. She lifted her head to look at him. "So to keep you all I have to do is get pregnant?"

"I'd prefer you didn't get pregnant, but I would never leave you alone and pregnant to go marry another woman."

She jerked away from him. "Why would you rather I didn't get pregnant? You don't want a child with me?"

He sat up and put an arm around her shoulders. "Because I wouldn't want you to think that was the only reason I stayed with you."

There was no doubting his sincerity. She took a slow breath. *You have to stop jumping to conclusions with him, Neida.* She leaned against his shoulder. "I'm sorry, Braden. It's just so depressing that you're determined to leave me for another woman."

"You know why."

"Yes. I know why and I even understand on a certain level, but my heart just aches."

"So does mine."

"But you're the only one of the two of us who has a choice. My only choice is deciding if I get hurt now or even more when you leave."

He sighed and allowed his arm to drop away from her shoulders. "You're right and I shouldn't have come." He rose.

She stared up at him while he slipped his cock back into his jeans and zipped them up. "Don't go," she said, rising.

He leaned against the door. "I can't seem to stop fucking up with you."

She adjusted her sweat suit before she rose to face him. She linked her fingers through his. "Don't do it, Braden. Please."

"If I didn't feel I had to, I wouldn't. But it feels like the right thing to do."

Oh hell! "Okay. Beg over." She pulled her fingers from his. "I'll go pack an overnight bag."

The look of relief on his face told her he'd expected her to change her mind. "But you have to promise me that you won't come near me again without a condom."

"You expect me to willingly go back to a condom after what we just shared?" He shook his head. "I'll promise not to make love to you raw again — if you say no at the time."

"Braden—"

He pressed his fingers against her lips to silence her. "As you've told me at least twice, you're an adult, Neida. If you don't want to have sex without protection, be willing to make an issue of it — before I get my cock inside your addictive pussy. Once it's buried deep inside your sweet heat, it would take an act of God to get me to pull it out before I come in you."

She stared at him. "So, what? You're telling me you're going to keep trying to have unprotected sex with me?"

"In a word? Yes. It'll be up to you to back me

down."

"That's not fair, Braden. Once you start kissing and caressing me, my capacity for rational thought quickly diminishes."

He slipped a hand into her pants and between her legs. "Then I guess my bare cock and I will get to enjoy more of this tight, hot, sweet and juicy, delicious pussy. Won't we?"

Her stomach muscles clenched at the raw intensity in his words and gaze. Instead of taking issue with him, she stretched on her toes and pressed her lips against his ear. "Yes—but only after hell freezes over." She nipped his earlobe and turned away.

He laughed and reached out to slap her ass twice. "An overnight bag isn't going to be big enough—unless you plan to walk around naked for the next two weeks—which is fine with me. If it's not for you, pack a suitcase."

With each cheek stinging, she sashayed away, swinging her hips. A smile curved her lips in response to the wolf whistle he let rip.

Chapter Sixteen

Braden and Neida spent most of their waking hours during the next three days making love. Although she clearly shared his depth of desire and he was fairly certain she loved him and had enjoyed their raw love making, she refused to allow him anywhere near her pussy during that time without a condom.

Every morning, he woke early to lie watching her sleep beside him. Each time he fell asleep with her in his arms, he wondered how he could possibly ever give her up. Each time he slipped inside her and felt her clinging to him and whispering his name as she came, he fell harder for her.

The thought of waking up next to her every morning and spending the rest of his life adoring her intrigued him. Made him ache with longing for it. How the hell was he supposed to walk away from her and marry anyone else? The feelings she invoked in him were so powerful that they overshadowed what he'd felt for Kania.

He stroked his hands over her large, beautiful bare breasts.

She made a sound in her sleep and maneuvered herself from her back onto her side, facing him.

His cell phone rang. Seneka.

Rolling onto his side, he got out of bed. He picked his cell phone up from the nightstand and quickly walked out of the room so as not to awaken Neida. "Neka."

"Actually, it's Autumn," his sister-in-law responded. "Neka's in the shower. Did I interrupt anything?"

He strolled through the unit to the kitchen where he poured himself a cup of coffee. "No. How are you, honey?"

"Great. How are you?"

"At the moment? Pretty good."

"Are you two coming tonight?"

"Coming where?"

"Tempest wants to show off Brandon and Malita again," she said of Layton and Tempest Grayhawks' young twins. To disguise the fact, she and Layton are having some friends over."

Braden suppressed a sigh. Who could blame Layton and Tempest for wanting to show off the twins conceived of their love? That's a feeling he wasn't ever likely to experience.

"You know how that goes," Autumn went on. "That could mean anything from one other couple to twenty. Neka and I are going. I'd love to meet your Neida there."

"I hadn't planned on going."

"Why not?"

"We don't have much time left together. I'm really not that interested in spending it sharing her with a horde of other people."

"I can understand but when else am I going to meet her?"

"Frankly, there's no reason why you should meet her at all, Autumn."

"Oh Braden. I was hoping you wouldn't say that. The guys tell me she's very important to you."

"The *guys* talk too damned much and you shouldn't listen to their gossip."

"Oh. I see.

"You see what?"

"That instead of being important to you, she's just an easy lay."

"The hell she is!"

"Then what's the harm in our meeting?"

"No offense, honey but I'd prefer you two didn't meet."

"Why?"

"Because she'll start to wonder about my feelings and imagine I think less of her than Neka does of you."

"Well? Don't you?"

"What the hell kind of question is that, Autumn?"

"It's difficult to view a man's opinion of you in a positive light when he tells you you're good enough to fuck but not to marry."

"Fuck you!" He snapped and ended the call before he surrendered to the urge to call her an interfering bitch. He was not going down that path again. In fact, it was time he erased the word from his vocabulary—at least when it came to women he cared about.

When she called back, he considered allowing it to go to voicemail before he finally answered. "What now, Autumn?"

She sighed. "The last thing you need is me making you feel bad. I'm sorry."

"Fuck! No. I'm sorry. I had no right to speak to you like that. Now I'll have to worry about Neka trying to kick my ass on top of all my other problems."

"This conversation is between you and me, Braden. But make no mistake, if he actually wanted to, he could kick your big ass."

He laughed. "You're probably right."

"Of course I am. You know it's not a good thing to

disappoint a pregnant woman. Don't you?"

"That's what I hear."

"Then I'll expect to meet her tonight."

"Yes—provided she wants to come."

"Please bring her, Braden."

"I'll do my best, honey."

Later that night, he shared a loveseat with Autumn while Neida danced with Seneka across Layton and Tempest Grayhawk's large living room. There were at least forty other people there, including Raven and several of the Grayhawk brothers and their dates.

"She's absolutely gorgeous, Braden."

He tore his gaze from the dance floor to smile at Autumn. Like Neida, she was a full-figured, pretty woman. Four years older and happily married to Neka, pregnancy had turned her pretty face into a beautiful one.

The noticeable swell of her stomach left him wondering how much sexier Neida's belly would look if she were pregnant with his child.

Autumn elbowed him. "Braden! You haven't heard a word I've said. Have you?"

"I'm sorry. What did you say?"

"Would you like to touch it?"

"Touch what?"

"My belly. You've been staring at it since we sat down."

He raised his gaze to hers. "Sorry. It's...ah..."

She tilted her head. "Would you like to touch it?"

"Would it bother you if I did?"

"People I barely know feel it's their right to come up to me and touch my stomach—whether I want them to or no. You certainly can as well."

He hesitated before he put his arm around her shoulders and gingerly touched her stomach.

"You won't break anything or hurt me," she said, placing her hand over his. "Touch it."

He inhaled slowly. How lucky Seneka was to be able to touch her belly whenever he liked—knowing his child was slowly growing inside her. A child they would shower with love as they raised him or her together. Soon, Neka would be able to feel his child moving inside her.

"Amazing huh?"

He raised his gaze to hers and smiled. "Yes. Totally amazing."

Autumn leaned close to whisper in his ear. "This could be your hand on her belly growing round with your baby."

Didn't he wish?

"Do you love her, Braden?"

"That's between me and her."

"I'll take that as a yes."

He stared at her.

She placed her hand against his cheek. "Oh Braden. Don't let her go. Please. You deserve to be happy too. Please."

"What I deserve and what I have to do, unfortunately, aren't the same thing, Autumn."

* * *

Looking around Seneka's shoulder as they danced together, Neida was startled to see Braden and Autumn smiling at each other, while he caressed her belly. She inhaled sharply.

"What's the matter?" Seneka asked.

She blinked at him, uncertain how to respond.

He studied her face briefly before he looked over his shoulder. He turned his attention back to her and continued dancing. "They're close," he said.

"Close? Seneka! What's going on between them looks a little more than close."

"It's not." He shrugged. "You might as well know they had a brief thing for each other while we were dating."

"And that doesn't bother you?"

"No. It wasn't anything much and besides, it ended before we were married."

"But…"

"I can see we need to talk." He stopped dancing, placed an arm around her shoulders and walked her over to another loveseat on the opposite side of the room from where Braden and Autumn sat.

He sat.

Neida stood staring across the room at Braden, who still had his hand on Autumn's belly and a look of wonder on his face.

Seneka took her hand in his and urged her onto the seat beside him.

She reluctantly turned to look at him. "Did they…were they intimate?"

"If by intimate you mean did they have intercourse, then the answer's no."

She moistened her lips. "Are you sure?"

"I'm very sure. It didn't go beyond a few heated kisses and caresses."

"On the mouth? He kissed her on the mouth?"

His lips twitched with amusement. "Yes. That's where a man generally kisses a woman he finds attractive."

"He found her attractive?"

"Of course he did. I've never asked but I'm fairly certain there might even have been some dueling tongues involved."

"Are you saying she dated both of you at the same time?"

"Of course not. She was dating me, but you of all people know Bray is a chick magnet. As you can see she's beautiful and he's a normal man so naturally..."

"So naturally what? They had to trade spit?"

He laughed and shocked her by leaning over to kiss her on her mouth.

She jerked back and stared at him. "What are you doing?"

"Showing you how meaningless a kiss can be. They never had intercourse and are now a very close brother and sister-in-law. End of story." He tilted his head. "Now, how close are you and I going to be, honey?"

"Not kissing on the mouth close!"

"No? How about a few pats on the ass close?"

"If you put your hand anywhere near my ass, you're going to pull back a nub!"

He laughed again. "I never could resist a challenge. Now you know I'm going to have to touch your luscious ass."

"My luscious ass? Don't you worry about my ass."

"I'm not worried about it. I'm just going to touch it."

"The hell you are!"

"I'm glad we agree, honey."

"Don't flirt with me and don't call me honey. You're a married man."

"No. I'm a *very happily* married man," he corrected.

Then act like it! She glanced at Braden, who had finally removed his hand from Autumn's stomach. But they were still sitting too close for her comfort. And Braden still had that look of wonder on his face.

"There's nothing going on between them beyond an in-law relationship," Seneka assured her.

Get a grip, Neida. You know he's right. There's no way Braden would feel as he does about you if he still had a thing for her. "Oh I know that."

"Do you?"

"Yes." She nodded. "I do but seeing him with his hand on her stomach like that and that look of wonder on his face threw me."

"This will be the first baby in our family since Shane was born so we're all very excited. Now that Bray's had his big paws on her belly, Raven and Shane will have itchy palms as well."

"And you wouldn't mind?"

"Of course not. We're a close-knit family and this pregnancy is a family affair. Everyone is relocating from the West Coast to this area so our baby will be surrounded by a loving family."

"If things go well and you end up pregnant, one of these days, we'll all be palming your belly."

"In your dreams!"

He smiled. "My brothers have almost as much emotion invested with this pregnancy as Autumn and I do."

If they were so close, why was Braden the only one expected to do his duty to their culture? She moistened her lips before she spoke. "I don't quite know how to ask this so please forgive me for just coming right out and asking."

"Go right ahead, querida. Ask me anything you like. If I can, I'll answer."

"Braden told me you were married twice—both times very happily."

"Yes. I loved my first wife as much as I love Autumn. I've been extremely fortunate to marry the only two women I've ever loved."

"That is fortunate. I'm wondering if you ever felt an obligation to marry for cultural reasons?"

"Instead of for love? When I was younger, I assumed I'd fall for a Native woman, but it just never happened. As you probably know, my first wife was Caucasian. We were very happily married until she died. Then I met Autumn. I knew the night we met, I wanted to marry her. Having been happily married once, marrying for any reason other than love wasn't in my game plan. Would it have been in yours?"

"Of course not! I'm just wondering why Braden feels he has to."

Seneka sighed and shook his head. "I think he feels a greater sense of cultural obligation because he's the eldest and he was particularly close to our father. It's a burden the rest of us have urged him to throw off. He deserves to marry for love—just as our father did. Unfortunately, trying to convince him of that isn't easy. You're our best hope of that."

"Then you'd better prepare yourself for disappointment. He still plans to go to Tulsa."

"So he says. I'm convinced you're just the woman to change his mind."

"What makes you think I can when Kania couldn't?"

"He told you about her?"

She nodded. "He still has feelings for her."

"I know but his feelings for you run stronger and deeper than those he has for her. He's not in love with her anymore."

"Do you think he's in love with me?"

"Don't you?"

"No. I don't."

He kissed her cheek, allowing his lips to brush her ear. "I wouldn't be too sure of that if I were you."

"Did he tell you he's in love with me?"

"No."

"He's hasn't told me he is either."

"That doesn't mean he isn't. I fell for Autumn almost instantly but got hung up on saying the actual words, which she needed to hear. I loved her long before I was able to tell her I did. Sometimes men find it difficult to put their feelings into words, but an astute woman won't automatically conclude she's not loved just because she hasn't heard the actual words."

She leaned away from him.

He arched a brow. "What's wrong?"

"Nothing. I guess part of me knows you're right about men and their inability to express their feelings."

"But?"

"But I'm just trying to wrap my thoughts around Braden having a thing for your wife."

"She wasn't my wife then. We weren't even engaged and for the last time, it meant nothing. Like this."

"Like what?"

"This." He bent his head and kissed her with enough force to make her start to part her lips.

Catching herself, she shoved at his shoulders and

jerked away. "What the hell do you think you're doing?"

"I *thought* I was kissing you. What did you feel?"

"Nothing!"

He arched a brow. "Nothing?"

"Nothing!" she insisted, feeling her cheeks burn at the lie.

"That's what I felt. Nothing. So what are you complaining about?"

"What?!"

"Did you want some tongue action or an interchange of spit?"

"Are you nuts?"

"Probably."

There was no probably about it. They were all nuts. She rose quickly.

To her sensitive ears, it seemed all conversation in the room had ceased. When she glanced around, she noticed Braden and Autumn looking in their direction. Her cheeks burned. Oh God. Had Autumn seen Seneka kiss her? And what did the other guests think? They must think she'd come on to him with his pregnant wife seated across the room!

Was it her imagination or had the music been lowered? No one other than Braden and Autumn seemed to be looking in their direction, but surely some of the other people in the room must have seen him kiss her.

"So what are you complaining about?" he asked, looking up at her.

"What am I..." She stared down at him, saw the amusement in his gaze and realized she'd overreacted to his tease. Relieved that he had no sexual interest in her, she laughed so hard that she didn't protest when he tugged at her hand and pulled her back down beside him.

He laughed too and put his arm around her shoulders.

She turned her face against his shoulder and continued laughing until tears rolled down her cheeks.

He lifted her chin and pressed a gentle kiss against the corner of her mouth. "If I weren't happily married, I might be insulted that my kiss meant so little to you."

She bit her lip and laughed again.

"Hey! That's enough of the laughing. Autumn tells me I can trade spit with the best of them. Sure you don't want to trade some spit?"

"Not with you," she said, wiping the tears away.

He nodded, a look of satisfaction in the dark gaze so like Braden's. "I'm very glad to hear that, querida. Dance?"

She nodded. "And while we dance, we can discuss your taking the money back."

"No. We can't. If you don't want it, leave it there to be eaten up by various fees. We're not taking it back, querida." He rose. "Now let's dance."

She got up and moved ahead of him.

He shocked her by slapping her on her ass.

She swung around to glare at him.

He laughed and slapped her ass again.

"Look you, if you touch my ass one more time—"

He caught her hand and turned her into his arms. "Shall we dance, querida?"

"Dance? You just slapped my ass. Are you serious?"

"Yes. I am."

"Why you—" She took a deep breath. "As a matter of fact, I'd love to dance, Seneka."

He smiled. "There you go, querida."

She heard a low whistle. She peeked around his shoulder. Raven, standing alone, lifted his right hand. After using it to outline the shape of a big ass, he made a slapping motion and winked at her.

Grow up, she mouthed at him.

Grinning, he made the slapping motion again.

The Elkhorn men were panty-dropping sexy, but they were all completely nuts. The sooner she realized that, the sooner she could get on with her life. She closed her eyes and pressed her cheek against Seneka's shoulder. "Shut up and dance."

He laughed and slapped her ass again.

Annoyed, she slapped his. Then laughed.

They laughed like two lunatics until Braden crossed the room to turn her out of Seneka's arms and into his. "I believe this is my dance, Neka."

"Braden," she whispered his name, rubbing her cheek against his shoulder. "This is what I want—to be in your arms." Always.

"I want it too, love."

She lifted her face to his with her lips parted.

He kissed her. The tender hunger in his lips vanquished any lingering doubts about his feelings for his sister-in-law or Kania. Neida knew she was the woman who made him ache with need. Whatever he'd felt for the other two women paled in comparison to what he felt for her.

Uncaring who might be watching, she slipped her arms around his neck and sucked his tongue into her mouth.

They spent the next ten minutes slow dancing and kissing until Tempest and Layton came over and asked if they wanted to go see the twins.

She nodded eagerly, surprised at the obvious reluctance she noted in Braden. Did he dislike children?

* * *

Braden and Neida left the Grayhawk's home just after one in the morning. She fell asleep on the drive back to his hotel suite. He couldn't vanquish a picture of Layton and Tempest, both speaking to their kids in Tsalagi before Layton picked them both up and held them in his arms.

The look of adoration on his friend's face as he looked at Tempest and cradled his children against his chest haunted Braden. The adoration and devotion between the four Grayhawks had been palpable. Although very young, it was clear to Braden that Brandon and Malita basked in the glow of knowing their parents loved them deeply.

Tearing his eyes away from the Grayhawks, he'd look at Neida. The look of hunger in her gaze seared his heart. They both knew they'd never share such a moment—even though they were as much in love with each other as Layton and Tempest were.

He parked his rental car in his assigned space, shut off the engine, and turned to wake Neida. When her lids fluttered up and she smiled at him, he longed to sweep her into his arms and beg her to marry him.

Instead, he pressed a quick kiss against her cheek before he got out and walked around to open her door.

Threading his fingers through hers, he locked and armed the car before walking inside. In the master bedroom of the suite, he slowly undressed her while she stood trying to suppress yawns. Although he longed to spend the night buried balls deep inside her, he pulled off his clothes and contented himself with cuddling against her back when they slipped into bed.

He lay awake long after she'd fallen asleep. With their remaining time together quickly dwindling away, he was loath to sleep. Finally, in the early hours of the morning, he fell into a restless sleep.

Chapter Seventeen

Warm, insistent kisses pressed against her bare breasts woke Neida the next morning. Cupping her hands over the back of Braden's head, she realized her pussy was already flooded as he sucked her right nipple into his mouth.

Her stomach muscles clenched. "Oh God, what a beautiful way to wake up," she whispered.

He lifted his head.

She gazed into his dark, desire-filled eyes. Clearly, she was having cock for breakfast. "I need to make a quick bathroom run," she told him. "Put on a condom while I'm gone."

He rolled away from her.

She slipped out of bed. Her pussy pulsed as she noted his semi-erect cock lying along the side of his thigh. "Won't be a moment," she promised and hurried into the bathroom.

When she returned, she found him lying on his back, massaging his cock with a condom on the bed beside him.

She stood in the doorway staring at him. He had such a beautiful body: big and sculptured with a thick cock made to stretch and delight her aching pussy. Rushing across the room, she got onto the bed, between his legs.

He quickly shook his head.

"Let's not go there again, Braden. I want to taste your cock before I feel it inside me," she whispered and bent her head to lave her tongue at the base of his shaft while closing her fingers around him.

He inhaled and exhaled slowly while she kissed a

path up the underside of his length. She loved the building tension in his body when she pressed her tongue against his urethra before she gently sucked the big head of him between her lips and into her mouth.

"Shit!"

She allowed him a few moments to savor the feeling before she compressed her cheeks and started to pump him while she sucked hard. Closing her eyes, she savored the taste and feel of his cock as it quickly thickened and lengthened in her mouth.

He curled his fingers in her hair and groaned.

The sounds of his pleasure heightened hers. Encouraged, she sucked harder, sliding a hand down to caress and massage his balls. Lost in a world of lust and love, she flirted with the idea of rising up his body and plunging her pussy down onto his bare cock until she felt his nuts pressed against her slit.

The delicious thought thrilled her so much, she sucked harder and deeper until he thrust his hips forward, sending his cock surging into her mouth. Before she had time to gag his hips jerked and jets of his cum shot into her mouth.

Keeping her eyes closed, she managed to swallow most of his seed before he gripped her shoulders and eased his cock from between her lips. She slid up his body, pressing herself into his arms.

He kissed her neck, sliding his hands down her body to cup her ass. He rolled them over so he lay on top of her. "Oh damn, I adore you more every day, love."

She pushes against his shoulders. "Why do you do that?" she asked.

"Why do I do what?"

"Why do you always call me love?"

He stared down at her. "Isn't it obvious?"

"Not to me it isn't. Querida and darling I get but not love."

"I call you love because I love you, Neida."

She pushed at his shoulders until he rolls off her. Then she turns her back to him. "Please don't say things you don't mean, Braden."

"I rarely do." He turned her back to face him. "And I do mean it," he said.

They stared at each other in silence for several moments before she realized what he meant. "Oh. I see."

"And just what do you think you see, Neida?"

"You love me but you're not in love with me."

"No. That's not what I meant. I am in love with you."

She shook her head. "No, Braden. Don't ask me to believe that."

"Why the hell not? It's true. I love you and I'm in love with you. I have been almost from the moment I first saw you."

Without any prompting from her, he'd finally said the words she'd longed to hear for what felt like ages. What should have been the most wonderful moment in her life felt like having a serrated knife plunged into her heart instead. "How can you expect me to believe you're in love with me when you're determined to marry someone else?"

"Don't give me any shit, Neida. You knew I had familial obligations before we became lovers. Those obligations make me love you more—not less."

She blinked. He was clearly serious. "Well, your

loving me isn't doing me any more good than it did your wonderful Kania who you also supposedly loved. So clearly, your affection isn't worth shit!"

He inhaled sharply before he clenched his jaw. Then he rolled onto his back and put an arm across his eyes.

His silence infuriated her. She slipped out of bed and stormed into the master bathroom. She took a quick shower before returning to the bedroom to pull her clothes on.

Although he sat propped up on the bed when she emerged from the bathroom, he remained silent.

In no mood for one of his silent stares, she stalked across the room to the nightstand and picked up his wallet. "I'll need your credit card to pay for the taxi home," she told him in a cool, angry voice.

He inclined his head slightly.

Damn him. Why didn't he try to convince her to stay or to make her believe that he really did love her? Only just resisting the urge to lean down to slap him senseless, she sucked in a breath, waving the card at him. "And you should consider yourself lucky if all I use this for is cab fare and not a wildly expensive shopping spree."

"If it'll make you feel any better, go right ahead and max it out. Hell, there are two more in my wallet. Max them out as well."

"I hate you!"

"That would sting if I thought there was a chance in hell that you actually meant it."

"I do mean it!"

"No. You're angry, but I know you don't mean it."

Damn him! She reached down to slap him.

He caught her wrist before her palm could connect with his cheek. "Oh no you don't!"

She tugged at her wrist. "Let me go!"

"You can max out my cards in a fit of anger but I'll be damned if you're going to slap me too. I won't ever hit you and you're not going to hit me."

So he thought she was just angry instead of angry and hurt? "Fuck you, Braden. You keep your money and your so-called love. Neither of them is worth anymore of my time! Go find yourself some unlucky Native woman and I'm sure you'll be swearing to love her too."

He released her wrist, his jaw clenching.

"When you marry her, I hope the two of you will share a long, miserable life together!" She tossed the card onto the bed and walked out of the bedroom, determined not to cry.

Braden rolled onto his stomach and closed his eyes. Certain he was about to lose another woman he loved, he felt as if a giant weight compressed his chest, making breathing extremely painful. *God help me. Please. Help me.*

He was still sprawled on his stomach with his face buried in one arm when he heard the door open. He dismissed his brief hope that Neida had returned. Hell would probably freeze over and his heart would be shredded into a million tiny pieces before that happened.

Moments later, he felt a hand on his shoulder. "Bray? I saw Neida outside. Are you all right?"

"Hell no I'm not all right."

"Do you want to talk about it?"

He rolled over onto his back and opened his eyes. "What's to talk about? I just did what I do best—hurt the woman I love and who loves me."

Raven sat on the side of the bed. "If she loves you—"

She'd never actually said she did, but he knew she loved him as deeply as he loved her. "There's no damned if about it. She does."

"Then she'll forgive you."

"For marrying another woman?" He sat up and glared at Raven. "Are you on drugs?"

Raven compressed his lips before he responded. "Hey, I'm not the one so determined to make myself miserable that I keep going out of my way to ensure I'll never be happily married. You're a first class fool if you don't go after her, Braden."

"When I want your damned advice, I'll ask for it. Until then, fuck the hell off, Raven!"

Raven shot to his feet. "Fine. Why should I give a fuck if you're too stupid not to keep driving away women who are too damned good for you anyway?"

"What?"

"First you let Kania, a woman whose shoes you weren't fit to touch, get away. Now you're doing the same thing with Neida. You're too much of an ass to deserve either one of them!"

He watched Raven storm out of the bedroom with a frown before he got out of bed to shower. Raven might be a bad tempered ass, but he was right. He couldn't allow his relationship with Neida to end on such an unhappy note for her.

* * *

Neida had breakfast out and took a walk along

Franklin Mills Mall before she headed home. During the ride on the train her cell phone rang. Her heart raced, but it wasn't Braden. "Hello?"

"Hi, beautiful."

"Mark! I didn't expect to hear from you so soon. Is everything ok?"

"They couldn't be better, beautiful. Thank you so much!"

"For what?"

"I received notification from the bank that you made me trustee. Oh Neida girl, I can't tell you how much good it's going to do for the kids who need it so much."

"How much good what will do?"

"Your gift! Do you have any idea how many kids I can help with $50,000?"

"I don't know what you're talking about."

"The trust I received in your name. Was it supposed to be anonymous?"

"I didn't send anything, Mark. I don't have $50,000." Unless she decided to keep the money Braden and his brothers had given her.

"Then who sent it?"

"I have no…" She trailed off recalling Braden's annoyance when she'd told him of her plan to send part of the money she'd been spending on her student loans to Mark once school started again. "He did it."

"Who?"

"Braden. It had to be him."

"We've never even met. Damn Neida, he must have it bad for you to do something like this."

"He says he's in love with me."

"He did? Congratulations, Neida. Give me plenty

of time so I can make arrangements to get back home for it."

"For what?"

"For the wedding."

"There isn't going to be one—at least not between him and me."

"$50,000 is a lot of money to send to a man he's never met. He must have done it for you."

"He's rich."

"Even still. There must have been other things he could have done with it. He did it for you. Make sure you give me plenty of warning. Please tell him how very grateful I am."

"I will. Never mind. I should tell him myself. Can I have his address?"

She gave it to him.

"Thanks. Now I have to go. Love you."

"Love you too."

When she arrived home, she immediately spotted Braden's rental car in one of her parking spots. It was empty. After a moment of indecision, she went inside and up to her floor. Standing outside her apartment door, she frowned. He wasn't in his car or in the lobby. So where the hell was he?

She opened her apartment door, went into her living room, and came to an abrupt stop.

Braden turned from her patio doors to look at her.

"How did you get in?"

He held up a pair of keys.

"I never gave you my keys."

"I noticed that."

"Then how did you get them?"

He shrugged. "Remember all those mornings you

slept late? I took them and had copies made."

"You had no right to do that!" She stormed across the room and attempted to snatch them from him.

"That's never stopped me before." He slipped her keys in his pant pocket and slipped his arm around her. "Despite what you think you know about me, I've never loved anyone more than I do you. Never Neida, but I feel like I have to do this."

"I know." She sighed. "Ah…thank you."

"I'm lost. What are you thanking me for?"

"Mark called me."

"The paragon?"

"Braden."

"Whatever. He called you and what?"

"And you gave him $50,000 dollars."

"Why the hell would I give my competition a penny?"

She stared up into his eyes. "You did it for me."

"Did I?"

"Yes. You did and he's not your competition."

"Isn't he?"

"You have no competition, Braden."

"Why not?"

She shrugged. "You just don't."

"Can't you say it?"

"Not to a man who's going to marry another woman."

"That doesn't mean I don't love you because I do."

She closed her eyes, pressing her cheek against his shoulder. "I don't want to hear anymore explanations about why you're going to marry someone else. Just hold me, Braden."

They spent the day together at her apartment,

ordering lunch and having dinner bought in. That night, they danced under the stars until she was too tired to move another step. Then they undressed and slipped into bed. He wanted to make love but she just wanted to be held.

He caressed and kissed her until she fell asleep in his arms.

* * *

In the morning she woke alone. A vase with a single red rose sat on each nightstand. An elegant jeweler's box and an envelope lay on the pillow where Braden had slept the night before. She sat up quickly and opened the box.

Inside laid, an exquisite gold key encrusted with rubies and sparkling diamonds on a fine gold chain.

Her heart raced as she opened the envelope.

My darling wyanet,

My father believed a man had two sets of keys he should jealously guard from all but his wyanet. One set was to his home. The other was to his heart. Please accept this key, which symbolizes the power you alone wield over my heart. Without saying a single word and with just an all too brief but powerful glance, you stole it so swiftly and surely you firmly locked it against all other women the first time I saw you.

If you believe in fate, know that you and I will meet again—in another time when we'll be free to spend the rest of eternity together.

Even as we follow painfully separate paths, know that I wish you all the best and hope you find the happiness you deserve in this life. Please believe that my heart now and will always belong exclusively to you. No matter where I go or who I go with, you will always hold my heart in the palm of your hand.

Until we meet again, please believe that I love you more than you can imagine. And I always will.

Yours, now and forever,

Braden

"No! Damn it, Braden, no!" She jumped out of bed and called Raven. "Where is he?" she demanded when he finally answered on the fifth ring.

He sighed. "I'm sorry, querida. Neka and I both tried to talk him out of it, but he caught a plane to L.A. His flight left 5:30 this morning."

"To L.A.?"

"Yes."

Not Tulsa. So there was time to make one last attempt to change his mind. "Can you get the Grayhawks to fly me there? I know a private plane must cost a fortune, but if you recall, I just happen to have $300,000."

He laughed. "Do you?"

"And since I never wanted it anyway, I'm willing to spend every single penny of it on the flight."

"That's very generous, but unnecessary. Just on the off chance that you might want to make another run at him, I have two seats booked on a flight to L.A. tonight at 5:20. Interested?"

"Yes. Of course. I'll pack a bag. You'll come pick me up?"

"It would be my pleasure, querida."

"I'll be ready in an hour," she said. "And thanks, Raven."

"For what?"

"For everything, including your kindness and

encouragement."

"You're welcome, querida."

* * *

Braden spent the seven and a half hour trip back to L.A. torn by conflicting emotions. Finally admitting to Neida that he was in love with her had lifted a burden from him. Even if she had believed him, how had she felt when she woke and found his letter?

What would she think and feel when she heard that he was engaged and eventually married to another woman? Would she flee to the arms of her ex who he suspected still loved her? What kind of life would she have working herself into bad health beside him in some impoverished and probably dangerous part of the world? Would she be happy with him? He wanted her to be happy.

He thought of his two prospects in Tulsa. He was so damned wound up he couldn't even remember their names. He couldn't recall the names of the two women he was considering for marriage. Something was wrong with that damned picture—something seriously wrong.

When he arrived home, he took a quick shower and then made the drive to his mother's apartment. For once she didn't seem particularly glad to see him. "Braden! There you are. I was just debating if I should call you. Come in."

He followed her into her living room. He walked over to her balcony before he turned to look at her, seated uncomfortably on her sofa.

"When I called Tulsa, I was surprised that you weren't there. You weren't home either. Were you in Philadelphia, Braden?"

He nodded.

She hesitated. "Did you see her?"

"Yes. I was with Neida, Mom."

"You were with her the entire time?"

"Yes. I spent all my time there with her."

"You were having a last fling with her?"

"That's what I told myself when I went to Philadelphia instead of Tulsa, but I knew in my heart that a fling with her was never going to be enough for me. I've always known she deserved so much more than that."

Her lips trembled. "I see."

"I hope you do, Mom."

"I thought we shared a vision, Braden."

"I thought so too."

She sighed. "Are we still on the same page?"

He shook his head. "No, Mom. We're not."

Chapter Eighteen

Braden spent an hour with his mother before he left. On the drive home, he called Shane, who was still in L.A. "I need a favor, Chief."

"Name it."

"I just left Mom and she needs a shoulder to cry on."

"Yours has been the shoulder of choice since Dad died, Bray."

"She's not very happy with me at the moment and she really needs one of us to be with her. That kind of leaves you since Ray's still in Philly."

"I see. I'm on my way."

Shane was a quick study and rarely asked unnecessary questions. He probably did see. "Thanks, Chief."

"She's my mom too. Leave it to me. Talk to you later."

He drove around for ninety minutes before going home. There he spent two hours working out. By the time he stepped into the shower, he felt physically tired and mentally and emotionally battered. With thoughts of Neida haunting him, he toweled off and fell into bed without dressing. Almost immediately he fell asleep and dreamed of Neida.

Braden walked through the house, imagining he could feel her in every room. Standing in the kitchen with his eyes closed, he ran his hands over the island. She might almost have been in the room with him. Shaking his head, he opened his eyes and walked to his bedroom.

His nostrils flared. Thoughts of her were so strong

her scent seemed to fill the room. Her soft warm hands might actually be trailing over his abs to his cock. He felt it closing around him. She then gently pumped him. Once she'd gotten him hard and roused, she slid her naked body up his.

Hungry memories enabled him to feel her rubbing her wet pussy against his fully erect cock, already secreting pre-cum before she gripped the base of it and pressed it against her slit. Then she pushed her hips forward.

The head of his shaft slipped inside her. Fuck! That felt real.

Braden snapped open his eyes.

Neida, naked and straddling him smiled down at him as she reached back to remove the key from her neck and place it on the nightstand. "I decided to come to collect the heart you said was mine, honey."

He stared up at her, momentarily speechless with joy.

Still smiling, she slowly pushed down her lovely hips. His bare cock shot into her warm, wet pussy. His bare cock. He gripped her hips and held them still. "Querida!"

Locking her gaze on his, she struggled to force the last few inches of cock inside her. "Release my hips, Braden."

"There's a condom in the top drawer," he told her.

"We won't need it," she said.

"Why the hell not?"

"Because there's no feeling in the world as delicious as your sweet, bare cock sliding in and out of my pussy. And I love you and want to enjoy that feeling over and over."

His heart pounded with joy. "You love me or you're in love with me?"

"It's both, Braden. I love you and I'm in love with you."

"Are you sure?"

"I'm very sure I love you and I want your seed. I want to taste it in my mouth, feel it trickling out of my pussy and my ass or anywhere else you want to put it."

He swallowed and struggled to contain the joy he felt. It was time he made it clear to her that this relationship wasn't going to be all about what he wanted and needed. "What about an unwanted pregnancy?"

She shook her head. "There was never a question of my not wanting your baby, Braden. I just didn't want to be a single mother."

"What's changed?"

"I have other options now."

His hands tightened on her hips. "Other options? What other options? You don't mean…"

"No, I don't mean abortion or adoption. Now please release my hips."

Braden wasn't sure what that left but he couldn't make himself care anymore. The woman he hungered for above all others had followed him again—clearly signaling she was going to fight for him. He slid his hands around her body to cup her ass as she forced the rest of his dick into her. "Fuck me," he told her.

She licked her lips and smiled at him, gently rocking against his groin. "Oh I'm going to, honey."

"Then stop talking and do it, love." He closed his eyes and groaned at the exquisite delight of having his bared cock buried so deep inside her tight, wet, heat.

The powerful emotions he felt rivaled those of the physical ones. Although sweet beyond words, the sex between them nearly paled in comparison to the absolute wonder and need he felt with her.

If by some cruel trick of fate, he was never able to make love to her again, he knew he would continue to cherish her. Continue wanting to protect her.

Placing her hands on his chest, she lifted her hips until only the head of his shaft remained inside her. Then, tortuously slow, she lowered her hips until his cock was again completely encased within her sweet pussy.

She sat on him, taking deep breaths.

He caressed her ass and then slapped each cheek. "Fuck me," he said again.

She shuddered, leaned over to press her tongue into his mouth, and ground herself against him.

He tightened his hands on her ass, pushing his dick up into her while tugging her ass down.

She moaned and tightened herself around him.

Hot, greedy desire filled him. Unable to contain his hunger any longer, he rolled them over, lay on top of her and devoured her mouth, sucking hard on her tongue while she jerked her hips off the bed to eagerly welcome his cock back inside her.

Powerful surges of pleasure thundered through him, setting his senses on overload. Sliding in and out of her now that they'd both acknowledged how they felt elevated their love making to an almost dizzying height. Having his physical and emotional need for intimacy with her satisfied at the same time gave him the most incredible sexual experience of his life.

Her soft sighs combined with the weight of her

large breasts pressed against his chest and her pussy gripping his cock made it difficult to maintain control. But the last time they'd been intimate, it had been all about him. Not this time.

With a supreme effort of will, he pulled out of her. Grabbing a pillow, he pushed it under her hips and positioned himself between her thighs with his mouth pressed against her slit.

Tilting her hips, he slipped his tongue into her pussy.

"Oh Braden!" She linked her legs over his shoulders.

He wanted to eat her slowly but he knew his control wouldn't last and he was determined to come inside her. He reached up to pinch and massaged her breasts as he devoured her pussy.

When she started to moan and pull at his hair, he slipped his tongue out of her and quickly mounted her, sending his cock surging deep into her pussy.

She clutched her hands on his ass.

Struggling to retain control of himself, he kissed her and plundered her pussy with a rapacious need until he felt a rush of moisture flood his cock. Then, he released the iron control he'd exerted over himself, held her hips still and exploded inside her.

He loved how, even in the midst of her climax, she kept tightening herself around him, as if determined to milk the last drop of cum out of him. With that done, he groaned and buried his face against the side of her neck.

She wrapped her arms around him. "Oh Braden. I love you," she whispered.

"I love you too," he said, rolling over onto his back

so that she sprawled on top of him with his cock still embedded in her pussy.

She lifted her head from his shoulder to look down at him. "So what are you prepared to do about it? I came to make sure you don't go to Tulsa. How long do I have to convince you that we belong together? That you're mine and I'm not going to let anyone else have you?"

"I am yours, darling. Because I've finally accepted that fact, I'm not going to Tulsa."

"Ever?"

"Well, we have relatives there so I'm not swearing off ever going there again, but I'm not going there looking for a wife."

She bit her lip. "Why not?"

"Because I love you and I'll be damned if I'm going to spend a miserable life married to anyone else. I'm all yours, Neida—if you'll have me."

She blinked rapidly before she climbed off of him and lay on the bed with her back to him.

He got up and walked around the bed to sit on the side of the bed. "What's wrong?" he caressed her cheek. "Oh come on, Neida. I've just blown the close relationship I had with my mother so please don't tell me you're having second thoughts."

She sat up. "You blew your relationship with her how? What did you do?"

He shook his head. "Blew is too strong a word. I should have said I disappointed her when I told her I was going to ask you to marry me."

She pressed a hand against her lips for several moments before she spoke. "But I don't understand. In the letter you left, you made it sound as if we were finished. If you really want me, why did you leave that letter?"

"Oh love, I'm sorry about that." He sighed. "When I left it, I was still in denial and trying to figure out a way not to disappoint my mother. So I still intended to end our relationship."

"What changed?"

"On the plane ride home, I suddenly admitted I couldn't do it. I'm a very decisive man. I know what I want and I go after it. I nearly always get what I want because I don't waffle. The fact that I kept waffling on going to Tulsa should have been a sure sign that I was in over my head with you. I would have realized that sooner, if my head hadn't been so messed up because I'm so in love with you."

She stared at him. Her lips trembled and tears streamed down her cheeks. "Oh Braden!" she leaned her head against his shoulder.

He slipped an arm around her shoulders. "Is that a good *oh Braden*? Or an I just realized you're too damned old for me, *oh Braden*?"

She jerked her head up and stared at him. "Just how many ways and times do I have to tell you I love you? I know your age and it's not an issue for me. There's no reason for it to be one for you. I adore you, Braden. That wouldn't change if you were twenty or sixty. I love you."

"I love you too." He knelt beside the bed, taking her hand in his. "Will you marry me, Neida?"

"Oh hell yes!" she said, slipped off the bed and into his arms.

"Yes?" He slipped a hand under her cheek and lifted her chin. "Yes?"

"Not just yes. Hell yes!" She sobbed, pressing her cheek against his neck.

He lifted her to her feet and engulfed her in his arms. "Damn, I love you."

"I love you too, Braden." She took several deep breaths before pulling out of his arms. "I'm sorry, honey."

"About what?"

"Your mother. I take it she wasn't happy?"

He shook his head. "No. She wasn't but she'll just have to learn to adjust. I love and respect her, but I'll be damned if I'm going to marry someone I don't love to please her."

"She's going to hate me. Isn't she?"

"Hate you? Of course not. Will you be her favorite daughter-in-law? Probably not. She had high hopes that I'd marry a Native woman. I crushed those hopes when I told her I was going to propose to you." He slipped his arm around her waist. "But she'll be civil to you and given time, you'll get to know the Jacqueline Elkhorn my brothers and I love and adore and are proud to call Mom."

She sighed. "So she is going to hate me."

"No! She's not a vindictive person. She'll just need time to come to grips with the fact that she's not going to have a Native daughter-in-law. Besides, she'll have more important things to do than hate you — like spending as much time with Autumn as possible. I'm sure Autumn must have mentioned that she experienced a certain level of coolness for a while. But once Mom realized how happy she made Neka, she warmed to her. All I ask is that you try to be patient with her if she seems a little distant to you at first. Can you do that for me?"

She nodded. "Of course I can, honey."

"And your mother, querida? How is she going to feel when you show up with a man almost fourteen years older and of a different cultural background?"

"She was very fond of Mark but she wants me to be happy. She'll take one look at you and know waiting for you was the right decision."

He drew her back into his arms. "Don't get the wrong impression, Neida. My mother wants me to be happy too. She was just hoping I'd be able to find that happiness with a Native woman. Please don't dislike her."

She lifted her head to look at him. "I can't promise to be warm and fuzzy if she makes it clear she doesn't like me, but I'll never be anything but respectful to her and I'll do my best to make her like me. And I'll try to bear in mind how her hopes for you have been dashed because of me."

"That's all I can ask."

"Just so you know, Braden. I'm predisposed to like her—just because she's part of the reason you exist."

"Small wonder I love you." He smiled and kissed her. "Now, I'm not getting any younger. How soon will you marry me?"

"I would have married you the moment we met, but don't think that's going to get me to settle for a hole-in-the-wall, slapped together wedding, Braden. I want the whole damn world to know you're mine. I want a big, white wedding with bridesmaids and ushers. Got it?"

He groaned. "Are you sure I can't convince you to marry me in two weeks so you can be pregnant a month later?"

She linked her arms around his neck. "I'm not marrying you in two weeks and I'm not getting pregnant until after we're been married for a few months. So don't think you're going to rush me." She stroked her fingers through his hair. "I want to enjoy every single moment of being engaged to you."

"Even if I'm in agony?"

She laughed. "That's the way the cookie crumbles, handsome. The wedding day is all about me." She rubbed her breasts against his chest. "But not to worry, darling. I plan to make the wedding night all about pleasing you in every way possible. My mouth, my pussy, and my ass will be yours to plunder and use anyway your big cock wants to."

"Yeah? Shit! Let's get married today!"

She laughed again. "Patience, Braden. We have the rest of our lives together to fall deeper in love with each other every day. I'm going to dedicate myself to making you happy and keeping you that way. I'll be your friend, lover, and anything else you want or need me to be."

"Fuck! Let's get married now!"

"Don't tempt me, honey. I want some time to work on making your mother like me a little. Let's say seven months from now?"

"Make it four and we have a deal."

"That would make it in December."

"Having you as my wife would be the best Christmas gift ever," he told her. "And we can spend your birthday month of January on our honeymoon."

"Oh Braden! You're sweet, sexy, and handsome. If we can arrange the type of wedding I want in such a short time, I'd love that, but since I'm only planning to do this once, I want to do it my way. Okay?"

He nodded. "Yes. Now how about a fuck?"

She rubbed her pussy against him. "Sounds good to me, honey."

He massaged her ass. "I love it when you call me honey."

She pulled out of his arms and stretched out on the bed. "I love it when you fuck me so I figure we're even." She patted the bed between her legs. "Now bring me my cock and come get your pussy, honey."

He still needed to find a way to get Raven to confide in him and to convince Shane to hold out for marriage with a woman he loved. He'd need to repair the damage he'd done to his relationship with his mother as soon as possible. And there was the problem of convincing his key personnel to relocate to the East Coast with him and closing the deal on his latest acquisition—which was proving more difficult than he and Raven had anticipated. But suddenly all of the problems that had weighed him down just hours earlier seemed insignificant. Because the woman he loved more than he'd thought possible loved him too and wanted to marry him and have his babies.

He slipped into bed and between her legs.

She smiled up at him. "Take what's yours and show me you're mine."

"I am, darling. I am," he whispered.

He shuddered as she reached between their bodies to press his cock head inside her.

Her tight, wet pussy, welcomed his bare cock. Her hands stroked down his back to clutch at his ass.

Oh shit. This was why he'd been born—to love and

adore this beautiful, sexy woman. As long as he had her love and passion, there was no obstacle he couldn't overcome. He would have to ask Layton to teach him to say *I love you* in Tsalagi. So he could tell her in four languages he was hers—now and forever.

Excerpt— Loving Large—Yours, Only And Always

By Marilyn Lee

Published by Marilyn Lee Unleashed

"Don't despair. When you least expect it, the hurt from Sam will dissolve and you'll fall head over heels in love again. It could happen at any time in any place. Just make sure you're ready to accept and embrace it when it happens."

Autumn Walker's mother's words flashed into her mind the moment she walked into the condo association meeting and saw him.

The man who caught her attention was tall, with long legs, wide shoulders, a narrow waist, and a taut ass. He might have stepped right off the cover of one of the Native American capture romances she and her friends had devoured as teenagers. She could easily imagine him bare-chested with long, very dark, silky hair pulled back from his face and hanging down his back as he sat astride a horse without a saddle.

Two women, who she suspected were more interested in spending time in his bed than they were in discussing proposed changes in condo fees, commanded his attention.

She stared at him, feeling herself going wet. What woman wouldn't want to be up close and personal with a man who was so sexy just the sight of him generated capture fantasies?

What she wouldn't give for the courage to strut across the room and join the two women clambering for his attention. She sighed. If only she were tall and slender with mounds of flowing locks like the women vying to hold his interest. But the handsome, sexy male who looked as if he'd just finished posing for the cover of a romance novel wasn't likely to be impressed with her five-foot, five-inch plump body or her dark brown skin. He probably preferred the tall, slender, blue-eyed blondes gazing so adoringly up at him.

Almost as if he felt her eyes on him, he suddenly turned his head, glanced briefly in Autumn's direction, looked away, and then did a double take. He arched a brow and locked his gaze with hers.

Embarrassed at having been caught staring, Autumn still couldn't look away from his dark, sexy, probing gaze. Her heart raced and the erotic imagination she'd struggled to control since her divorce quickly flooded her mind with visions of standing naked before him while he ran his big hands all over her body. Her cheeks burned at the delicious thought of feeling his smooth palms spanking her naked, dark ass cheeks until they burned with heat.

Oh to feel him lubing her up before he gripped her hips and fucked her ass, slow and deep. She bit her lip, going wet as she mentally savored the thought of him cupping his hands over her breasts as he thrust in and out of her rear.

She wore a pretty pink dress with a skirt that ended just below her knees. He could easily push it up to expose a hot pink thong. Once he pushed that skimpy piece of fluff aside he'd have easy access to both her ass and her pussy.

He arched a brow while the corners of his sensual lips slowly curved upward into an appreciative smile. His gaze shifted down to her breasts for several long moments before he looked into her eyes again.

Autumn caught her breath. Was she imaging things or did she detect a hint of interest in his gaze? He had definitely checked out her breasts.

Both blondes glanced at Autumn. One then touched his arm. The other placed a hand against his chest.

I guess they're telling you he's off limits. As if you need that warning.

The object of all three women's desire turned his attention back to the women at his side.

Autumn released a sigh of disappointment, still unable to tear her gaze away from him. He was so sexy.

He spoke briefly to the two women before turning his attention back to Autumn.

She swallowed and stared into his almost hypnotic eyes. He must be interested in her.

The women spoke to him again, seemingly determined to reclaim his attention.

Briefly turning his gaze back to the women, he flashed a smile and spoke to them.

Autumn watched in amazement as he then quickly strolled towards her, ignoring the women's efforts to keep him at their sides.

She swallowed and moistened her lips while her heart hammered against her ribcage.

He stopped a foot or so in front of her. He extended his hand. "Hello." He had a deep, sexy voice.

"Hi."

"I'm Seneka Elkhorn."

Seneka Elkhorn. Nice name. Nice voice. Nice body. Sexy as hell man.

She held out her hand.

A shiver of anticipation danced down her spine when his fingers closed over hers. She imagined him whispering sweet nothings in her ear in that deep, velvety voice as he caressed her bare skin with the big warm hand cradling hers.

"And you are?"

She blinked. "I'm sorry. What?"

"What's your name? Mine's Seneka Elkhorn."

Get a grip, woman and stop gawking as if you've never met a drop-dead gorgeous hunk. "Autumn Walker."

His eyes lingered on her bare left hand. "Autumn is my favorite time of the year."

"Oh…is it?"

"Oh yes." He smiled. "I see you're not wearing a ring, but is there a Mr. 'She's All Mine So Back Off' lurking somewhere?"

She'd never been happier to be divorced and commitment free. She shook her head. "Not anymore."

His smile widened. "No? This must be my lucky night."

His lucky night? Lost in a haze of erotic fantasies, she racked her brain for some witty remark that would titillate and entertain him while making him want to get to know her.

She stole a glance at his left hand. Bare. Thank God.

The association president went to the podium. "Good evening, everyone. We have a number of issues on the agenda so please find seats so we can begin."

Autumn stifled a groan. Why did the blasted

meeting have to start on time? She reluctantly withdrew her hand from his. "I guess I'd better find a seat."

He slipped a hand under her elbow. "Yes. Let's do that."

His fingers on her bare skin sent a tingle through her. She turned back to face him, hoping she'd managed to conceal her emotional turmoil from him. "I see a seat—"

"A seat?" He nodded toward two empty seats on the other side of the room. "There are two over there. Join me?"

She hesitated. Contemplating flirting with him as they waited for the meeting to start was one thing. Sitting with him might be too close to a line she'd never crossed before. Her divorce from Sam still stung. The reason he'd divorced her hadn't changed enough to make a difference in her life.

"Autumn," his fingers tightened on her elbow. He leaned down until his lips were a breath away from her ear. "I won't hurt you," he promised softly.

She stared up into his dark eyes. Why did she feel as if he'd read her mind and knew of her hurt? "What?"

"You can trust me, Autumn."

Trust didn't come easy. Sam had broken her heart, injured her pride, and damaged her self-esteem. When Sam left her, she'd decided lost love hurt and that love in general was overrated. Since then she had managed to remain romantically unscathed by channeling all her time and energy into preparing her students for careers in math and science.

Some of her students had done very well. She

found satisfaction in celebrating their triumphs with them. Her life wasn't exciting. It was safe. Safety was important.

He caressed her elbow. "You can trust me, Autumn."

Her desire to accept his word and trust him gave her pause. She knew nothing about him except that she found him more sexually exciting than any man she'd ever met. He seemed to want to spend at least an hour or so in her company. An hour wouldn't make much difference to him but it might act as a balm to her wounded ego.

She smiled up at him. "Okay."

"Great." He gave her a slow, warm smile before he led her over to the two empty chairs on the other side of the room. Once she was seated he sat so close to her, his thigh pressed against hers.

She attempted to draw her thigh away from his.

He responded by shifting in his seat in a manner that allowed him to press his thigh against hers again.

She inhaled sharply and glanced at him.

He arched a brow and ensured she was even more aware of him by sliding an arm along the back of her chair. He leaned so close she felt his breath on her cheek. "Relax, Autumn. I don't bite—at least not in public."

She blushed and turned her attention back to the front of the room. If he touched her, she wasn't sure how she'd respond.

He didn't.

Nevertheless, she spent the entire meeting wondering if he were as aware of her as she was of him. His thigh pressing against hers seemed to indicate he was yet each time she stole a glance at him, his attention was on the podium. Later, she couldn't remember how she'd voted on the proposed condo fees.

After the meeting ended, he turned to look at her. "So you're all for increased condo fees?"

"What makes you think that?"

He shrugged. "You raised your hand when the president asked for a show of hands of those in favor of the higher fees."

"I did?"

His lips twitched. "You did."

"Oh…hell!"

He laughed. "It would probably have passed anyway. Now for a really important question, do you have any plans for the rest of the night?"

"No.

"Will you have a drink with me?"

The thought that she might somehow parlay the drink invitation into a night of wanton and uncommitted sex, excited her senses and helped relax her inhibitions. "I'd like that," she admitted.

"So would I." He smiled.

He smiled a lot and lord what a warm, intimate smile. He was so handsome it was difficult not to stare at him.

"Are you ready, Autumn?"

After three years of celibacy she was more than ready to subject herself to any situation that would increase the possibility of their ending up in bed for the night. As improbable as she'd thought it before the meeting started, she was now convinced he shared her sexual interest.

She nodded. "Yes, I'm ready."

Marilyn's booklist:

Marilyn Lee Unleashed

Holiday Heat: Secret Lover
A Cheating Situation
Primal Lusts
My Mother's Man
Blue Desert Heat I
Blue Desert Heat II
Blue Desert Tales: Courtesan Seduction
Beauty Is Alisha Hoover?
Falling For Sharde
Nice Girls Do
The Dare
Fantasy Knights
Fantasy Knights 2 — Endless Love
Large, Shy And Beautiful
Where You Find It
Naughty Girls, Inc — No Commitment Required
Loving Large — Yours, Only And Always
The Quest — Hunter's Passion
Daughters of Takira — One Night In Vegas
Daughters of Takira 2 — Kyla's Awakening
Daughters of Takira 3 — Revelations
Any Time Any Place
Soul Mates
Secondhand Lover

Some Like It Male
Yesterday's Secret Sins
Marilyn Lee Omnibus I
Marilyn Lee Sampler
Marilyn Lee Sampler 2

<u>Red Rose Publishing</u>
Sister's Keeper
Finding Love Again
Betrayed By Love
Song of Desire
It Had To Be You
One Sweet Night
Tempting Neal
In Blood And Worth Loving
Eye of the Beholder
Night Heat
A Thing Called Love
Summer Storm
Skin Deep

<u>Ellora's Cave</u>
Night of Sin

Bloodlust series:
Conquering Mikhel Dumont
The Talisman
The Taming Serge Dumont
Forbidden Desires
Nocturnal Heat
Midnight Shadows

All In The Family

Moonlight series:
Moonlight Desire
Moonlight Whispers

Long Line of Love series:
Night of Desires
Love Out Loud
Only One Love

Teacher's Pet
Trina's Afternoon Delight
Branded
Road To Rapture
The Fall of Troy
Full Bodied Charmer
Breathless In Black
Playing With Fire
White Christmas
Quest II – Divided Loyalties
Quest III – Return to Volter

Changeling Press

Moonlight Madness
Bloodlust – Nighttime Magic

Loose Id, LLC

Dream Lover

Marilyn's homepage: http://www.marilynlee.org

Email: marilynlee@marilynlee.org

Marilyn's Bio:

Marilyn Lee lives, works, and writes on the East Coast. In addition to thoroughly enjoying writing erotic romances, she enjoys roller-skating, spending time with her large, extended family, and rooting for all her hometown sports teams. Her other interests include collecting Doc Savage pulp novels from the thirties and forties and collecting Marvel comics from the seventies and eighties (particularly Thor and The Avengers). Her favorite TV shows are forensic shows, westerns (Gunsmoke and Have Gun, Will Travel are particular favorites), mysteries (loves the old Charlie Chan mysteries. Her all time favorite mystery movie is probably Dead, Again), and nearly every vampire movie or television show ever made (Forever Knight and Count Yorga, Vampire are favorites).

Marilyn has won numerous writing accolades, including a CAPA award for Bloodlust: Conquering Mikhel Dumont and the following Lub-Dubs Awards for 2009: Lifetime Achievement Award, In Blood And Worth Loving (Best erotic novel and best sci-fi/fantasy/paranormal Award.

She loves to hear from readers who can email her at Mlee2057@AOL.com or who can visit her website, http://www.marilynlee.org. She has a Yahoo! Group called Love Bytes that readers can join by sending an email to: marilynlee-subscribe@yahoogroups.com